A

I looked at Scott. He had heartbreaker written all over him. I wondered if Emily was right. Had I pushed guys away so I wouldn't get hurt? In my fantasies, I had a great job and had a man I loved and lived happily ever after with him. In real life, people got fired from jobs every day and men were always leaving their wives for other women. The fantasy world was so much safer.

"We should go join the others," I said. I started toward the living room. In the doorway, Scott took me by the arm. I turned to look at him and my eyes followed his, looking up to see the mistletoe hanging overhead. He smiled and cocked his eyebrow.

I couldn't say I wasn't terrified, but this time I didn't let myself think about all the potential pain and heartbreak that might lie ahead. I just leaned in and kissed him. It wasn't my fault. It was the danger of mistletoe . . .

Books by Theresa Alan

WHO YOU KNOW

SPUR OF THE MOMENT

THE GIRLS' GLOBAL GUIDE TO GUYS

GIRLS WHO GOSSIP

THE DANGERS OF MISTLETOE

GETTING MARRIED

Published by Kensington Publishing Corporation

The Dangers of Mistletoe

THERESA ALAN

KENSINGTON BOOKS
KENSINGTON PUBLISHING CORP.
http://www.kensingtonbooks.com

For my husband,
Burton James McLucas,
the very best gift ever.

Acknowledgments

Thanks to Sara Jade Alan, as always, for her suggestions on this manuscript. Thanks also to Margie Lawson, Diana Rowe-Martinez, and Mary Webster for their help with brainstorming and keeping me sane.

Chapter 1

Amber

Twenty-eight days before Christmas

The night began with a simple philosophical question—is it possible to eat yourself into a cheese-popcorn coma?—and ended with reindeer-print boxer shorts draped over the lamp and a total stranger passed out and coiled up like a conch shell on my couch.

When I got home from work, I found a package waiting for me in the entranceway of my brownstone walk-up apartment building. It was a present from Aunt Lu. Every year around Thanksgiving she sent a giant vat of popcorn in a decorative tin. In theory this was a nice gesture, but for a single woman who had no self-discipline whatsoever, this was actually a very dangerous gift. Brimming with excitement (I loved presents! Even ones that would make my thighs bloat up like the cheeks of a chipmunk at a nut convention!), I took my booty, raced up the rickety green stairs to my apartment, tore off my many layers of winter outerwear, and opened the box to reveal a tin that was bisected with a sheet of spongy cardboard to separate the two flavors: cheese and caramel. I sat on the couch, turned on the television, and began shoveling cheese popcorn down my throat from my popcorn trough. The first few bites were ecstasy—the decidedly unwholesome neon-orange cheese powder melted on my tongue in a manner that was thoroughly delightful. Soon, however, I was no longer actually tasting anything; I was merely shoveling food down my throat as if my snack was a timed event and the buzzer would go off at any moment. I was riding a giddy wave of excess and loving it. At some point I realized my stomach was rumbling and I felt slightly ill, but there was more cheese popcorn to consume and I was powerless to stop myself from bringing yet another bite to my mouth. It was only when my doorbell zapped that I put a lid on the tin, dashed to the sink to wash off the radioactive orange powder from my fingertips, and temporarily concluded my popcorn orgy. I peeked out the window to see my girlfriend Chrissie standing on the steps below with an entourage of cute guys.

Wasn't it every single girl's fantasy to have cute guys simply show up at her doorstep? It was up there with winning the lottery without having to buy a ticket. And the crazy thing was, it was something I fantasized about a lot. Every time I got home from work, I would have a small flutter of hope that my life might have changed while I was gone—I'd have a message from a new client who would end up becoming my husband or I'd get a steady gig at a salon so I didn't have to make money exclusively with clients I found on my own. Or maybe there would be a message from that guy I met at the coffee house last week and suddenly I wouldn't be a romanceless, sexless schmuck anymore. Or I'd come home to a letter with a giant check in it from some mysterious tax rebate or something. The fact that none of these things ever happened did nothing to diminish my hope that something exciting was just around the corner. And look, here I was, with a bevy of cute guys suddenly on my doorstep.

I took stock of my appearance: I was wearing my hair back in a ponytail, which was somewhat unfortunate. It could look cute in a ponytail, but lots of guys told me my hair was my best asset—it was long, wavy, and butterscotch-colored—so I usually wore it free when trying to impress. But if I pulled it out of the elastic band now there would be an unfortunate telltale crimp, so the ponytail stayed. Other than that I didn't look too awful except for the bright orange powder glittering across my chest. I quickly brushed it off and bounded down the stairs to open the door. (My building was too old for fancy advancements like being able to buzz friends inside.)

"Hi," I said.

"Merry fucking Christmas," Chrissie said cheerfully. She held aloft a fifth of spiced rum. I sensed danger.

"What are you doing here?" I asked.

"Are you going to let us in? It's freezing out here."

"Oh. Sure. Come in. Um, my place isn't clean since I wasn't expecting . . ."

"Your apartment is never clean. Never fear. We won't judge you."

I stood back and let my guests in. "I'm Scott," said a good-looking guy in a baseball cap and navy blue Patagonia ski jacket. With his dark hair and caramel skin he looked like Kelly Ripa's husband what's-his-face who used to be in *All My Children*.

"Yo. I'm Vince," said another dark-haired guy.

"Brian," the blond guy said.

No one said anything for a moment. I was trying too hard not to look at Scott again in any obvious or carnivorous way. Finally I realized they were waiting for me in the arctic cold. "Oh . . . I'm Amber. Amber Taylor. Follow me."

"We brought rum for the eggnog," Chrissie said as she charged up the stairs. Chrissie's long strawberry-blonde hair curled in Shirley Temple corkscrews. I imagined that when her hair was wet it must have reached her ankles. She had *tons* of it. She often attempted to push at least part of it out of her face with a headband or a network of barrettes, but tonight she wore it loose and it bounced as she walked.

When everyone was in my microscopic apartment, Chrissie began rooting through my cabinets for a pitcher to whip up a deadly concoction of eggnog and rum.

I went to massage therapy school with Chrissie. Being a massage therapist is my twenty-eighth "career." I've also been a sushi deliverer, the personal assistant to an eccentric writer, and, of course, cliché of clichés, an unemployed actress. I came to New York to pursue acting, but I couldn't even get parts in unpaid theater roles let alone roles in movies or on TV. As much as I enjoyed rejection and poverty, when the office I was temping at offered me a full-time position in event planning, I pretty much gave up on acting and took it. I'm not a detail-oriented person, and event planning is all about detail, but I managed to do all right on the job for almost two frazzling years. Amazingly, I only messed up at work a few times, and my getting fired wasn't about my mistakes: half the company got the ax due to a severe budget shortage.

Still, when I got laid off I felt like I'd gotten a divorce—betrayed and hurt. It was worse than breaking up with a boyfriend. I'd worked so damn hard for the company, and my reward for my sixty-hour weeks was getting canned without a dime in severance pay and no place to go. I packed all my things into a box and walked out of the office feeling like I'd been cheated on. After reeling from being let go, I simply couldn't bring myself to get another job doing the same thing. Anyway, being an event planner had never felt like a calling.

I needed a job that made me feel like I was making a difference. That's why I went to school to be a massage therapist. If a person was in pain, it affected every other part of his or her life. In this field I could help people feel better physically and spiritually. I enjoyed being a massage therapist, but since I was just starting out, the money wasn't exactly rolling in. Plus, I was still paying off my student loans from getting a bachelor's degree in theater (*What* was I thinking? A degree in button-making would have been more lucrative), culinary school (which I sort of flunked out of due to the fact that cooking school teaches you not only how to cook, but how to calculate how much food to buy and how to run a successful restaurant—no one told me there would be math involved in cooking school!), and massage school. Despite the fact that I gave the federal government a hefty chunk of my monthly salary, I was on the you-will-die-well-before-you-can-pay-off-your-student-loans payment plan. Though I wasn't making much money, at least I knew that as my own boss, I could never get fired again.

As Vince, Scott, and Brian made themselves comfortable in my living room, I said, "Um, so how do you guys know Chrissie?"

"We met atta bar," Vince said, shrugging not just with his shoulders but with the entire length of his arms, his palms facing up, as if to say, *You know how it goes.* "Brian and Scott, these are my guys."

I nodded just as the phone rang.

"Excuse me for just one sec," I said, walking only a few feet into what passed as my bedroom. "Hello?"

"Tell me you have your ticket." It was my sister, Emily.

"I haven't *exactly* bought my ticket yet."

"Christmas is a month away. You should have bought your tickets weeks ago. Prices are going to go through the roof."

Emily, of course, *would* have had *her* tickets back in July even with a wedding to plan and a house to buy. "Well, you know, sometimes if you wait you can get those last-minute bargains."

"What are you going to do if you don't get a last-minute bargain?"

I exhaled at the same moment Chrissie thrust a cup of eggnog in my hand. The girl was a tornado— an unstoppable force of nature.

I mouthed the word "thanks" to Chrissie. Aloud I said, "Emily, don't you think it's a little silly to spend hundreds of dollars so we can see each other for just a couple of days?" I took a sip of the spiked eggnog, which could better be described as rum with a splash of eggnog. It nearly singed the hair off my head, it was so high octane.

"Of course. It's ludicrous. Christmas is ridiculous in every way. But if you don't come, Mom will kill you."

I moaned. Emily was right. "You're right. I'll never hear the end of it."

"Never."

"But I just saw all of you at your wedding in August."

I had no money in my savings account whatsoever, and I had abused my credit cards so badly I couldn't even charge a ticket to Denver. Why had I ever left home to move to New York? Everything was so much harder out here. My rent on this five-hundred-square-foot hovel nearly bankrupted me while Emily just moved into her first home. Her place was three times the size of mine, yet she paid two hundred dollars less on her mortgage payment each month than I did on my rent.

"We're your loving family. It's not like we can see each other only once a year. And let me reiterate my main point, which is that you'll never hear the end of it from Mom if you don't come home for Christmas. You know she's psychotic about the importance of this holiday. She will torment you every day for the rest of your life if you don't come."

"She will, she will." My mother really could be a broken record at times. When I lost my job in event planning, she would call day after day and tell me to get a real job. I'd think, *Mom, I get it. I'd like to find a real job, too*. Then, three minutes later she would say the same thing in a different way. Something like, "You know, you could work in an office and wear pretty suits. Wouldn't that be nice?" *Yes, Mom, if only I could find a job I'd love to wear pretty suits.*

I huffed into the phone. It was so unjust to be thirty-two and still letting my mother tell me what to do. "Why is she so weird about it? We're not religious. We're not traditional. I don't get it."

"I don't know why, but the point is that she'll make your life a living hell if you don't get out here. Even if you make it to every Christmas for the next thirty years, Mom will be pestering you about how you broke her heart because you didn't make it to the first Christmas I'm hosting in my life."

"You're right. You're right." I took another sip of my eggnog-flavored rum. I loved my mother, but she could be such a pain. Still, making her happy made my life so much easier. How the hell was I going to miraculously come up with the money for a plane ticket? Maybe I could sell some of my organs off. Did I really *need* two lungs?

"Plus," Emily continued, "Mom said she's going to make some big announcement."

I paused. "What kind of announcement?"

"I don't know."

"What do you think it could be?"

"I don't have a clue."

"You think she and Mork are getting a divorce?" ("Mork" was our nickname for our mother's husband, Jesse Moss. He looked just like Robin Williams in his Mork days, with straggly longish hair. That, combined with his obsession with suspenders, had caused us to call him Mork ever since Mom began dating him way back when Emily was twelve and I was ten. How were we to know Mom was actually going to marry the guy? Mom didn't know about our secret nickname for him. We loved him, but secretly we were happy he was her second husband and not our dad because we both preferred having the surname Taylor rather than Moss.)

Emily made a noise that roughly equated to, "I don't know."

"Well, she's too young to retire and anyway she loves her job," I continued. "Maybe she's secretly gay. Maybe we're really adopted. I know! We're secretly wildly wealthy and Mom and Dad hid the money from us when we were growing up because they didn't want to spoil us but now we're going to come into our inheritance!"

"Yeah, right. Anyway, don't you want to see Luke's and my new house?"

"Why won't she tell us the secret early?"

"Because she wants us all there in person."

"We're going to become wealthy, I just know it. I bet she's won the lottery and is buying a boat and going sailing around the world and taking us with her!"

Emily sighed in exasperation. "Just get your ass out here."

"Fine." I sniffed. "I'll keep checking Priceline and hope for a miracle."

"Why don't you just ask Mom for the money?"

"Because I can't bear to have her lecture me on how it's time that I got a husband and a 'real' job. I'd thought that with you getting hitched she would lay off, but no, it's only made her even more determined to get me married off. She acts like I'm beating men away. I'm *trying* to find some-one."

Mom did sort of have a point: the truth was, I got asked out a lot. I was the queen of the first dates. The problem wasn't that the guys didn't like me but that I didn't like them. There was never that spark I longed for. It was nice having men take me out to expensive dinners and shower me with gifts, but I wanted to find a guy who made me light up when I saw that he'd left a message on my voice mail or sent me an e-mail. Usually I cringed when I got a call from a guy because I knew I'd have to give him that "I'm not into you" speech.

"If I don't find the right guy soon, my eggs will have rotted away and I'll never have kids. But I can't just marry the first sperm-carrying male who crosses my path."

"Since when have you been all hot and bothered to start having kids?"

"It's the holidays. They make me think about what my life is going to be like twenty years from now if I never get married and have kids. Mom will be dead and I'll be all alone for the holidays."

"You'd always be included in my Christmas."

"It's not the same. I'd be the pathetic spinster tagalong. It's too depressing. The other day, I saw a commercial for *The War of the Worlds*. It's a movie about Earth getting attacked by aliens, and when we're under attack, all the families come out of their houses and hug each other while watching the battle rage. Don't you see, Emily? If we get attacked by aliens, I won't have any family to hug and console. You and Mom are all the way in Colorado. I'll be all alone."

"Amber, if we get attacked by aliens, you'll have bigger things to worry about than whether you'll have family to hug while the planet is being destroyed in a blaze of alien fire. Anyway, you get asked out on dates all the time. You either turn them down flat out or only give them a few dates before you give them the ax. How are you going to find someone if you don't give anyone a chance?"

"If you don't feel it, you don't feel it."

"This has everything to do with your fear of commitment. This is just like you flitting from job to job."

I groaned. "I told you, I couldn't get work as an actress, I got laid off from being an event planner, and the other jobs were just too mind-numbing for words. You sound just like Mom."

I could picture Emily clearly. She would be wearing freshly washed pajamas—actual pajamas rather than a tank top and sweats like normal people—her straight honey-brown hair would be perfectly neat in a sleek bob that cradled her face. Her nails would be short and neat and trim, and her skin would be flawless as always because a zit would never dare try to break out on her face because Emily simply didn't tolerate disorder.

"I'm sorry if I sound like Mom, but it would behoove you to think of her wrath if you don't get your ass out here."

My stomach rumbled irritably and I felt a sharp pain. I moaned and clutched my unhappy gut.

"Spending time with your family won't be that bad," Emily protested.

"No, that's not it. I got my yearly tin of popcorn from Aunt Lu and I devoured like half the cheese popcorn in a single sitting. You think popcorn is some light and healthy treat, but I've looked at the nutritional information on the bags of cheese popcorn at grocery stores, and the stuff has a jillion calories and is loaded with fat. Yet I'm utterly powerless to resist."

"I know. I could eat the entire thing of caramel popcorn in a single sitting. When I got the tin in the mail, I refused to open it. I'm waiting for my office holiday party and I'm going to give it away to the person I'm the secret Santa for."

"Wow. What willpower. If you were here, I'd gladly give you all my caramel popcorn."

"If you came out here for Christmas I'd give you all the cheese popcorn."

"No. The last thing on this earth I need is more. Thanks anyway."

I really did want to figure out a way to get home. I was dying to see Emily and Luke's new place, and

I always liked hanging out with Emily and Mom. Plus, now that Emily was a stepmother, I had a stepniece and stepnephew I couldn't get enough of.

"I assume you're not going to Dad's this year for Christmas, either?" Emily asked.

Since our parents were divorced, we always had two different Christmases. I usually missed the one with Dad because he was understanding about the difficulty of me flying to California the weekend before Christmas and then flying to Colorado the next weekend. (Mom always got the actual holiday; Dad got the weekend before, mostly because he understood that the important thing was to be with your family, not the exact calendar day you did it.) Also, I'd never been particularly close to Dad. He always worked a lot when Emily and I were young and now that I was an adult, we just didn't have much to talk about. He didn't get my world and I didn't get his. It wasn't that we didn't get along, but our relationship was formal and distantly polite.

"Nope. Dad even offered to pay for my ticket, but I told him I can't afford the time off from work."

"Then you definitely need to come out here."

"I know. I miss you."

"Oh, by the way, don't forget to send Luke a card. It's his birthday next week."

"Of course I won't forget." I *had* forgotten; thank goodness she'd reminded me.

"What was that sound?"

"I have some friends over."

"Ahh. I'll let you go, then. I love you. But promise me you'll be here for Christmas. I had to suffer through Thanksgiving with Mom and Mork and Luke's mother all by myself. I can't bear to be on my own for another holiday."

"I'll do my best. I love you."

"I love you, too."

After hanging up the phone, I rejoined my guests in the living room. I sat on the floor because Vince and Chrissie were on the couch. Brian and Scott sat on the two chairs from my microscopic kitchen table. I owned very little furniture as I couldn't afford it and didn't have room for it anyway. The television was propped on two cement blocks covered in a batik blanket. That was all the furniture I had except for the mattress in my coffin-sized bedroom and a small used dresser for clothes. My place was messy and cluttered, but I blamed that on the matchbox size of the place.

"How do you two know each other?" Scott asked Chrissie and me. He sat with his legs parted with his hands on his blue-jeaned legs. He had an easy confidence about him.

"We went to massage therapy school together," I said.

"So you're a message therapist, too, huh?"

"Yep."

"Do you give happy endings? Chrissie claims she doesn't," Scott said.

Immediately, my jaw involuntarily clenched and I felt a wave of irritation. If you were going to make a living as a massage therapist, you had to be ready for some guys to think you were little more than a prostitute. A "happy ending" was something that apparently enough female massage therapists offered their male clients that some men came to look forward to them. I'd only had to deal with a few men with hard-ons and unrealistic expectations, but the stereotype of massage therapist as prostitute irritated me to no end.

"No," I snapped.

"There's no reason to get defensive," Scott said. "I just think a massage is incomplete if you ignore that area. It would certainly help a guy relax."

"He can go relax that part of his body anytime on his own. Did you ever notice how you can't tickle yourself and you can't really massage yourself, but on that area of your body, things work just fine when you're solo?" I took a defiant swig of my eggnog-rum and nearly stripped the lining of my esophagus—it was like drinking Drano.

"It's better if somebody else does it, though," Scott insisted.

I glared at him. Unfortunately, he was so good-looking, I found it difficult to maintain my righteous indignation. Plus, I realized I was allowing myself to become irritated. *Nobody makes you angry; only you allow yourself to become angry.* How many times had I read that in one of my eight zillion self-help books? Reading these books was all part of my plan to become a better human being who was at peace with humankind and in a perpetual Zen state of mind and all that kind of shit.

As I looked at Scott and tried to calm myself, I realized he looked familiar.

"Scott, have you and I met before?

"Scott was in that Verizon commercial," Chrissie said. "Do you remember it? It was the one where . . ."

"Oh, yeah, I remember you! I know the commercial you're talking about," I said excitedly.

Scott's face flushed. "The residuals helped me pay my rent for the last few years."

"That's so cool. I feel honored to have a semi-famous actor in my apartment."

He shrugged. "It's been a while since I've gotten any work."

"Still, it's great that you got the part. I tried to be an actress and failed miserably. You must be so proud."

"He's being modest," Chrissie insisted. "He was in a couple movies, too. Have you ever heard of *Red Rose?*"

"Uh, no. Sorry."

"Don't worry about it. It was in the theater for like, ten minutes." He shrugged.

"You were in a movie. That's awesome," I said, genuinely impressed.

I was distracted by Chrissie's shriek as Vince pulled her onto his lap and thrust his tongue so far down her throat he could probably taste whatever she'd had for dinner swirling around in her stomach.

This was Chrissie: making out while I was stuck staring at two strange men and feeling decidedly awkward. I glanced at Scott again. Scott was so comfortable in his skin, so confident. I really wanted not to like him. He had that sort of alpha-male arrogance about him that successful businessmen, college athletes, and men who have always had power seemed to have. But I found that Scott's sureness of himself was strangely intoxicating.

"Ah, so Brian, what do you do?" I asked, trying to ignore the porno audition taking place on my couch.

"This and that."

I cleared my throat. This was going to be harder than I thought. "Uh-huh. Are you from New York originally?"

"No."

"How long have you been here?"

"A while."

I nodded, then stood. "Why don't I get us some more drinks?"

"I'll help." Scott followed me to the kitchen. "I hope I didn't offend you with my comment. I was just kidding."

"No, not at all." I became very busy mixing the rum and eggnog.

"That's a really cool necklace." Scott gently caressed my pendant; the pads of his fingers grazed my collarbone. The heat from his touch shot through my body; I shivered involuntarily.

"It's a goddess symbol."

"Are you a goddess worshipper or something?"

"Not really, not exactly anyway, no, uh-uh." My tongue was stuck on some channel of stupidity. "I just believe there is a power that women have, and when I'm going through tough times, I can tap into that energy. Does that sound New Agey and weird?"

"No. I get that. I believe that everything gives off energy. You know, vibrations that can be either negative or positive. It's like how electrons bounce from person to person, from this counter to you, from the counter to the glass. If you give off positive energy, you attract it."

"Doesn't positive attract negative?"

"Maybe, but I like my way better."

I smiled. "I do, too." I was slightly taken aback to hear his theory. He was classically handsome, and I tended to think that guys who were that attractive didn't think about much more than getting drunk and laid. Plus, I liked his idea. It was the what-goes-around-comes-around philosophy, and I personally believed that if you did good things, good things would happen to you.

He returned my smile. I nearly whimpered with longing.

When we returned to the others, Chrissie finally came out of her lip-lock with Vince. "You know what this party needs? Music!" she said.

I surveyed my CDs. In recent years, most of what I'd added to my music collection were compilations of chanting by yogi masters and meditation gurus. All I can say is thank goodness I had crappy taste in music during my misspent youth (which, granted, was only a few years ago), and I had some suitably pop-sounding party-mix CDs.

The next few hours involved a great deal more rum and conversation on topics I suspect were less than high-brow.

When I woke in the morning, I found myself on the floor in the living room with carpet lint up my nose. Brian was curled up naked on my couch, and a pair of red boxer shorts with smiling reindeer was draped over my lamp.

Why oh why was Brian naked? I bolted upright and did a quick status check—I appeared to have all my clothes on. Of course, clothes could always be put back on, so that didn't necessarily mean I was safe. Please, please tell me I didn't sleep with Brian the Monosyllabic Wonderboy.

Further reconnaissance revealed Chrissie and Vince in various states of undress on my bed, as if my bedroom karma wasn't—pardon the expression—already screwed enough.

Scott, I noticed, was nowhere to be found.

I looked around for telltale condom shrapnel or worse, a used condom lying like a smooshed sea snail in a sad and gooey heap. There was no sign of condom detritus, which meant either I was in the clear or in worse trouble than I thought.

"Chrissie!" I hissed in a whisper. "Chrissie!"

She lifted her head and cracked open one eyelid about a nanometer. "Huh?"

I waved frantically to indicate I wanted her to come over to me. Wrapping the sheet around her, she staggered over. Her hair looked like Medusa's might have if Medusa had just been shocked by a bolt of lightning.

"Why is there a naked man on my couch?"

Chrissie's gaze followed the direction my finger was urgently pointing.

"Brian? Brian's just one of those guys who goes a little crazy once you get a few drinks in him. He started singing 'Rudolf the Red-Nosed Reindeer' and doing a striptease."

"I didn't mess around with him, did I?"

"He passed out not long after the striptease."

"Thank God."

Chrissie woke up the guys and told them it was time to get going. After my houseguests sheepishly dressed and departed, I straightened up a little.

If only the disaster that was my checking account could be cleaned up so quickly. I was afraid, however, that it wasn't going to be quite that easy.

Chapter 2

Emily

Twenty-seven days before Christmas

Was there a twelve-step program for idiots? If not, perhaps I should start one. "Hello, my name is Emily and I'm a total idiot. I came to admit that I was powerless to overcome my stupidity and my life had become unmanageable."

What was I thinking offering to host the holidays this year? It was a fit of delusion. Momentary dementia. Perhaps I was the victim of a drive-by lobotomy. In any case, I clearly wasn't thinking straight.

I think when I made the offer at Thanksgiving, I was thinking, "Luke and I just bought our first house. I want to show it off. I have a good idea, why don't *I* host Christmas?"

After my relatives and in-laws all enthusiastically agreed to the idea, the reality of what I had done began to set in. What sort of fool agreed to host Christmas right after she'd moved into a new house? Now I had to rush through finishing painting all the walls, getting new carpeting, and replacing that god-awful burgundy ceiling fan from 1968 that had pink flowers painted on it. Not to mention the fact that we needed new towel racks in the bathroom, new knobs on the cabinets, and a bed for the guest room so our guests had somewhere to sleep. Meanwhile, I'd have all the normal Christmas insanity of gifts and wrapping and decorations and parties. There was Luke's birthday to celebrate at the beginning of the month and a weekend trip to my father's the week before Christmas so we could do the whole divorced-family multiple-Christmas thing. On top of all this, I was still getting used to married life and trying to become a full-time mother to Luke's children from his first marriage.

Perhaps God would be merciful and I'd be run over by a truck tomorrow.

As I sat at my kitchen table with my to-do list in front of me—with strict deadlines I had to meet to get everything done by December 25th—I realized the enormity of my folly.

My life had already been turned upside-down. One moment I had been a single girl who spent my evenings alone with the TV or a book (or, occasionally, a date), and the next minute I was a wife and mother of two. Since meeting Luke and the kids, I suddenly had the music to SpongeBob Square-Pants stuck in my brain as I drove to work, when only weeks earlier I'd never even heard of Sponge-Bob SquarePants. (It was very disconcerting to be caught by fellow drivers jamming away to the SpongeBob theme song while stopped at a STOP sign, I assure you.) My life right now was complete chaos. Until Luke and I finished painting, we couldn't fully unpack, so we were living like we were camping, tripping over unpacked boxes and unable to find anything we were looking for. It was killing me to live like this, but for now there was no other choice.

Luke and I met two years ago at the animal shelter where I used to volunteer on weekends. (When I started planning the wedding and then looking for a house, I stopped doing volunteer work for the time being. Hey, these days I was busy helping raise two kids to not grow up to become ax murderers. I figured I was doing my part to benefit society.)

Luke brought his daughter, Claire, to the shelter to get a puppy because a year after her mother died in a car accident, Claire still had a lot of anger, and Luke thought a puppy might cheer her up. When Luke and I met, the attraction was immediate. I believe I may have begun salivating with lust, and a little voice in my head was saying, *Holy Hottie, Batman!* Our gazes locked and, as we discussed different breeds and the best way to care for them, our eyes never strayed. When he and Claire left that day with the golden-furred mutt named Lucy, a huge bag of dog food, a leash, a water bowl, and a department-store's worth of dog toys, I was crushed. I'd never had such an immediate carnal attraction to anyone, and the thought that I might never see him again nearly killed me. All week at work all I could think about was Luke, his adorable tow-headed daughter, and his brown-eyed son Josh, who was just two at the time. When Luke returned a week later on the premise that he just wanted to let me know how things were going with the new puppy, I couldn't stop smiling: I knew the attraction was mutual. Before he left he asked me out to dinner. On that first date I knew that whatever it was between us went far beyond mere lust. We were married this past August and moved into our first house a few weeks ago.

Now I had a full house with a husband, two kids, and a dog named Lucy.

Though our wedding wasn't extravagant, between that and buying a new place, we didn't have enough money to do all of the improvements on the house that we wanted to do, but I felt compelled to do them anyway because we were hosting Christmas.

My mother and sister wouldn't judge me if the house was still in shambles, but Luke's mother was a different story. I wouldn't say Gwen was shallow, but appearances mattered to her. She was the kind of woman who loved to point out when I looked tired or had put on weight. Worse, she was always comparing me to Luke's first wife, Elizabeth. *Elizabeth was a great cook. Elizabeth did such a good job of balancing motherhood with her career as a therapist. Elizabeth kept such a neat and well-decorated home.* Blah, blah, blah.

I realized it was ridiculous to compare my maternal and domestic skills to those of a dead woman. I should have been blissfully happy—I'd found the man of my dreams, I finally owned my own home, and I had two gorgeous kids. Unfortunately, the man of my dream's mother couldn't stand me, my home was in shambles, and my two gorgeous kids hated my guts. No, that wasn't really true. Josh liked me all right. Claire *used* to like me. Then Luke proposed and I was no longer going to be "Daddy's friend," but "Daddy's wife." That changed everything.

As I scanned my to-do list and silently prayed I would die young—the next ten minutes or so would do nicely—I heard the door open. Luke was home with the kids. Four-year-old Josh had chubby, Campbell's Soup–kid's cheeks and eyes like melted chocolate just like his father. Seven-year-old Claire had blonde hair like her mother, her father's dark eyes, and wisdom beyond her years: Claire knew that I didn't know what I was doing when it came to raising kids. Children could smell fear, and I was filled with it.

Luke and I took turns picking them up from the Montessori school they attended, which had a daycare for Josh and an extended afternoon program for Claire. Josh toddled in with his little brown suede pants and jacket with fleece trim and a tan knit hat that covered one ear. The other side had become skewed, letting his other ear peek out. He looked adorable, like a little brown baby bear.

"Hello, you cute little chubster."

"Hello, Emily."

When Luke and I first started dating, the kids naturally called me Emily. At our wedding, some great uncle said to Claire, "What do you think of having a new mommy?" She had replied with crossed arms and a stomp of her foot that I was *not* her mommy. Josh followed her lead and also continued to call me Emily, not Mom. I was OK with it. I figured that I had to earn the right to be called Mom.

"Hi, Claire," I said.

She nodded in acknowledgement.

I helped Josh take off his coat and hat. To Luke I said, "OK, I made a list of everything we have to do around the house. I was thinking we should go to Home Depot tonight to buy paint and order carpet. I'm going to ask Mom to watch the kids. I thought we could do the painting this weekend."

Luke sighed and nodded. I knew he was beat;

he was putting in twelve-hour days at work. I felt bad, but it was probably best that we just killed ourselves now and got everything done so we wouldn't have all these tasks looming overhead.

I was just reaching for the phone to call Mom when she called me. This wasn't so much a telepathic connection as it was habit. Mom called every night. If the kids did anything cute, I'd report on that. Mom would tell me about her day at work and talk about the weather. Sometimes I got the feeling she thought there was some law that required we speak for a certain length of time each day whether we had anything to say or not. She would tell me that she had to go pick up her dry cleaning or something, and I'd think, *You know, that's not all that thrilling—you don't have to tell me about every second of your day. A simple highlights-only version would be just fine.*

"Hi, Mom, I'm glad you called. Luke and I need to go to Home Depot tonight and it would make our lives much easier if we didn't have to bring the kids. We might be there a while and the kids will get restless. Would you mind watching them?"

"Of course not."

"You're a lifesaver, thank you." When I had been single, living so close to Mom and her husband, Mork, had often been a drag. I'd be about to have sex with a hot guy on my couch (it didn't happen often but it happened), or I'd be hunkered down in my pajamas ready to surrender my brain to TV and relax after a hard day when she'd show up at my door unannounced. I asked her approximately a million times to please call first, but she wasn't broken of the habit until one time she walked in and found me having sex with my boyfriend (see, I told you it happened sometimes).

But now that I suddenly had kids, it was nice having some backup handy. The kids only had a few distant cousins on their mother's side of the family. Luke's father had passed away many years ago and his mother and stepfather, Jay, lived three hours away, so Mom was really the only help we had.

"Thanks. I'll get some dinner into them. Do you think you could come by in about an hour?"

"Sure thing. What did you do with yourself today?"

"You know, the usual." I worked as an actuary for an insurance company, which essentially meant that I crunched numbers all day. My job was to anticipate risk. I took data about a person's health and decided what his or her insurance premium should be. I'd been a math major in college and being an actuary was one of the few careers other than being a math teacher that my degree had prepared me for.

"Have you talked to your sister? Has she gotten her ticket to Colorado yet?"

"I did talk to her and she's working on buying her ticket as we speak."

"Is she going to your father's this month?"

"No, she's missing Christmas with Dad again this year." I knew that on the other end of the line, Mom was suppressing a smile. She and Dad had split up more than twenty years ago and she'd been remarried for more than a decade but, like Amber, she'd never really forgiven Dad for the divorce. Plus, my mother was slightly psychotic about Christmas. She'd grown up poor and had seven brothers and sisters, so she'd been lucky to get socks and hand-me-down sweaters that were four sizes too big for her on Christmas morning. As an adult, she made up for the crushing holiday disappointments of her childhood by lavishing presents on Amber and me. Unfortunately, Mom favored quantity over quality when it came to gift giving. I appreciated the thought, but let me explain it this way: if I got genital herpes and a bladder infection for Christmas, that would be an improvement over the presents she gave me last year. "How was your day?"

"Well, I wanted to take a step class at the 24 Hour Fitness, but I got stuck on the phone with the insurance company. Remember when Jesse had to go to the hospital for his back?"

"Yeah."

"Well, I got a letter saying that the insurance company hadn't paid it. I was on hold for twenty minutes, only to find out it *had* been paid after the letter had been sent out. Then I wanted to pay some bills, but I kept getting distracted . . ."

This was about the time I started zoning out. As I popped some Tater Tots and chicken nuggets in the oven, I began mentally reviewing everything Luke and I needed to get at Home Depot. *Handles for the cabinets. Paint. Brushes. Tarp . . .*

Focus! This is your mother. She's kind enough to watch the kids, the least you can do is listen to what she has to say.

". . . and then I sat down to pay the bill just as the phone rang. It was a telemarketer. She was selling . . ."

I wonder how much carpeting the house is going to cost us. What color should we paint the living room? I can't wait to get these icky old knobs off the cabinets . . . Ahh! I'm doing it again.

"I tried to go back to paying the bill, but just then . . ."

It was no use. I could only partially catch what my mother was talking about. At some point I realized she'd stopped talking.

"Really?" I ventured. It seemed like a safely vague thing to say.

"You seem a little preoccupied."

"Sorry. I'm just working on cooking dinner."

"I'll let you go, then. See you soon."

"I love you."

"I love you, too."

I hung up the phone and got the broccoli ready to steam. I could get the kids to eat broccoli if I covered it in cheese. It was the only way I knew to sneak a few vegetables down their throats. I'd smother broccoli in toxic sludge if I thought they would eat it. They refused asparagus, salad, lima beans, and carrots, but broccoli they would eat . . . for the time being, anyway. Though I'd only lived with them for a month, Luke and I had been dating for two years and I'd come to expect that one day the kids would suddenly announce they refused to eat broccoli in any form and I'd need to find a new stuff-nutrients-down-their-throats tactic. For a time, Claire had been obsessed with canned mandarin oranges and would consume no other fruit. Assuming canned fruit was better than no fruit at all, I bought her twelve cans, which she devoured in a week. So I bought twelve more, and she abruptly decided she never wanted to eat another mandarin orange again in her life. I had twelve cans collecting dust in my pantry at this very moment (because you couldn't pay me to eat canned produce). I kept them around for the same reason I held on to last year's fashions—I never knew when they might become popular again.

Ordinarily I would make something different

for Luke and me (believe me, if I never had to eat broccoli with cheese or another chicken nugget, I wouldn't be the least bit upset about it) but in the interest of saving time, I decided Luke and I would just eat with the kids tonight. (I can't say I was sorry there would be fewer dishes to do, either. Who knew having a family would involve so many dishes?)

The kids ran into the kitchen, screaming at each other about something, but I was trying to finish cooking while contemplating whether I wanted to pick up the ringing phone or not. Luke and I had caller ID on our phone upstairs but not on the one in the kitchen. I thought it might be Mom so I answered.

"Hello?"

"Hello, Emily. It's Gwen."

Remember how Jerry always reacted when he saw Newman? I felt about like that. Unlike Mr. Seinfeld, however, I responded in a cheery voice. "Hi. What's up?"

"I wanted to talk to you about Christmas."

I closed my eyes, bracing myself. "What did you want to talk about?"

"I just was a little worried about Christmas dinner. I was thinking that I could help you with the cooking."

"Thanks, but I've got everything under control."

"It's really no bother. You know how much I like to cook."

"If you want to bring an appetizer and a bottle of wine or something, that would be great, but really . . ."

"Have you thought about catering? My friend Lorraine is an excellent caterer."

Catering? Luke and I couldn't afford to feed our guests mac and cheese for Christmas dinner, let alone afford a caterer. "That's a good thought, Gwen, but . . ."

"You *really* should think about it. I know it's a little pricey, but it'd be worth it. Wasn't I right about the chocolate fountain?"

"The chocolate fountain was nice," I agreed, although it had also been appallingly expensive. Luke and I had paid for our wedding ourselves, so we'd tried to keep things simple to keep costs low. Unfortunately, Gwen wanted to use our wedding to grease the palms of her many, many business contacts, so she'd harassed Luke and me endlessly to use the services of her associates (services we didn't want or need). One such acquaintance had a business where she brought chocolate fountains to events like weddings and parties. The chocolate fountain had cost more than twice what our wedding cake cost us. With a chocolate fountain, twenty or more pounds of chocolate were melted down and sent through a contraption that looked like a steel Christmas tree, though you couldn't see the metal, just the chocolate pouring down it in creamy waves. Guests speared pound cake, strawberries, and so on with little wooden skewers and then drenched the cake or fruit in the flowing chocolate. It was tasty and elegant looking, but not worth putting yourself into debt over.

"What about for Christmas Eve?" Gwen said.

"What about Christmas Eve?"

"Jay and I were planning to come that day."

"You were?"

"And we'll need something to eat. Why don't Jay and I take all of you out to dinner? Your mother and Jesse are of course invited, too."

"Gwen, thank you. That's a really nice offer. I'd appreciate that."

As I attempted to talk with Luke's mother—always a frazzling experience on its own, let alone when at the same time I was making dinner—the kids' conversation, which thus far had been nothing more than a dull background drone, escalated into a full-blown shouting match.

Josh: "But you said!"

Claire: "Did not."

Josh: "Did too!"

"I'm sorry, Gwen, what did you say?"

"What's going on over there?"

"Claire and Josh are squabbling. You know how kids are."

I looked down to see Josh's brown eyes looking earnestly up at me. "Emily?"

"Gwen, hang on a moment, will you?" Turning to Josh, I covered up the mouthpiece and said, "What?"

"Claire lied to me. Yesterday she said she would play with me tomorrow. It's tomorrow now and she won't play with me."

"I don't want to play your stupid little kid games!"

"OK, Josh, sweetie, I'll play with you just as soon as I get off the phone with Grandma Gwen."

He exhaled with exaggerated exasperation, rolling his eyes. Clearly, I wasn't getting his point. "Claire is a liar! She should be punished. You are not supposed to lie."

I took my hand off the mouthpiece. "Gwen, can I call you back in a little while? The kids are being a little rambunctious."

"With a little practice, you'll be able to manage the children just fine."

I closed my eyes and bit my lip. *Breathe. Inhale.*

Exhale. Remain calm. "It was good hearing from you, Gwen. We'll talk soon." I hung up the phone and turned to the kids. "Dinner is ready so go sit down."

"Claire is a liar."

"We'll talk about this after we eat. You don't want your dinner to get cold, do you?"

Luke walked into the kitchen at that moment.

"Perfect timing," I said, giving him a quick kiss on his soft lips.

We sat at the kitchen table with our simple meal. Sitting on the floor looking hopeful was our mutt, Lucy, the dog who had brought Luke and me together in the first place. Her tail slapped the tile floor and she looked at me plaintively with beseeching brown eyes as she waited for one of us to drop some morsel of food that she would then lick up in a blur of fur and wagging tail and pink tongue. For some reason, Luke and I were incapable of just simply calling her Lucy. Luke called her Lucy Pants and I called her Lucy Girl. We didn't talk baby talk to her, but we did use funny voices and tones that were much more enthusiastic than those we greeted one another with. Every time Lucy came to us with her tail wagging and her ears at attention, we greeted her with lots of exclamation points and inane questions. "Lucy Girl! Lucy Girl! What are you doing? Huh? What are you doing? Are you being a good girl? Are you such a good girl? Yes, you are!"

"Nothing for you, Lucy Girl. Nope. Nothing for you!" I said. Turning to Claire I asked, "What did you learn in school today?" I popped a chicken nugget in my mouth.

Claire's blonde hair liked to curl, so even though I brushed it each morning, about eleven seconds after I finished, it looked like she was trying to grow dreadlocks. I couldn't bring myself to cut her hair short, though. I thought the Street Urchin look was cute on her anyway.

"I learned about Egypt. I learned lots about it. We learned about the zombies."

I laughed. "I think you mean the mummies."

She furrowed her eyebrows. "Yeah. The mummies. That's what I said."

I immediately wiped the smile from my face. "Oh. Right. Sorry. I must have misheard you. What else did you learn?"

Before she could answer, Josh announced, "I'm all done." He'd barely made the slightest dent in his meal. The kid was going to perish of anorexia and Luke and I would get carted off to prison for child abuse.

"Josh, you haven't eaten any of your broccoli," Luke said.

"I not hungry."

"Please just eat a few bites so you can grow big and strong," Luke pleaded.

As the intense negotiations got under way, I looked at Luke, my partner in all this, and smiled. I loved watching him with the kids. I still couldn't believe how lucky I was to have found him. I'd spent so many years dating men who were good-looking, smart, and successful, *wishing* that I could feel head over heels in love with them but never actually feeling that way. I'd been in three long-term relationships before Luke. The first guy, Brett, I'd dated through college. When he started talking marriage, I broke up with him, saying we were too young, which was an entirely reasonable excuse, though the real truth was that even though I liked him, I knew he wasn't the guy I wanted to spend my life with. I met Dean at a wedding in Denver. He lived in Portland. Because we only saw each other one or two weekends a month, each time we saw each other, it was exciting and new. That excitement made it easy to pretend we were genuinely in love. But as soon as he began talking about transferring to Denver so we could be together all the time, I knew I'd been lying to myself and broke it off. A year later I met Chad at a dinner party. With Chad, I even got so far as to let him move in with me. After the initial throes of romance wore off, I began to sense that something wasn't quite right. I loved him and tried my hardest to make things work, but eventually I realized that as much as we cared about each other, "forever" just wasn't in the cards for us. I was devastated when I realized I had to break up with him, but I knew that mere companionship wasn't enough. I wanted the real thing. True love, no compromises.

I'd started to worry that it wasn't going to happen for me, that there was something wrong with me—maybe I was too picky, maybe I was too emotionally cut off, maybe my parents' divorce had ruined the concept of romance for me and made me overly cautious. Then I met Luke and felt such an immediate sense of lust and attraction, I realized it wasn't any of those things. It was simply that until I met Luke, I hadn't met the right guy. I hadn't felt that curious combination of pheromones and physical attraction and emotional connection with any other man.

It seemed like now that I'd found love and was happily married, all my problems should be over. Instead, I was suddenly living in terror—terror that I would lose Luke. It wasn't logical, but love's like that—it makes you crazy. Instead of thinking of Gwen as a stereotypical nightmare of a mother-in-law, I worried that if she didn't grow to like me, she could somehow drive a wedge between Luke and me. My parents' divorce hadn't soured me on the idea of marriage, but getting a divorce was out of the question. I'd experienced enough of that nightmare to last me a lifetime.

After dinner, Luke cleared the table and I mopped up Josh's face, which looked like a Jackson Pollock painting. There was a knock at the door— Mom. Mom had a key to our place, but ever since she'd walked in on me having sex with Chad, she knocked first.

"I'll be right there!" I called and walked to the door. "Hi, Mom."

My mother was a petite, roly-poly woman with shoulder-length white hair and a jovial smile. Both my sister, Amber, and I were tall and thin like Dad, but we had our mother's smile.

"Thanks for coming over on such short notice." I gave her a hug.

"No problem, dear. You know I love spending time with the kids."

"We should be back by ten at the latest."

Mom already knew the drill on bedtimes and homework. I took her coat and watched as Claire and Josh ran up to give her a hug.

Luke and I said our good-byes, pulled on our coats, went out to the garage, and climbed into Luke's silver Honda Insight. As he drove, I studied my nails, which were in a pitiful state. "I broke a nail," I said, as if I were trying to win a contest for Most Boring Conversationalist. "I broke it really low, so it hurts." I found that sometimes in an effort to fill in gaps of the conversation, I said whatever thought flickered through my mind, regardless of how outrageously dull those thoughts might be.

"I'm sorry."

I shook my head. "I'm becoming my mother," I said. "Talking just to talk."

"You're not that bad."

"Every night when she calls me, when we hang up I look to see how long we talked for and how many precious cell phone minutes I've used up. Inevitably it's only about six or seven minutes, but it feels like we've been talking for hours."

"I find that talking to parents is always onerous." This was why I loved Luke—he used words like "onerous." What could be sexier than a man with a large vocabulary?

Luke parked the car and we walked into the giant box of a store. I got a cart and we headed to the paint section.

"OK," I said. "Let's figure out the living room."

Luke pulled a strip of sample paint colors out from the rows of bookmark-sized samples. "Isn't this a nice color?" Luke asked, pointing to a dark hunter green.

"For a minivan, yes. For a room in our house, no."

"I thought you said you wanted to paint the living room an earth color."

"I do. But I don't want it to be so dark we feel like we're in a cave. What about this?"

"That's the color of snot."

"That is not the color of snot, you brat."

"What about this?"

"Has your color blindness ever been diagnosed? You should probably see a doctor about that."

"Very funny."

"What about this?"

"Well, it's not intensely awful, but it's not great."

Back and forth, back and forth we went. And that was just the living room.

By the time we'd bickered our way through all six rooms that needed painting, I was ready to go home and take a nap.

But we were just beginning. We spent the next two hours in intense discussions over carpet color, handles for cabinets, lamps, towel holders, you name it. Luke and I actually had similar taste, thank goodness, but I'd spent thirty-four years of my life being able to decorate my living space exactly like I wanted. Having to compromise was taking some getting used to.

When we got home, I paused to check in on the kids. Claire was sleeping partially on her stomach and partially on her side, her little butt in the air, her blonde curls tangled in a halo around her head. I smiled. She looked like an angel.

Funny how deceiving looks can be.

Chapter 3

Amber

Twenty-six days before Christmas

I'd finished my massages for the day and was puttering around my kitchen with a rumbling stomach searching for culinary inspiration when the shrill ring of the phone startled me.

"Hello?"

"Have you bought your plane ticket yet? Please tell me yes," Emily said.

Emily was my best friend in the world, but I didn't want to deal with this right now. "The cheapest ticket I can find is five hundred dollars. I can't afford that."

"What if Mom and I chipped in to help you buy your ticket? That could be our Christmas present to you."

"Emily, that's nice of you, but no. You'll say that that will be your only gift to me, but I know you. You always buy me presents even after vowing that you won't. Last year you bought me that expensive blouse even after we promised we wouldn't exchange gifts, remember?"

"Only because I wanted to, but this year I'll just send a check, I swear."

"Emily, I'll figure something out, I promise." Emily and I both thought that it was silly to buy a bunch of gifts people didn't need. We subscribed to an it's-the-thought-that-counts point of view. But even though we had these lofty values, the need to give gifts and spend money on Christmas presents had been engrained in our heads since we were little kids and it was a hard habit to break. "I *am* dying to hear Mom's secret. She'll tell us even if I don't come, right?"

"I don't know."

"I've got to know what it is. Do you have any ideas?"

"Not really."

Emily had many great qualities, but an inspired imagination wasn't one of them. The more I thought about it, the more logical the lottery win seemed. On Christmas morning Mom would give Emily and me enormous checks, and I'd be able to pay off my credit cards and live happily ever after. I couldn't wait!

I opened my cabinet looking for something to eat. The cans of tomato soup and the jar of peanut butter held no appeal. Neither did the mac and cheese nor the canned chili. My freezer had a few frozen dinners that had been there since the Ice Age and my refrigerator was a barren wasteland with only some ketchup and tonic water to clutter the landscape. I closed the door and sighed. "I woke up to a naked man on my couch yesterday morning."

"Congratulations."

"No, it wasn't like that. It was one of those, 'Oh, God, how much did I drink last night?' situations. Fortunately, my friend Chrissie assured me we didn't sleep together. He's apparently one of those guys who gets a few drinks into him and goes nuts and feels compelled to take off all his clothes and dance around naked."

"Your life sounds like so much fun. My life is all chicken nuggets and spilled drinks."

"My life isn't that exciting, trust me. I'm the one who is jealous of you. I can't wait to have kids." I looked at my empty refrigerator and messy apartment. What kind of mother would I be? "What am I talking about? I can't even keep my tiny apartment vacuumed. How could I possibly keep a small human alive?"

Emily laughed. The sound made me instantly feel better. This was what it meant to have a sister—it meant having someone who could make me laugh even when life seemed just too hard.

"I'm just faking it, to be honest with you. I have been going out of my mind trying to get this house in order and learning to cook. I think I'm going to take a cooking class and a baking class, maybe pottery and flower arrangement classes, too."

"And with what time are you going to do all this, little Miss Susie Homemaker? I think the important thing is that you actually have time to hang out with your kids and husband, not that you're a master chef with a spotless house and award-winning garden."

Emily sighed. "I have to get this house in order. Do you know how much carpeting we looked at? There's Berber, that means large loops with a textured surface; texture, that's cut yarns; frieze is tightly twisted cut yarns with a shaggy surface; plush means cut yarns with a velvety surface; multi, that's multiple yarn colors; loop, which has short, dense loops, with a smooth surface; then there is . . ."

"Emily, it's really not necessary for you to teach me about carpet styles."

"And we haven't even started talking about colors . . . and kinds of installation. And let's talk about tile . . ."

"Emily, no offense, but this is *so* not interesting."

"You're saying I'm boring?"

"No . . ." I hedged. "It's just that you used to be able to talk about other things than cooking and carpeting."

"Fine. I didn't mean to bore you. I'll let you go."

"Em, come on. I'm just saying."

"I should get going anyway."

"I love you, Em."

"I love you, too."

When the phone rang a minute after I hung up, I assumed it was Emily calling back to tell me something she'd forgotten to say.

"Hello?"

"Hi, dear."

Mom.

"Hi. How are you?" I sprawled across the couch, bracing myself for the lecture I knew was coming.

"I'm fine. Listen, Emily told me you haven't bought your plane ticket yet."

"I'm just waiting for some last-minute deals to come through."

"Don't do what you did with your college applications."

Unbelievable. It had been more than fourteen years since I'd had to apply to college, and she was still holding it against me that I was late turning in my applications way back when.

It was all because my sister was this insanely organized person. While I had a shoebox stuffed with important papers, Emily had a filing cabinet with neatly labeled color-coded folders that contained every bank statement, credit card bill, and receipt she'd ever gotten. It went without saying that Emily never bounced a check or paid a bill late. She was hugely annoying in that way. In some ways Emily and I were a lot alike—our laughs, our mannerisms, the way we talked—but in other ways we were so different it was a wonder we could possibly share the same genes. Emily set goals for herself and would never give up until she'd mastered whatever she set out to do. As for me, I tried lots of different things and if it turned out I wasn't good at something, I didn't feel like a failure. I didn't need to have a big house or be a famous actress with Academy Awards to prove to myself I was worthy.

Part of me wanted to say, "What if I didn't make it out there for Christmas?" But I couldn't get the words to actually come out of my mouth. I couldn't admit to Mom that I didn't have the money. I would just have to get a part-time job or take out another credit card or something.

"Christmas is a very important time. Your family is the most important thing in the world."

"Yes, Mom, I know."

"We need to be together. This is the first time your sister has ever hosted Christmas. You wouldn't want to disappoint her, would you? Anyway, don't you want to see their new house?"

"Mom, I said I was going to be there. I promise. You don't have to keep convincing me."

My mother had worked in sales for years and years. She knew how to relentlessly wear a person down. It was much easier just to agree with her right away.

"Emily is doing such a good job juggling everything. The house needs a lot of work and I think it's been hard for her to balance work with suddenly becoming a full-time mother of two, but you know Emily, she always rises to the challenge."

"Yup. That's Emily." I looked out the window. It got dark so early these days. There were strings of Christmas lights lining apartment windows and signs for a Chinese take-out restaurant and a pizza place. In the distance there were Christmas trees twinkling with lights and billboards lit up with spotlight brightness. There were times in New York when all the lights and neon signs were an ocular orgasm.

"How's your work going?" Mom asked.

"Oh. You know, it's been good. I'm just trying to build up my client base."

Mom exhaled. "I worry about you. Being self-employed like that. What about health insurance? What if you don't get enough clients to pay your rent? I just don't understand why you refuse to get a real job. Is a little security such a bad thing?"

"Mom, I'm an entrepreneur. You should be proud of me."

"I didn't say I wasn't proud of you. I said I was worried about you. I'm worried about your finances."

"I'm doing fine financially," I lied.

"Are you, Amber? Are you really?"

"Mom, I'm doing fine. I promise."

"If you need help buying your plane ticket, you know I can help you."

"I don't need any money."

"I have something very important to tell you and your sister."

"Yeah? What is it?"

"I'll only tell the two of you when you are together in person."

"What does it have to do with?"

"I won't tell you until Christmas."

"What if for some reason I didn't make it out there?"

"I thought you just assured me that you'd be here. Are you going back on your word?"

"No. I'm just saying hypothetically, what if I didn't make it out there? When would you tell us?"

"Maybe never. Anyway, you said you'd be here so what are we even talking about this for?"

I exhaled. "I don't know, Mom. I don't know."

Though I loved my mother, I found her exhausting. I must say that when I hung up the phone, I wasn't in a very Zen frame of mind.

I needed to get some food into me; then I'd be able to think straight. Since I had nothing in the house that sounded remotely appealing, I put on my coat, scarf, and gloves, and threw my checkbook and a calculator into my purse and headed to a nearby coffee shop for a sandwich. I strategically set myself down at the bar next to an empty bar stool to allow for a hunky man to sit down beside me and sweep me off my feet into happily ever after.

I ordered a sandwich and a black coffee and opened my checkbook and attempted to balance the row of numbers into my calculator, trying to make sense of it all. The problem was that any attempt at balancing a checkbook on my part was ridiculous. Emily had taught me to write down every check I wrote, every deposit I made, and every withdrawal, which I did, but somehow when I did all the addition and subtraction, it never quite matched up to what the bank said I had. I suspected the bank was pulling numbers out of its ass, but since I couldn't figure out what was really going on, I was essentially playing financial roulette. After getting laid off and being out of work for so long, my credit card debt had spiraled totally out of control.

What I did know was that I did not have five hundred dollars for a plane ticket to Denver. I'd already bankrupted myself buying a bridesmaid's dress and flying to Denver in August for Emily and Luke's wedding. And I couldn't think of a single friend who had five hundred bucks to lend me. Dad would lend me the money, but I hated borrowing money from Dad even more than I hated borrowing it from Mom, even though he made about four times more a year than she did. I didn't like feeling indebted to Dad.

I couldn't let myself worry about this right now. Something was going to happen. Some force in the universe was going to look out for me. Everything was going to be all right.

I took hold of my goddess pendant between my thumb and forefinger. I pictured Scott's fingers touching it, lightly brushing my collarbone. He had to be seeing someone. No one that good-looking could be single. Still, it wouldn't hurt to ask Chrissie . . .

My aimless fantasies were briefly forgotten when a man sat on the bar stool next to me. I felt a shiver of excitement, fixed a smile on my face, and then I looked at him. He was about a million years old. At least in his sixties. Oh. Boo.

I hated when reality got in the way of my fantasies. In my fantasies, I'd fall in love with a man a few years older than me (but unlike the guy sitting next to me, he wouldn't be old enough to qualify for senior citizen discounts). He'd be an established professional with a spacious, gorgeous penthouse apartment that I could move into. I'd cook gourmet meals and work part time as a massage therapist. We'd have a dog that I'd take on long walks. I missed having a dog.

I took a sip of my black coffee and smiled, thinking about the dog Emily and I had when we were little. We got Clyde when Emily was six and I was four. He was a mutt and not the brightest dog in the world, but he was ours and we loved him. He could sit and shake "hands," but that was the only trick he could do. "Fetch" was far beyond his talents. We'd throw a ball, he'd race after it, then he'd come back without it. Frankly, he sort of reminded me of myself: well intentioned but never quite getting things right.

Right around the time our parents were separating, Clyde got out of the yard and was hit by a car and killed. It was a time of huge upheaval in our lives. In a span of just a few weeks, our dog had been killed, our parents separated, and suddenly Emily and I had to leave our large house with a yard and our own separate rooms and share a bedroom in a tiny condo. I got through it by throwing myself into poetry, after-school drama classes, sewing, and arts and crafts. Emily got through it by focusing on her schoolwork.

It wasn't a big change for us not to live with Dad because he traveled so much for work anyway, but there were other huge differences in our lives. Before the divorce, if Emily and I needed new gym shoes or school clothes, Mom just took us to a store and we were able to buy whatever we needed. After the divorce, Mom took us to Target instead of department stores and gave us a strict budget. Suddenly we had to decide whether it was more important to have underwear without holes or socks without holes because we couldn't afford both. Before, when we went grocery shopping, Emily and I could pick out whatever we wanted. After, Mom bought only what was strictly necessary. Instead of steak or fish and chicken for dinner, we'd have hash and eggs, pasta, or waffles. Even with all the cutbacks, Mom was constantly sitting at the kitchen table hovering over her checkbook with a calculator and a pencil and a furrowed brow. Mom had never been a worrier before—she'd always put a smile on her face and kept a positive outlook on things. After the divorce, it was like she'd been taken over by an alien being, a woman who only knew how to feel anxiety and sorrow. Worse, every night through the paper-thin walls of our condo, Emily and I could hear Mom crying herself to sleep.

On weekends when Dad was in town, we'd go visit him in his big new house. He'd take us out to fancy dinners and to the movies and he never once got a stressed-out look on his face when we asked him if we could go out for ice cream—he didn't need to worry about what a couple of ice-cream cones would do to his budget. Visiting Dad was like going on a minivacation from worry.

Before my parents separated, my bedroom had been pink and frilly, with lace bed shams and lots of posters of cute boys. Emily's room had pale blue walls and white furniture and nothing remotely flowery or girly. When we suddenly had to share a room in Mom's condo, trying to compromise on how to decorate it had us at each other's throats. After an impressive amount of arguing, Emily and I finally agreed to put up posters of animals. At the time, our love of animals was the only thing we had in common.

I'd always been a slob, and I swear if it was possible for an eight-year-old to have a heart attack, Emily would have been well on her way due to the stress of sharing a room with me. Emily kept her clothes hanging in the closet exactly half an inch apart. I primarily kept my clothes in a heap on the floor. The only thing Emily liked about the situation was the fact that she got the better bed because she was older. We had a trundle bed so we could conserve space in our tiny room, though the point of that was lost as I was much too lazy to ever go to all the work of folding up the mattress and frame and putting it under Emily's bed. (Which, of course, drove her nuts.)

As kids we fought and yelled and screamed all the time. Then, at night in bed in the dark room when neither of us could sleep, we talked about our lives and our dreams and laughed for hours.

I missed her. I didn't want to spend Christmas all by myself. And I wanted to know Mom's secret.

All I needed was a miracle.

Chapter 4

Emily

Twenty-four days before Christmas

So I was sucking my husband's dick and wishing he'd stop taking his time and get on with things already. *Come on.* There was really nothing to do down there but let my mind wander, and all I could think about was how much I had to do and it was stressing me out and I was not at all turned on. Finally my jaw was getting sore and I just wanted to get on with things so I could shower and get to the office. I climbed on top and moaned a few times. Still he kept going.

"Did you come?" he asked.

"It felt really good." *It* could mean the sex itself, so I wasn't lying exactly.

Mr. Energizer Bunny still kept it up. I was going to have to take action. "I think I'm not going to have any . . . more." OK, damn, I did lie to him. But this was an emergency.

"Are you sure, babe?"

"Mmm hmmm."

"This is for me?"

I smiled. I could usually only pull off two orgasms, but Luke would keep going until he was sure I was orgasmically tapped out. Under most circumstances I found this the height of consideration, but every now and then I longed for a quickie.

He came about two seconds later and I gratefully rolled off him. I lay there for just a moment in the darkness. The hard thing about winter was how little daylight there was. I knew that I was lucky to live in Colorado. If I lived somewhere like Iceland or Sweden, I'd get almost no sunlight at all during the winter. When Luke finally finished up, it was six in the morning and funeral-black outside. I took Lucy for a quick walk, and when I left the house at seven for work, the sky was still a steel gray. My body had a hard time waking up in this weather; my internal clock got all confused and wondered why I wasn't still sound asleep beneath the covers.

That five-minute walk with Lucy was probably the only exercise I'd get all day. I'd lost twelve pounds before the wedding and got into the best shape of my life. Then came the honeymoon—all that drinking and eating plumped me right back up again. I'd felt so good about my body before the wedding—perhaps a little too good. I'd actually think to myself, *I'm so skinny and pretty!* Never in my life had I thought *I'm so skinny and pretty!* But for a while there, I felt amazing. It wasn't even that hard to do. I just exercised a little more and watched what I ate. (Huh, who knew it could be that easy? An entire industry would crumble if people could remember the top-secret formula to losing weight was to simply eat less and exercise more.) I wanted to keep that confidence, but during the holidays, it was impossible to watch what I ate and I had no time for the gym. My yoga mat and elliptical rider in the corner of the bedroom simply mocked me—they were statues, never moving.

Work was dietetically dangerous at this time of year. There were cookies and brownies everywhere. I was already oozing out over the top of my pants. (Amber called it "Done-lap disease," as in "My belly done-lap over my pants.") The madness had to stop.

This morning when I got to the office, I was greeted by a plate of homemade pumpkin bread, sliced and ready for the taking. I looked longingly at it but, thinking of the holiday party that night, I decided to save my calories.

"Hi, Emily."

I looked up to see Janice, a coworker who was about my age. "Janice, hi."

"How are you?" Janice asked, pushing up her glasses. She had long dark hair that she'd worn in the same plain style since she was in fifth grade. Ours was an unlikely friendship. She was passionate about online gaming, board games, and *Star Trek*—all things I couldn't care less about. When she talked about gaming or Trekkie conventions my eyes started to glaze over, but there was something so genuine about her I was drawn to her despite our differences.

"I'm good, thanks. Busy, of course, but good. Life is really stressful right now, but I'll live."

"You know what really helps with stress?"

"What? A nanny? A maid? A million dollars?"

She smiled, "Yoga."

I nodded, thinking of the mat in the corner of

my room that perpetually taunted me. "I used to do a little yoga. I loved it but somehow never managed to find the time to actually go and do it."

"I go three times a week. You can take a class for only seven bucks if you ever want to come with me sometime."

"That sounds good. Maybe I will. You going to the party tonight?"

"Yep."

"Will I get to meet Hank?"

She sighed. "I'm not sure. These sorts of things terrify him."

I nodded. She'd been married to the guy the entire time I'd known her and I'd never met him. She'd even had to come to my wedding solo. Weddings were hard enough when you knew lots of the people there; they were downright painful when you were all alone. But as far as I could tell, she couldn't get Hank to leave the house unless he was dressed like Mr. Spock and going to a Star Trek convention.

"Well, I'll see you tonight." I gave a little wave and made my way down the corridor to my office.

My office was Spartan and neat. All the offices had large windows so management could spy on us when we had our doors closed. We looked like dioramas at the Natural History museum—office workers in their natural habitat.

All the offices were gray—gray carpet, gray computers, gray desks and chairs. It was the color scheme of a graveyard. I think the point was to remind us that every day we worked here brought us one step closer to death.

I hung my coat on the back of my door, stuffing my gloves in the pockets of my black pea coat and draping my scarf over the hood. As I waited for my computer to boot up, I looked at the close-up of Luke that I had on my desk. He had a strong build, sexy smile, captivating eyes, and dark hair that was just long enough that you could run your fingers through it with satisfaction.

It felt strangely comforting to be at work. At least here I knew exactly what I was doing and I was good at what I did. I liked the clean world of mathematics where there was always only one right answer. With children, there was only chaos theory.

I spent the morning going through files and typing data into the computer. Late that morning my boss stopped by and peeked his head into my room. Ralph had recently celebrated his fiftieth birthday. He had a round face, gray hair, and glasses, and he was always laughing at things that no one else found funny.

"Emily."

"Good morning, Ralph."

"Good morning. You know those files I asked you to have done by next Friday? Is there any possible way you could get them done by—"

I quickly pulled the files from my drawer and handed them to him. "Already done. Here you go."

He shook his head and laughed. "I knew I could count on you."

I smiled, waved, and watched him go, feeling a sense of satisfaction. I'd gotten a job here right after college and worked here ever since. Most of my friends changed jobs every two or three years. Amber usually got a new job every two or three months. There were times when I thought about making a change, but I liked knowing everyone and everything about my job. I'd gotten regular raises and promotions ever since I'd started here. I thought some people—like Amber—moved around and switched jobs because they assumed that with a new job or new apartment or new boyfriend, life would suddenly be better when, most of the time, all life would be was a little different.

The day went by in a flash, and before I knew it I was waving good-bye to Janice.

"I'll see you in a couple of hours," I said.

"See you soon."

At home, I showered and did my hair. I inspected my appearance in the mirror. Like my sister, my hair was naturally wavy. Unlike Amber, I straightened it with a straightening iron to impose some order on it. Except for the fact that Amber wore her hair long and wavy and I wore mine short and straight, we could have been twins. We were the same height, more or less the same weight, and we had the same full lips that disappeared into thin, straight lines when we got angry.

When it was about twenty minutes before we had to leave, it occurred to me that Luke wasn't beside me shaving and getting dressed. I walked downstairs to find him unshowered and wearing grubby jeans and a T-shirt watching a rerun of *The Simpsons*.

"Honey?" I asked.

"Hey, what's up?"

"We have to leave in twenty minutes."

"Leave for what?"

"My office holiday party. I've only mentioned it about a thousand times."

"That's tonight?"

"Yes, that's tonight. Mom is going to be here to watch the kids in about ten minutes."

"Oh, man. I really don't feel like going out right now."

"Well, that's really just too bad, isn't it? Half the

reason I married you was so I'd never have to go to an office holiday party alone again, so get your ass into the shower and into some sexy clothes pronto."

"*Half* the reason?"

"At least half. Maybe as much as sixty percent. Now get a move on."

"You're not dressed yet," he pointed out.

"I know what I'm wearing, though. It will take me five minutes to get dressed and five minutes to get my makeup on."

"Yeah, right," he said.

"What's that supposed to mean?"

"I mean I'll believe it when I see it."

"Do you want to bet on it?"

"Sure. If I win I get a blow job."

"I give you blow jobs all the time."

He laughed.

"What's *that* supposed to mean?"

"Nothing, nothing."

"I went down on you just this morning."

"That was the first time you'd done that in six months. These days oral sex comes around less often than a lunar eclipse."

Had it really been that long? Huh. "What do I get if I win?"

"Sex with me."

"Puh-lease, I can have sex with you anytime I want."

"Are you saying I'm easy?"

"Yeah, I'm saying you're easy. If I win, I get a night of dinner and dancing."

"Hmmm . . ." he pretended to mull it over. "Deal."

I raced upstairs and dressed in a black silk blouse, black skirt, and heels. I wore the small diamond posts that Luke got me for Christmas last year and a silver necklace.

I was finishing putting on my makeup when Luke emerged from the shower.

"Well, well, well," I said. "Lookie here. I do believe I'm completely ready to go and yet here you are, naked as a newborn baby."

"Maybe I just won't go."

"Oh, you're going, mister. You're going."

It only took Luke a few more minutes to get dressed, and we really weren't running late at all. I didn't want to get to the party the second it started anyway. The important thing was that I got to successfully antagonize Luke.

The doorbell rang. "That'll be Mom. You ready?"

He nodded. Together we went downstairs to the front door and I let Mom in.

"You look beautiful, honey."

"Thanks, Mom."

"Luke, you look very handsome."

He gave her a hug and kissed her cheek. "If it were up to me, I'd be on the couch in my sweats watching reruns on TV."

She laughed as the kids appeared in the doorway.

"Good night, kids. Be good for Grandma Moss," I said.

"You look pretty, Emily," Josh said.

"Thank you."

"Can I touch?" Claire asked.

"Are your hands clean?"

She held them out and I inspected them. I extended my arm and she gently stroked my silky sleeve. "Good night." I kissed her forehead and then kissed Josh good-bye. "Mom, there's a frozen pizza in the oven and I rented a couple of movies for the kids. The movies are on the coffee table."

"Have fun," she said.

I pretended not to notice Luke roll his eyes.

This would be the first of many parties we'd attend this holiday season, including Luke's birthday. Thinking about all the events we had lined up seemed both fun and daunting. Inevitably the night of the event I wanted nothing more than to stay home in my pajamas in front of the TV, and the same was true tonight. Once we got there, checked our coats, and entered the twinkling ballroom, however, seeing my coworkers—the women in their glittering jewelry, the men in their dark suits—infused me with a sense of excitement. For a few hours, thoughts of all I needed to get done in the next three-and-a-half weeks deserted me.

As Luke served himself a small plate of appetizers, I began talking to a woman from another office, whom I'd met several times before. I really liked her. She was funny and down-to-earth and every time I saw her at some social event, I remembered how I meant to cultivate a deeper friendship with her and see her much more often than I did. The only problem was, I couldn't remember her name. I'd met her far too many times to ask her now. I thought it began with an "L," but Liz didn't seem right. Linda? No. Lydia? No. Crap.

"How's the new house?" she asked me.

"Oh, it's wonderful. We're pretty much moved in. We're getting new carpet and this weekend we're going to paint, so it's starting to feel like home. How are things going for you?"

"Good. Busy. You know how it goes."

"Are you looking forward to the holidays?"

She rolled her eyes. "I'm looking forward to them being over."

"That's how I feel."

Luke wandered by and lingered behind me. I knew he was there, but since I didn't know the name of the woman I was talking to, I couldn't introduce them. *Go away! Go away! I don't know her name! Move along!* I tried to send the message telepathically, and it seemed to work, because he moved on after a minute or two. I realized this woman, whatever her name, probably thought I was already having marital problems after only being married for a little over three months, ignoring my husband already.

Another woman approached us. "Hi, Lorraine," the woman said.

Lorraine! Her name is Lorraine! That's right! Luke, you can come back now, I can introduce you!

"Hi, it's nice to meet you. I'm Emily."

"I'm Alice." She took a long sip of her drink. It looked like either Sprite or ginger ale.

"Are you having fun?" Lorraine asked Alice.

"Are you kidding? I'm having a blast. It's such a relief not to be at work or at home. It's so nice to be able to dress up and not worry about having spittle all over my blouse."

"Alice just had her third baby," Lorraine explained.

"Congratulations."

"Do you have any kids?" she asked.

I nodded, answering the question affirmatively for the first time in my life.

"How old are yours?" Alice asked.

"Seven and four."

"Aren't those adorable ages?" Alice took another sip of her drink. "I think I like them best when they're infants, though. Babies are a lot of work, and the sleep deprivation is nearly driving me off a cliff, but it's such a magical thing to breastfeed, to watch them sleep, to see the way their eyes drink in the world around them."

"Um, yes, babies are magical." Luke and I hadn't talked about whether we were going to have any more kids. Sometimes I thought I wanted the experience of having my own, but the two I had were nearly putting me in the loony bin, so it was hard to imagine caring for a newborn, too. "You know, I should go find my husband. It was nice meeting you, Alice. Lorraine, it was good seeing you again."

I stopped and helped myself to a plate of fattening foods on my way to see Luke, who was talking to Janice. I devoured the finger foods quickly, not taking the time to taste them.

I walked up to Luke, looping my arm through his and kissing his cheek.

"Janice, hi," I said. "No Hank?"

She smiled. "He said he was going to shop online tonight for some Christmas presents for me. I finished my shopping months ago." A woman after my own heart. No wonder we got along.

"I always try to get my shopping done early," I said. "But it never works out. Like my mom will say she's dying to buy herself this expensive face cream, and she always ends up buying it for herself before I can give it to her. It's maddening."

"Giving is fun, though," Luke said.

I nodded. "I think it's a lot more fun than getting gifts, especially when the gifts you get are crap."

Luke and Janice laughed.

"When I was ten years old," I said, "I foolishly told my family that I liked wolves. I got wolf-themed gifts for the next twenty years even though I was over my obsession with wolves after about four minutes. I have about fifteen sweatshirts with wolves silk-screened on them that are so heavy and thick they make me feel like an astronaut in a space suit. I was ten for God's sake. Those were the days when I could still listen to Michael Jackson without getting nauseous. What did I know?"

We talked a little bit more and then I told Janice that Luke and I had a big weekend of painting ahead of us and said we should get going.

"I'll see you Monday," she said.

"Have a good weekend," I said, waving. Luke and I headed for the door.

"I'm sorry about not introducing you to Lorraine. I've met her at least five times and I could not for the life of me remember her name."

He laughed. "I figured as much; that's why I left."

A man who could pick up my telepathic signals. Now *that* was a catch.

As we got our coats, Luke said casually, "Hey, I told you about that childhood friend Mom wants me to meet for lunch, didn't I?"

"Ah, no. What childhood friend?"

"Oh, just this girl."

Luke hit the elevator button. I studied his expression.

"What girl?"

"Just some girl I knew in grade school."

"What's she like? When's the last time you saw her? Is she married?"

We stepped into the elevator and Luke hit the button for the ground-floor parking garage. He watched the numbers light up as we descended floor by floor. "She was nice in grade school. She moved to South America when we were in junior high. The last thing I heard about her was that she was working in mergers and acquisitions in England. I don't know if she's married."

"Your mother didn't say? When are you meeting her?"

Luke looked at me and smiled. "You're not jealous, are you?"

I tried to feign indignity. "Of course not. I'm just interested. So?"

"So what?"

"When are you meeting her?" I revealed more exasperation in my voice than I'd intended.

"Monday."

Luke hit the automatic unlock button to the car and opened the passenger side door for me. As I was about to step in, he leaned in and whispered, "What are you wearing under that skirt?"

I didn't want Luke to know how much his lunch date bothered me. Just because we were married didn't mean we could no longer talk to people of the opposite sex. I tried to sound coy. "Wouldn't you like to know?"

"Yes, I would."

"Well, maybe, if you're a good boy, I'll let you find out."

I trusted Luke, but I didn't trust his mother. As we drove home I imagined Gwen slipping the rape drug into Luke's drink when he dined with this "childhood friend" (a professional prostitute, no doubt) and this evil woman would have her way with him, take explicit photos, and do her best to break us up. I knew this scenario was ludicrous, but crazy thoughts filled my head until the wine caught up with me and I nodded in and out of consciousness. At some point I vaguely noticed that Luke was carrying me up to bed, taking off my shoes, and slipping off my dress, kissing the tops of my breasts gently.

"Go away," I mumbled as Luke tried to paw at me. "Tired. Sleepy."

The last thing I remembered was the sound of Luke sighing.

Chapter 5

Amber

Being a part of the arts scene in New York had both its good and bad qualities. One of the perks was that I got to hang out with people who were creative and intellectual and interesting. Plus, every now and then I got comp tickets to cool plays, dances, and performances. I once got to see Cirque du Soleil for free and I'd seen more bands and concerts at no charge than I could count. The bad part, however, was the sort of dilemma I found myself in now.

I was trapped in a sparse audience in a dank theater, suffering through my girlfriend Nadia's . . . I wasn't even sure what to call it. It was part performance art and part literary reading and part experiment in torture. I'd spent the last hour jabbing my right thumb nail into my left palm in an effort not to fall asleep. In an audience of twelve, snoring would be a bit obvious. Anyway, the pain in my palm was preferable to the pain of what I was seeing onstage. It had started with a long scene involving Nadia slowly cutting an onion and crying; she then did some sort of interpretive dance with the tears still in her eyes, the point of which was utterly lost on me. Next she did a reading from *The Canterbury Tales* in its original Middle English. Nearly every word was completely unrecognizable. I couldn't remember if I'd enjoyed reading *The Canterbury Tales* in high school (or was it college?), although I suspect not. I was never big on books published before 1900. Anyway, whether or not I liked it when it had been translated into a form of English I could more or less understand, having her drone on in a language that sounded like every word involved hocking a loogie was an exercise in agony.

I'd come out to see her tonight because I support my friends, but I also had another motive: I didn't want to spend the night alone.

I had a lot of girlfriends, but there seemed to be some sort of mystic cycle in which they always got boyfriends at the same time and forgot I existed. If I'd had a boyfriend, we could double date, but since I was single, I made for an awkward third wheel. I'd spent the last couple nights alone in my apartment feeling sorry for myself. Yesterday two of my clients canceled their appointments at the last minute, and seeing $160 plus tip that I was counting on fly out the window crushed me. I knew that everything would be all right in the end, but I couldn't help but wonder how exactly things would turn out.

I was usually pretty good about being on my own. I could entertain myself by dancing around my living room or meditating or drawing or trying a new recipe, but last night I felt acutely alone. My family was far away, I had no boyfriend, and my girlfriends couldn't always be counted on when I needed them. If I couldn't find a way to make it home for Christmas, my loneliness would be even worse because I'd be the only person on the planet eating tomato soup for Christmas dinner. It was a scenario that was far too pathetic to even consider.

A sudden spattering of applause jarred me from my daze and I looked up to see Nadia bowing. She walked offstage and I sat up in my seat, sighing deeply. The bulk of the torture was over. Now came the after-party hell.

I stood, picked up my jacket off the back of the tattered red velour chair, and shuffled my way out to the corridor to wait for Nadia to emerge from backstage. I recognized several of the people milling about waiting for Nadia from her other performances. I smiled and said hi and asked them what they were up to. One woman with short blue hair and a nose ring had a photography installation at a prestigious gallery. Another was in an off-Broadway play. When I told them I'd opened my own massage studio, their expressions fell—I knew they were thinking that I was a quitter and a failure and a sellout because I wasn't acting anymore. The thing was, I used to love acting in high school and college and I wasn't bad at it. But at some point, I'd fallen out of love with it. Even when I got parts, the frustration of dealing with late nights when I had to wake up the next day to go to a day job that actually paid got old. I admired people who loved it enough to persevere, but I just wasn't one of them. It was too spiritually and emotionally taxing. I loved the years I spent onstage and didn't regret them, but that time in my life was over and I wasn't sorry about that, either.

Nadia, ever the drama queen, took her time coming out to build up the suspense.

"Hi."

I turned to see a man I hadn't met before. He was about forty and his hair was just starting to go gray at the temples. He was exactly my type: slightly older, casually but nicely dressed, not at all smarmy-seeming. "Hi," I said.

"You're an actress too, right?"

I shook my head. "Nothing as glamorous as that, I'm afraid."

"A model?"

He'd had me going there for a moment. I couldn't tell you how many men tried to hit on me with that you-must-be-a-model crap. If you were tall and thin and not completely hideous looking, all men pretended like you looked like a model. "Nope. Wrong again."

"So what do you do?"

I didn't need another reaction like the one Scott had given me a few nights earlier, so I decided to be purposely vague. "I'm a small-business owner."

"What kind of small business?"

"It's in the health industry."

"That's wonderful. I happen to be an entrepreneur myself. I own a few nightclubs, a few here and a few in Europe."

"That must be fun."

"It keeps me busy. So, how do you know Nadia?"

"We took some classes together at college. How do *you* know Nadia?"

"I'm her stepbrother. I'm Dad's oldest son from marriage numero uno."

"How many have there been?"

"I've lost count."

I smiled.

"My name is Anton by the way."

I extended my hand to shake his. "Amber."

"It's nice to meet you, Amber. Are you going out with everyone after this?"

I shrugged.

"I hope you do. I'd like to buy you a drink."

"Thanks, but I have a boyfriend."

"My loss. Maybe I'll see you around."

He walked away and I could hear Mom and Emily's voices in my head telling me that I should have given him a chance. Maybe I should have. It would've been nice to go out with a handsome, successful man for at least a few dates, but I could already see how things would turn out: We'd go out a few times, and he would be nice enough but nothing amazing, he'd cheat on me at the first chance he got . . . What was the point? Anyway, I didn't feel that spark. You need the spark.

Nadia finally emerged from backstage. Gareth, a painter, was the first to hug and kiss her and gush about how great the show had been.

Gareth was one of those men who was so gay he was a caricature of gayness, as if he were making fun of being gay. "I *love* Chaucer." He clapped his hands. "The language is so stunning. 'Whan that Aprill with his shoures soote / The droghte of March hath perced to the roote, / And bathed every veyne in swich licour / Of which vertu engendred is the flour;' . . . Oh! I love it!"

When a half dozen or so well-wishers had finished congratulating her on her performance, I took my turn. "Nadia, it's good to see you." I kissed her cheek. From her smile, you could tell that she didn't need anyone to tell her just how great she was—she knew. We'd been friends ever since we'd taken classes together at NYU. We had nothing in common except a mutual appreciation of acting and theater, but when you spent countless nights staying up late and memorizing lines and striking sets with someone, you formed a bond regardless. "You looked great up there." It was the only thing I could think to say that wasn't a lie. She really was a beautiful woman in an unusual, exotic sort of way. Her straw-colored hair, her amber eyes, her tanned skin, and her topaz makeup combined to make her look like she'd been dusted with gold.

"Amber." She squeezed me. "You look great, too. You're coming with us for cocktails, right? I want to catch up on everything that's going on in your life."

"I'd love to but a friend of mine is leaving for Africa tomorrow and I have her going-away party I need to make an appearance at." The truth was that I couldn't spend money on eight-dollar cocktails. The friend-going-to-Africa story just came out of my mouth from nowhere—I still had some actress in me after all. I needed a good story to get me out of going. Nadia would never accept that I was too broke. Instead she would insist that I come anyway and she'd have other people buy me drinks. Then the other people would think I was a mooch and I *hated* that.

"Oh, I'm sorry to hear that, but I understand. Don't be a stranger, 'kay?" With one last parting kiss on the cheek, she moved on to another well-wisher.

I slipped on my coat and went into the frigid December weather. I was twenty blocks from home and decided to hoof it. The fresh, cold air felt good, and it was nice to stretch my legs after having them scrunched up for the last two hours.

I didn't realize that I'd fallen into a trance until the twinkling lights of a storefront window jarred me from my daze. A white glass angel looked right back at me. There was something about her kind eyes and smile—she seemed to want to assure me that everything was going to be all right.

I awoke the next morning knowing what I had to do. The only way I'd ever be able to afford a ticket home was if I got a part-time job. I could use a little extra money anyway. There had to be some kind of last-minute seasonal work I could get. I could wrap presents or work as an elf at Macy's or something.

I didn't have any massage appointments until the afternoon, so I decided to spend my morning looking for work.

I stopped at three bookstores and asked for applications. The first one threw me because it asked for the names and phone numbers of references from previous jobs I'd had. I only worked as a sushi deliverer for about a month before the early mornings nearly killed me (you had to get the sushi delivered by five in the morning; my sleep cycle never adjusted and I went around pathologically tired the whole month). I worked for the writer for several months, but I didn't have his phone number on me. Anyway, Rex Feder was a cantankerous old guy. He liked me, but he was not the gushing or enthusiastic sort you wanted to get a recommendation from. I worked as a waitress at a bar for three hideous months, and somehow I doubted that would help me get a job. And my managers at the software company where I'd worked as an event planner had all been laid off when I'd been canned. I decided to put down my teacher from massage school, Chrissie, and my sister (using Luke's last name only, even though Emily hyphenated her name to Taylor-Garrett). Chrissie was sort of a colleague, and I thought my teacher liked me. At least I had all of their phone numbers.

At Macy's, I asked to see the manager, who was a severely pregnant woman wearing a T-shirt dress. Her outie belly button poked out from her stomach against the cotton dress like a small penis. "Hi, I'm interested in becoming one of Santa's elves," I said, trying not to stare at her enormous belly.

"We've already chosen our elves for the year," she snarled. If I were as pregnant as she was, I'd be cranky, too. Still.

"Oh. Well, here's my application just in case. By the way, I have experience as an actress."

She rolled her eyes. "You and everybody else in New York. Besides, you're too tall."

"Oh. Well, thank you anyway."

I filled in applications at virtually every store I came to. Filling out applications was time-consuming and irritating. When I got my job as an event planner, I felt like I'd really arrived as an adult because I was finally getting a job where I needed a résumé and a cover letter, not an application. Yet here I was thirty-two years old and turning in applications once again.

I looked at my watch and realized I was going to have to rush to make my one o'clock massage appointment when I passed by a little shop called the Cheese Haus. There was a HELP WANTED sign in the window, so I paused.

The store looked like an upscale deli, with a wide selection of cheeses and sausages. It was decked out to look like a little slice of Germany—it had a cutesy, folk-kitsch sort of look, with old German signs on the wood wall and pictures of German castles and smiling Germans hoisting beer steins the size of buckets.

A man and woman were standing behind the counter looking supremely bored. The guy was skinny and wore a red vest and a black hat with a feather in it. He looked dorky in his uniform, but the woman, who had to be in her forties, was in a serious pit of fashion despair, wearing a puffy-sleeved white shirt with a flower design running up and down her right and left sides like suspenders. She wore a flouncy blue skirt and had a ring of flowers atop her head. She could star in a movie called *Heidi's Adventures in Hell.*

"Hi," I said. "I'm looking for a job."

The woman appraised me sternly. "We're not looking for someone who is just going to work here for a month or two. We're looking for someone who's interested in the long term."

"Oh, that's what I'm looking for, too. I was just looking for something part-time, though."

"The position is part-time." Again, she looked me up and down, as if trying to figure out if I was some sort of sausage bandit or cheese thief. "Here, fill this out."

She pulled an application form out from under the cash register and I did as I was told, aware all the while that I was going to be late for my appointment if I didn't hurry. "Here you go," I said with a smile. "I hope to hear from you!" I turned to leave.

"Hang on a second," the woman said. She turned her attention to my application. "Tell me, Amber, why is it that you want to work for the Cheese Haus?"

For a paycheck, you idiot. Do you think it's my lifelong

dream to hawk dairy products? "Well, I really enjoy working with people, and I'm a huge fan of all sorts of cheeses. I could eat cheese all day."

"Do you have any retail experience?"

"Ah . . . not exactly, but I do have experience as a waitress. I'm good at asking people what they are in the mood for and making recommendations based on that."

"When can you start?"

"Uh, well, can you tell me what the pay is?"

"Twelve dollars an hour."

Ugh. After taxes that would be about zero dollars an hour. Still, if I worked here for the next three weeks, I'd earn enough to get a plane ticket home. "I can start tomorrow."

"You're hired."

"Great," I said.

But somehow, I didn't really mean it.

Chapter 6

Emily

Twenty-three days before Christmas

The next morning I awoke early and roused Luke.

"It's Saturday. We have to get painting!"

He groaned and popped a sleepy eye open to watch me as I dressed in an old pair of sweats and a T-shirt.

"You have entirely too much energy," he said accusingly. "Too bad you didn't have any of that last night."

"Yeah, well, sorry." I wrapped a bandanna around my head to keep my hair out of my face. "I'll see you downstairs."

Josh and Claire were on the couch watching morning cartoons.

"Do you want to build a fort today?" I asked.

"Yes!" Josh said.

Claire ignored me. I wanted to be annoyed, but she looked too adorable with her tangle of blonde curls, her pink pajamas, and her pink bunny slippers.

"Well, Daddy and I need to paint today. The living room is going to be covered in a tarp, so I thought we could build a fort in your room. We can bring the portable TV in there and you can watch movies. How does that sound? Claire? Claire?"

"I'll just play in my room," Claire said at last, still not meeting my gaze.

"That's fine. Josh, do you want to build a fort?"

"Yes!"

"Come on, follow me. We'll go to your room and build a special place just for you."

Josh's room was small, and the medium-dark blue walls made it seem even smaller. The color was one I could live with for the time being, though.

Josh had a red race-car bed and I'd assembled shelves for all his books and toys. Unfortunately, despite my best efforts, keeping Josh's room tidy was a lost cause.

I spent a few minutes helping Josh build a fort out of pillows and blankets. Then I brought in the portable TV/DVD player that Luke kept in the garage and popped in a *Finding Nemo* video.

With the kids temporarily occupied, I went back down to the living room armed with the special kind of tape that wouldn't stick to paint. Luke came down the stairs wearing sweats and a T-shirt. "What room do you want me to start on?" he asked.

"This room. Help me move the furniture away from the walls."

When that task was done, I began laying out the tarp, carefully sealing it to the baseboards. "You want to help me start taping around the doorknobs and window frames and stuff?"

"There's nothing I'd like to do more."

We'd forked over twenty bucks for a roller brush that we filled with paint. Using that, Luke was quickly able to get the bulk of the wall covered with base paint, leaving the edges for me. I hadn't counted on just how much work the edges entailed. I wanted to be careful not to get primer on the ceiling or along the window ledges. Even though the edges were taped, I painted cautiously.

With the smell of paint fumes and the transformation in the air, I felt a sense of purpose and excitement and possibility for, oh . . . about a minute. In no time, my arms were so tired I was afraid they might fall off. And this was only the first of five rooms.

Still, as I worked, I felt an assuring sense of satisfaction in beautifying a place that was mine. Finally, for the first time in my life, I was no longer a renter or a tenant but a homeowner.

Unfortunately, the whole time I worked, I saw everything I did through Gwen's eyes. In my head, I heard her voice finding fault with everything I did. The color wasn't right, I wasn't doing a professional-enough job, the texture was out of date . . .

I'd lived with her biting remarks every day for months when I'd been planning the wedding. According to Gwen, the location for the reception wasn't elegant enough, the food wasn't classy enough, the photographer wasn't the very best. Everything I did was wrong. She continued to haunt me even now.

I yawned. I wasn't getting enough sleep. That always happened when I had far too much to do and too little time to do it.

I bet Luke's first wife, Elizabeth, never got so stressed out that she lost sleep. Claire was always asking Luke about Elizabeth and, according to him, Elizabeth could do no wrong. She was patient and kind and artistic and selfless. She was beautiful. She was twenty-eight years old when she died in a car crash. Her car slipped on black ice and she'd gone off the road and flipped over several times. She would forever be twenty-eight years old and wrinkle-free.

Luke and I worked steadily all day but didn't get nearly as far as we'd hoped.

That night, we ordered in a pizza and ate it on our bed because it was one of the few rooms in the house that didn't reek of noxious paint fumes. Opening the windows didn't seem to help the fume issue any—it only made our house bitterly cold.

We brought the portable TV into our bedroom and the four of us sat on the king-size bed with paper plates and napkins like we were having a picnic.

"Please, please be careful not to get any pizza sauce on the bed." I watched Josh bring the pizza to his lips and knew my pleas were futile. The slice of pizza looked about as steady as a whirling top on a tightrope.

"Isn't this fun?" Luke asked. "It's kind of like we're camping."

"My arms are so sore it hurts to bring the pizza to my lips." I could barely keep my eyelids open. Every part of my body was sore. My eyelashes ached. My toenails throbbed. My back felt like I'd recently gone diving off a hundred-story building.

When we'd polished off the pizza, Luke gathered up the empty pizza box and paper plates and brought them downstairs. I fell back on the bed and hoped I'd never have to move a muscle ever again.

"Emily, would you read us a story?" Josh asked.

I looked at Josh and Claire's expectant gazes and forced myself to sit up.

"Sure."

Reading them bedtime stories was one of the things I enjoyed most. It was fun to ham it up as I read different characters' voices, and it was the one time of the day when Claire and I always seemed to hit it off.

"What book do you want me to read?"

"Why don't you tell us a story," Claire said in a tone that sounded like a challenge.

"You mean, make it up?"

She nodded.

"Tell us a story! Tell us a story!" Josh agreed.

"Oh. OK. Come here," I said, indicating that they should come up beside me. They wedged themselves in on either side of my body.

"Come on, let's get you guys all snug under the covers. There we go. All right." Creativity had never been my strong suit. Amber was the artistic one in the family. She'd always been writing and directing plays for the neighborhood kids to perform for an audience of maybe two other kids and a few squirrels. She would make purses out of ripped-up jean shorts or old lunchboxes. She made her own jewelry and clothes. Not me. But how hard could it be to tell a good story, really?

A long time ago, there lived an old woman with a secret. She lived in a large old house that was surrounded by woods on all sides. Sometimes she got lonely in that big old place. It was so quiet in there, the only sounds were the mice in the basement gnawing on the floorboards.

"What's gnawing?" asked Josh.

"Uh, it's like chewing." He nodded, contented with this answer.

Sometimes, just to get out, the old lady would walk through the woods. On the other side of the dense forest, there was another house where a little girl named Clarisse lived. Clarisse had no mother, for her mother had died giving birth to her. Clarisse's father worked all day bringing lumber in from the woods. Clarisse, like the old lady, was often lonely.

The old lady liked to hide behind the trunks of the trees in the forest and watch little Clarisse play. Sometimes Clarisse would run through her backyard flying a brightly colored kite, her long blonde tresses sailing behind her like ribbons.

"What's tresses?" Josh asked.

"Oh, sorry, it's another word for hair." He nodded and I started again.

Every day the old woman would walk through the woods and hide behind the trees and watch the little girl grow up.

But one day, as the old woman hid and watched Clarisse kick a big, colorful ball around the yard, her foot slipped in the dirt. The sound was quiet—just a crunch of a leaf—but at that moment, Clarisse felt the hairs on the back of her neck stand up straight like guards on the march. She sensed that someone was watching her, and when she turned and saw the old lady, her knees trembled with fear. Clarisse had heard rumors about the old lady—all the kids talked about her. Everyone said she was a witch. The schoolchildren were almost as scared of her as they were of the three-headed monster that lived near the lake.

Clarisse didn't want the old woman to know how scared she was, so she demanded, "What do you want, old lady?" in her most stern and assured voice.

"Nothing, child. I'm just a lonely old woman."

I made my voice tremble, as if I were speaking into the blades of a fan.

"I like watching you play. It reminds me of when I was a little girl."

"Well, I don't like you watching me," Clarisse said.

"I will go then, my child." The old woman turned to walk away.

"Wait," Clarisse called. The old woman turned back to her. "Are you really a wicked old witch like people say?"

"It is not true that I am a witch. But I know things. I have certain powers. I could help you, my child, for I know the ways of the world."

"What makes you think I need any help?"

"I know that you are scared of the creature that lives near the lake," the old woman said.

For a moment, Clarisse wondered if the old woman could read her mind. Then she realized it was just a lucky guess on the old woman's part. What small child wasn't scared of a three-headed monster that had long ropes of green snot dangling from all three sets of noses?

"Oooh!" Josh said, laughing. I knew the green snot would be a crowd pleaser.

On their way to and from school each day all the children had to walk by the cave where the three-headed monster lived. The three-headed monster hadn't eaten any children recently, but the word was that the monster could snap at any moment. It might get a craving for little kids once again.

"That's a lucky guess, old woman. Who wouldn't be scared of a three-headed monster?" Clarisse asked.

"I can help protect you."

Clarisse paused. She was definitely interested. "How?"

"Magic."

Clarisse had always liked the idea of magic. She couldn't do any herself but, oh, how she longed to. "What sort of magic?"

"I will give you these three magic pebbles." The old woman opened her palm.

Though Clarisse was several feet away, she could see that there were three colored pebbles in the woman's gnarled hand.

"What's gnarled?" Josh asked.

"Uh, it's like all twisted up, like this." I twisted my hands up and made an ugly face. Josh nodded sagely.

One pebble was blue, one was green, and one was purple.

"Any time you need any help," the old woman said, "toss one of the pebbles into the air. The moment you toss it into the air, think very hard about what it is you need help with. When the pebble lands, help will come to you. But be careful how you use the three pebbles. Once you toss them into the air and they land, they will no longer have any magical powers."

Clarisse eyed the old woman suspiciously. She wondered if it was a trap. If Clarisse got close enough to the old woman to take the pebbles, maybe the old woman would grab her or cast a spell on her. Of course, thought Clarisse, if the old woman really was a witch, she could have cast a spell on her already.

As if the old woman could read Clarisse's mind, she said, "I will leave these here for you. Take them if you wish."

With that, the old woman disappeared into thin air, but the three pebbles remained hovering in the sky just where the old woman's hand had been. Clarisse's eyes grew wide. She'd never seen anything like it. She looked around to see if she was being watched, but she didn't see anyone. Her heart pounded as she approached the pebbles that were floating on air. As quick as a blink, she grabbed all three pebbles and stuffed them in her pocket.

"Well, kids, that's it for tonight."

"What?" Claire asked, her eyes bulging. "But what about the pebbles? What does she do with them? Is the old lady really a witch?"

I smiled, pleased with myself. "All will be revealed in good time."

"But I won't be able to sleep all night. I need to know what happens!" Claire insisted.

"You'll find out everything soon. I'll tell you more another night. Now come on. Let's brush your teeth and get you to bed."

I helped the kids brush their teeth and helped Josh with his pajamas. I tucked him into bed and gave him a hug. The feeling of his tiny arms around me was like getting an injection of happiness—it instantly put a smile on my face.

"Good night, my little Snuggle Muffin."

"Good night, Emily."

I went to Claire's room next. She was already in bed. I felt like we'd bonded a little over the short story, and I was feeling a little high from my small victory.

"Good night, sweetheart," I said, reaching down for a hug. She hugged me back, but her hug was perfunctory, like I was the smelly old uncle she had to force herself to hug to be polite.

It made my heart break a little, a tiny fissure that made my insides feel bruised.

Chapter 7

Amber

Twenty-one days before Christmas

Somehow, in my blind pursuit of a few extra bucks, it didn't occur to me that I, too, would have to wear a ridiculous outfit like the ones worn by the people I met when I first came to the Cheese Haus.

When I showed up for work, Leigh, the woman who hired me, handed me a uniform. I went to the back where there was a unisex bathroom with a few lockers and tried it on. The dress was two sizes too big and yet too short lengthwise for my tall frame. It looked both slutty and sloppy at once.

I peeked out of the bathroom. "Leigh?"

She cocked an eyebrow in response.

"Do you have anything longer? Maybe a couple sizes smaller?"

"That's all we have. Here. Here's your wig. Put this on."

"Wig?" She handed me a blonde wig and a

wreath of flowers. I had so much real hair I had no idea how I was going to be able to hide it all under the shoulder-length wig, but I pulled my long hair into a ponytail and wrapped it in a low, tight bun, and the wig went on all right. The wig only came down to my shoulders but it was so full of waves and curls it was like having a small child draped over my skull. I put the wreath on top of it all, looked in the mirror, and sighed. *It's just until Christmas. It's just three weeks. Think of it as another acting job.*

The thin young man who'd been at the store the other day was behind the counter, smiling as if this were the most fun he'd ever had.

"Hi!" he said cheerily.

"Hi."

"You look great!"

"Mmm."

"My name is Bob."

"Nice to meet you. I'm Amber."

"Amber!" Leigh barked. Unlike Bob, she wasn't smiling. "Come here."

Leigh instructed me to sample various cheeses.

"We have your usual cheddars and port-wine cheddars, but we also have some specialty spreads and flavors like chocolate cheese. Here, have a taste." She cut a chunk of cheese and speared it with a toothpick.

"It's delicious," I said. "How do you two stay so thin around this stuff?"

"Believe me, after a while, the last thing on earth you want to eat is cheese," Bob said, chuckling. I stared at his big white teeth for a moment, wondering if I'd missed the humor, then I realized that the socially appropriate thing to do was smile.

Over the next two hours, I tasted so much cheese a dairy dam blocked my intestines until my stomach bloated out like a balloon from the Macy's Thanksgiving Day Parade. Fortunately, my over-sized dress hid my swollen stomach.

Leigh showed me how to work the cash register and familiarized me with the stock. She asked me to dice up a couple bricks of our smoked cheddar, pierce the cubes with toothpicks, and arrange them on a tray. This was well within my abilities and, as I worked, I tried hard not to think about the fact I had a college degree.

I spent the rest of the afternoon standing out-side the shop with samples of cheese. I smiled at everyone who passed, but many people looked at me as if I were trying to force arsenic down their throats and swindle them out of their retirement savings. *It's just free cheese, people, get a grip.*

"Would you like to try some smoked cheddar?" I asked a passing woman.

The harried-looking woman didn't even say no or shake her head—nothing. I felt somehow both invisible and yet conspicuous.

I stood with my tray and watched the mobs of people bustling by. The mall was a fluffy wonder-land of lights and candy canes and life-size teddy bears. Christmas trees and outsized gingerbread men were everywhere.

Every now and then a person would take a bite of cheese, tell me it was delicious, maybe ask a cou-ple questions to feign interest, and then tell me they'd be back to buy some (and, then never re-turn). The worst were the teenage boys who felt compelled to mock me. Even some adults couldn't help but comment on the costume. Fortunately I

had a background in acting and kept right on smiling. I decided to look at the experience as an opportunity to work on my meditation skills and
focus on being a more Zen and focused individual,
not letting the slings and arrows of outrageous idiots bother me. I'd just pretend to be happy despite the faint homicidal urges whirling inside me.

Remember, there is magic and goodness in the world.
You just have to be open to seeing the miracles.

I was afraid that the miracle here would be for
me to successfully restrain myself from impaling
passing shoppers with cheese-threaded toothpicks.

I was not a huge fan of work of any kind, but if
you had a job where you were forced to wear a ridiculous outfit, that was a special kind of hell. Unless, of course, you were in theater, then costumes
were okay, but even then they weren't always great.
Once in high school I'd had to wear a bee costume
and buzz around onstage in front of all my hormone-
raging peers. That had been traumatizing, but the
humiliation I'd felt back in high school was nothing compared to the nightmare coming my way—
someone I knew! I didn't know him well, but this
was an embarrassing enough gig without the
added horror of bumping into someone I recognized.

When I saw Scott, and Scott saw me, it took us
both a moment to remember where we knew each
other from. It took him an extra second since I was
in my blonde wig and preposterous outfit. He was
with a blonde girl wearing a jacket with fur trim.
The girl was pretty, but she looked like she partied
too hard. She was just a little overweight, and it was
the kind of unfortunate extra weight that didn't
make her curvier, it just gave her face a saggy, too-

many-chins sort of look. She looked tired and her hair was all scrunched up in the back like she had just taken a nap and forgotten to brush her hair when she woke up. With a little rest and a hair-brush, she could have been very pretty.

Scott smiled once he figured out why I looked familiar. God, he was cute. He was just wearing jeans, a pale blue sweater, and a ski jacket, but he looked like a model for American Eagle Outfitters. It wasn't unjust enough that I had to wear this outfit and be seen in public by someone I knew, but that someone had to be a total babe. Why did life work this way?

There was nothing I could do but smile back, so that's what I did.

"Amber?"

"Scott. Hi. Care for a taste of smoked cheddar?"

"I didn't know you worked here."

"I'm just working here temporarily to bring in a little extra cash for the holidays."

"Nice outfit," the blonde girl said with a sneering smile.

I smiled extra cheerfully. "Thank you."

Scott took a cube of cheese and slid it off the toothpick with his tongue. "It's good. This is Stephanie."

"It's nice to meet you," I said. "Would you like to try some?"

She gave me a look as if I'd suggested she sample a plate of earthworms. "No thanks."

"We have specialty baskets you can send home for the holidays," I said.

"My family lives in California and they're always dieting, otherwise I'd be happy to buy some." Scott plucked another piece off of my tray.

"Don't worry. I don't work on commission. I don't actually care if you buy any cheese."

He chuckled. "An honest salesperson. I love it."

The way he smiled at me seemed decidedly flirty, but maybe that was just the way he was. He wouldn't be flirting with me right in front of his girlfriend, would he?

"We have a lot of shopping to do," Stephanie said, suddenly irritated. "We have to get going."

"It was good to see you again," Scott said.

"It was good seeing you, too. Merry Christmas."

I watched them go. They weren't holding hands. They weren't walking that closely together. Maybe they were just friends. I wondered if Scott was working on a play. I could read lines with him. Maybe there would be a kiss . . .

I shook my head. Why was I thinking like this? Scott was way too cute for me. He was obviously the kind of guy who would play the field. He'd say whatever it was he thought he needed to say to get a girl in bed and then he'd dump her.

I looked at my watch. Time appeared to be moving backward.

Eventually I managed to get rid of all my samples. I went inside to help behind the counters. At least inside I didn't feel quite so conspicuous. *Come on, six pm Come on, six pm!*

When at last the next shift arrived, I felt a momentary flurry of excitement that was quickly extinguished when Teresa and Roxanne dawdled in the back while changing into their uniforms. I continued to stare at my watch. It was now 6:04. Did they know what it had taken me to hold out till six? Did they? *Did they?*

When I finally went to the back to change, Bob was just coming out of the locker room.

"Do you want to get a drink?" he asked.

I realized that all I had waiting for me was an empty apartment. The apartment might not seem so empty after a drink or two. "Sure. Give me just a second."

I changed into my street clothes, freed my real hair from its tight bun, and put my uniform in my backpack.

I followed Bob to a nearby bar and we slid into a booth. He smiled at me. "Are you a student?"

"I actually just finished going to massage therapy school. I've started giving massages, but money is just a little tight right now."

A waitress stopped by our table. She was young and had dark hair and silver shimmery eye shadow.

"What can I get you?" she asked.

"I'll have a Long Island Iced Tea," I said. "A big one."

"Me too," Bob said.

"You need menus?"

"I don't," I said.

Bob shook his head.

When she left he said, "Do you advertise?"

I shook my head. "It's all word of mouth."

"Do you work out of your home?"

"I rent a small little space in a building with a bunch of other people. There's an astrologist and a fortune-teller and a few therapists."

When the waitress returned with our drinks, I reached for my wallet. "I'll get it," Bob said. "I always get a bunch of extra cash around the holidays."

"Oh. Thank you, that's nice of you." I took a long sip of my drink.

"You have very pretty eyes," he said. "What color are they?"

Hmmm, that's interesting that he's talking about my eyes. "Hazel." The intensity with which he looked at me was somewhat unsettling. *Calm down. He's just being friendly.*

"What do you do when you're not giving massages or selling cheese?"

"I like old movies. I like to cook. I meditate."

"I like board games. Do you like board games?"

"They're all right, I guess. Really the only time I play games is when I'm home with my family for the holidays. But games are good, sure."

"Do you have a boyfriend?"

"Not at the moment."

"What happened to your last one?"

I thought about Steve. He was a sweet computer programmer who was fifteen years older than me, though he didn't look it. He was nothing but kind to me, always looking out for me. When my closet door broke, he fixed it, when my bike got stolen, he bought me another. I wanted so badly to love him back but there was something about him that I just couldn't trust no matter how nice he seemed.

I shrugged. "It just didn't work out. How about you?"

"My last girlfriend was mean."

"How so?"

"She cheated on me three times."

"Ouch. That is mean."

"You'd better believe I went to Planned Parenthood and got tested after we broke up."

Why are you telling me this? "I'm sorry you went through that. Relationships are tough. You have to find someone you connect with and have things in common with and are attracted to. Attraction can be such a tricky thing."

"I'm very attracted to you."

Oh. Boo. He *wasn't* just trying to be friendly. He was hitting on me.

"Maybe you and I should catch a movie sometime." He gazed at me over his glass.

"Do you mean like as a date?"

"Nah, no. Just friends."

Yeah, right. "Uh, maybe. I'm actually on kind of a strict budget until after Christmas."

"I'll pay."

"That would be too much like a date and I never date coworkers." Lie Number One.

"That's what friends are for."

Why did men make it so hard for you to let them down gently? "You know, I'm really busy until after the holidays. I have a massage to give in half an hour so I really have to run." Lie Number Two. I slurped down the rest of my drink. "It was really good talking to you." Lie Number Three. "Thanks for the drink. I'll see you tomorrow."

"I can't wait."

The next day at the Cheese Haus, I started out working with Bob behind the counter. Leigh had the day off. Apparently she'd been putting in twelve-hour days, so now that I was on the "team," as Leigh said, she was finally able to take a break. Bob looked at me with a goofy smile that sent my gag reflex into high alert.

Ringing up people's orders was no problem, but I lived in dread of having to do a void. Most of the time I was able to get Bob to do an exchange or a void, but sometimes he was busy with another customer and I had to do it myself, with no success. I got the feeling that if the customers had their way, they would happily disembowel me on the spot.

"I'm sorry, I'm new," I kept saying. Though Leigh had shown me how to do a void, I always left out one crucial step, which messed up the entire thing. The customer's increasing irritation made me more nervous and I messed things up even worse, until I had no choice but to call Bob over where he would look at the jumbled receipt and ask me in a tone that bordered on awe, "What exactly did you *do?*"

I was grateful when Leigh came in that afternoon and I found myself once again standing in front of the shop attempting to get people to try our specialty garlic white cheddar when I saw a woman coming toward me like a shark fin when you're all alone in the middle of a large ocean: Donna Bennington, my former nemesis when I worked at the software company as an event planner. Donna was about my age and she'd wanted the job I had, so she reveled in pointing out my mistakes to anyone she could. She somehow managed to do it in such a subtle way she never looked catty. The only good thing about the layoffs was that she got laid off, too. I'd hoped I'd never have to deal with the likes of Donna Bennington again, but if I did, I wanted to be in a place of dazzling success—I would have a huge diamond engagement ring, a handsome fiancé, a great job, and no money problems. I certainly did not want to run into her while I was wearing an ill-fitting Fräulein costume looking like an Alpine farm girl about to go milk some cows.

"Oh, my God! It's Amber Taylor! How *are* you?"

I went temporarily blind by the spotlight beam of her enormous diamond ring. "I'm good."

"What are you up to these days?"

"I just landed a part in a play," I said. The lie came out as reflexively as a sneeze. As soon as the words were out of my mouth, I thought, *Where the hell did that come from?* I hadn't so much as auditioned for a part in years. "The role is about a down-on-her-luck actress who finds work around the holidays working at a cheese shop. I'm here doing research." It was the most ridiculous story ever concocted, but Donna played along.

"Really? That sounds fascinating."

"Yeah. And I've started my own business, which keeps me busy when I'm not onstage. It's going very well." *Shut up. Shut up. Shut up.*

"In event planning?"

"No, I never really enjoyed working in that field."

"I always thought it was a strange career for you. You always were a little flaky. In a good way."

How could you be flaky in a good way? "What are you up to?"

She held out her left hand as I knew she'd been dying to do from the second she stopped to talk to me. "I'm getting married in May!"

"Your ring is beautiful."

"I know!" She giggled. "How about you? Do you have a special guy in your life?"

"Yeah. He's another actor. He's been in a number of commercials and a couple movies." Though I'd never made a cent as an actress, I clearly had no problem playing a part.

"That's great. Well, I should probably let you get

back to your 'research.' I have lots of Christmas shopping to do!"

"Have fun."

I waved and smiled as she walked away. The way she said "research" had a definite twinge of skepticism to it. I knew it was just my wounded pride that was getting to me, and it didn't matter what Donna Bennington thought of me. So my massage therapy business hadn't really taken off yet and I was only getting a few clients a day . . . At least I had direction these days. I had a career, a calling, my own small business. This cheese thing was just for a few weeks.

I decided I'd given away enough samples and went back inside the shop. "Hey, Bob, when's payday exactly?"

"Friday."

"Yes!"

"I wouldn't expect a check, though."

I took my place behind the counter beside him. "Why not?"

"It usually takes a couple weeks for them to get you in the system. So you should get a big paycheck the Friday after Christmas."

"Excuse me? *After* Christmas?"

"Sorry."

My heart sunk. I was no closer to having the money for a plane ticket than I had been before I'd put myself through all this shame and humiliation. How could I have been so stupid? Why didn't I ask when paychecks came *before* I accepted this job? Donna was right: I was a certifiable flake. I couldn't wait to curl up under a blanket at home in my pajamas and cry myself to sleep.

When my shift finally ended, I walked home in a

world that was cold and gray. I trudged up the stairs of my brownstone apartment, my feet heavy as anvils. Inside I kicked off my boots, took off my coat and mittens, and began peeling off my clothes as I made my way to the bedroom. I dug through my dresser to find some sweats to put on and came across a strip of condoms. I couldn't remember when I'd bought them, and a glance at the expiration date let me know that they were best used by two months ago. Great. It was official. My sex life had expired.

With a heavy heart, I walked over to the garbage to toss out the ancient, cobwebbed condoms just as the phone rang. I didn't want to answer it because I suspected it was either Mom or Emily calling to harass me about whether I'd somehow managed to find a plane ticket that I wouldn't be paying off until I was sixty, but they'd just keep calling me until they drove me into an insane asylum, so it was probably just better to answer the phone now.

"Hello?"

"What's wrong with you?"

I sighed. "Hi, Chrissie. Nothing. I'm just in hell. I took a stupid job at the Cheese Haus to pay for a plane ticket home, but I found out that I won't get my first paycheck until after Christmas. What kind of idiot doesn't ask about when she'll get paid before she accepts a job? It's really hard to get through life when you're a moron. Anyway, now I have no way to get home for Christmas, and my mother and sister will probably disown me."

"I think you're being a little dramatic."

"No, Chrissie, I'm not. You don't know my mother. She hasn't let Emily or me spend a single Christmas with my father since they divorced, and they got separated when I was six years old. She'll begrudgingly let us spend Thanksgiving with him every few years, but Christmas is all hers."

"Didn't your sister just get married? Maybe she can spend Christmas with her husband's family and you guys can celebrate the following weekend or something."

"Luke's family lives in Colorado, so both my family and his family will be together. Mom refuses to celebrate Christmas the weekend before or after. She's not usually so illogical, but she's psycho about Christmas. She grew up really poor and now that she's more financially comfortable, she spends every Christmas lavishing gifts on us to prove to herself that she's made a success of her life. It's all about childhood issues she has yet to resolve, I'm telling you. Anyway, I don't want to be by myself for the holidays."

"Oh, sweetie, we'll figure something out. You know I'd lend you the money if I had it, but you know what my checking account is like."

"Thanks, but I wouldn't take your money even if you had it." I thought again about the secret Mom said she wanted to share with Emily and me. She didn't have a good track record when it came to these sorts of things. Once when she'd gone on a business trip, she promised that she would come home with gifts for Emily and me. The "gifts" turned out to be used tubes of generic ChapStick. Not even a good flavor like cherry, but some sort of bubblegum scent that was gag-inducing. On another trip, she did the same thing—talking up the gift she was going to surprise us with on her return. She surprised us all right, by bringing us each a rock. They were pretty, shiny rocks but, hello, a rock is a rock. Still, the optimist in me hoped that this time, the surprise would be worth the anticipation.

Chrissie and I talked a little more, then I hung up the phone. I thought again about the dusty, old condoms. I knew lots of guys who would be happy to sleep with me. Unfortunately, I wanted more than that. I wanted real love, a real connection. That made matters considerably more difficult.

Chapter 8

Emily

Twenty-one days before Christmas

I had to take the day off from work so the installers could rip up the old, faded carpet and exchange it for the pretty, new tan carpet Luke and I had picked out. I felt guilty about taking the time off, but it gave me some time to take care of getting Christmas cards in the mail and getting the house straightened out now that we were done painting. I was relegated to the kitchen to work since all the other areas of the house had the carpeting being ripped out. It was an odd feeling of being a stranger in my own home—I felt like I was in the way no matter where I was and I couldn't relax and be myself with the two large, young installers working away at my flooring.

I sat at the kitchen table with a mug of coffee, several boxes of Christmas cards, and a ribbon of stamps in front of me. The kitchen and bathrooms were the only rooms not carpeted, so I was pretty much marooned here for the day.

There were so many things to worry about when it came to sending holiday cards. I liked cute cards that weren't religious and weren't too Christmasy so as not to offend our Jewish or agnostic friends. I didn't want anything with Santa winking or angels playing harps. I shopped at specialty-card stores because I lived in fear of buying cards at Target or Hallmark and sending out the same thing as a half a dozen other people I knew. The problem with shopping at little boutiques was that each set of twelve cards cost approximately the equivalent of a three-week trip to Europe. Luke and I had a list of one hundred and three friends and family to send cards to, which meant that I needed nine boxes of cards.

I'd once thought that you could never have too many friends, but now that I needed to get holiday cards addressed and mailed, I realized it wasn't true. Luke and I had far too many loved ones. At thirty-five and thirty-four, Luke and I were still young, which meant we still had years and years of making even more friends. By the time we were seventy, I was going to have to start addressing holiday cards on New Year's Day if I wanted any chance of finishing by Christmas. Our only chance was to develop a friend attrition rate that would keep our circle of acquaintances manageable. We could only hope that some of our loved ones died young or that we got in bitter feuds with them so that they became our sworn enemies.

I needed to decide whether to include a little family newsletter or just scrawl a personal message on each card. I personally liked newsletters with Christmas cards because with some friends and family, the only time I heard what was going on in their lives was when they told me in their Christmas letters. Plus, it seemed like a waste to spend all that money on postage and cards and just sign the card *Love the Smith Family,* or whatever.

Writing out a little message on each card would take centuries, so a small newsletter was the way to go. But that meant I'd need my laptop and printer. I made my way through the landmine of carpet installers. One of the guys was an overly smiley redhead whose chipped tooth peeked out every time we passed.

"Excuse me, sir, could I just grab a couple things from the study?"

"No problem."

I grabbed my laptop and brought it out to the table, then returned for the printer and a stack of paper.

I sat down at the computer and opened up a Word document. I paused a moment, thinking about my year. It had been crazy and incredibly stressful but also thrilling. I needed to think of the best way to express this.

> *Happy holidays! As you know, this was the year Luke and I got hitched. We were so happy that so many of you could be there for our big day. It was a beautiful ceremony on a beautiful day.*

Did that make it sound like I was bragging? I'd better say something that made it sound like my life wasn't perfect.

> *Luke and I had a wonderful time on our honeymoon in Puerto Rico. It was beautiful and much less expensive than other tropical locales like Hawaii and the Virgin Islands.*

Good. Demonstrating that money was a concern to us showed that our life wasn't a fairy tale.

We especially liked exploring the caves in Río Camuy Cave Park and the rain forest in El Yunque.

Dogs and cats ran around everywhere and they looked like battered soldiers or pirates with missing eyes and scars and the occasional lost limb. That was the only downside to Puerto Rico—it made me a little sad to see all those scruffy animals in desperate need of a Humane Society. Someday when Luke and I hit the lottery and can devote ourselves to charity work, starting a Humane Society in Puerto Rico will be one of the things I do.

Another exciting thing that happened for Luke and me this year was that we bought our first home. We love the neighborhood and the house has lots of character—meaning it needs lots of work! It's not exactly a crumbling fixer-upper, but Luke and I have been hard at work sprucing the place up and making it our own. It's been tiring and stressful but also exciting.

Luke is still working as a software engineer for the Laboratory for Atmospheric and Space Physics. He writes software to help scientists collect data on weather patterns. I'm still working as an actuary, and our jobs are going well for both of us.

Claire is seven now. She recently started second grade and is excited to go to school every day, as she loves to learn. Josh, who turned four this year, can't wait until he's old enough to go to school with her.

Luke, Claire, Josh, and I hope all is well with you and yours. We wish you happy holidays and a wonderful New Year!

When I was done composing the letter, I printed off one hundred and ten copies. I waited to feel a sense of satisfaction, but I realized it was only the beginning. I still had to fold all these letters into the cards and address and stamp all those envelopes . . . I just wanted to crawl into bed.

As the newsletters printed, I called Amber.

"Hello?" she answered.

"I need your Christmas list. Please. Christmas is three weeks away. I beg of you. I'm going to Dad's the weekend before Christmas, so this is my only weekend to shop. You know me. If I don't get this done soon I'll get so stressed out I'll combust. I'll end up buying you some random crap and you'll be horribly disappointed, and then you'll feel guilty that I spent a bunch of money on junk you don't even like, and then how will you live with yourself?"

"Are you sure you're not secretly a Jewish mother or a Catholic priest or something? Because you are all about laying on the guilt."

"Just do it. I'll talk to you soon, okay?"

"Love you."

"Love you, too."

I hung up and then dialed Mom and gave her the same guilt trip. The kids were easy. They'd basically been waiting all year for this opportunity, and the endless deluge of commercials on cartoons gave them lots of ideas. The grown-ups were a bigger challenge.

When Luke arrived home with the kids, I gave him a long, deep kiss hello.

"Were the carpet guys so sexy they got you in the mood?"

"Ha, ha, very funny. No. They weren't even a tiny bit sexy. I just got lonely being here alone today. Anyway, I just wanted to wish you a happy birthday."

"You already did."

"That was on the phone. I wanted to do it in person."

I gave Josh and then Claire a hug.

"So"—I tried to make my tone casual—"how was your lunch with . . . What was her name?"

Luke sifted through the mail. He looked at me, pausing as if processing what the words I had just said meant. "Carol? Lunch was fine." He tore open an envelope.

"So, what's she like?"

Reading the letter he shrugged. "The same."

"I'm sure she's changed a little since junior high. Is she pretty? Does she have any kids? Is she married? Divorced?"

"She's all-right looking. She's divorced. No kids. I talked to Mom today," Luke said.

Was he deliberately trying to be obtuse, or had lunch with his old friend really not been a big deal? *All-right looking*—what did that mean? I needed more specifics. I couldn't help but imagine her being an Angelina Jolie look-alike. Whenever we saw a movie with Angelina in it, Luke temporarily lost several dozen IQ points. Why was this Carol divorced anyway? I just *knew* it was because she was an uncontrollable sex addict.

"Mom said she'd like us to come down for my birthday," Luke said. "She'll make us dinner."

"She wants us to drive all the way to Pueblo? That will take up our whole day. This is my big weekend to do Christmas shopping. I can't get it all done in one day. And the kids . . . They'll go stir-crazy being locked up in the car for that long. Can't we meet each other halfway?"

"We already arranged it. You know what Mom is like."

Only too well. "I'm sure your mom can understand that sacrificing an entire day with two little kids trapped in the car for six hours isn't exactly convenient. Anyway, it's *your* birthday. She should be going out of *her* way, not us."

He sighed. "I should have talked to you first."

"Yes, you should have." I sighed.

It was his birthday, so I wasn't allowed to get mad. I forced myself to smile.

"Are you ready to hit the town to celebrate your birthday?" I'd been planning for Luke's birthday for the last couple weeks and I wasn't going to let Gwen ruin our fun.

"What should I wear?" Luke asked me. "I mean, should I dress up?"

I smiled. Whatever clothes he was wearing he wouldn't be wearing for long. "Something nice but comfortable."

I had packed each of us an overnight bag—we were going to spend the night at a hotel downtown. In my bag I'd included a strapless black silk merry widow with garters, a black thong, stockings, and black heels. I'd bought the outfit back when Luke and I were first dating but had never gotten the chance to wear it. I'd meant to pack it for our honeymoon, but in all the wedding-day confusion, I completely forgot about it. I couldn't wait to have an entire night with Luke knowing that no little kids might interrupt us, crying about how they'd seen a monster and had a bad dream, so could they sleep with us? When Luke and I first started dating, he would get a sitter for the kids and he'd come over, we'd romp ourselves senseless, and then he'd have to leave early to take the babysitter home. When we knew things between us were looking long term, he decided it was all right for me to hang out with the kids and sleep at his place. It was great to be able to spend the whole night with him, but our sexual exploits were frequently interrupted by either Claire or Josh and it changed the way we had sex. I learned to come quietly and I never felt comfortable getting completely naked, let alone putting on some trampy lingerie. I was looking forward to being able to just let go tonight. On our honeymoon the kids stayed with Mom, and Luke and I were on our own and able to have sex three or four times a day. But it seemed like that had been years and years ago. We'd been much too busy these last couple months to act like proper newlyweds, and tonight we were going to set things straight.

Mom arrived and she said all the right things about how great our new carpeting looked and how much better things were looking since we'd finished painting. She was right. The house was really starting to come together. Luke and I kissed the kids good-bye and begged them to behave. I drove Luke to the hotel. When I pulled into the hotel's parking garage, he gave me a look.

I raised my eyebrows up and down. "Mom will be staying for the night."

He smiled.

I parked and pulled the bags I'd packed out of the trunk.

"Naughty girl," Luke said.

"Not yet. Pretty soon, though, I hope."

The champagne was already chilling when we got up to our room.

"Pour us a couple glasses and get naked. I'll be right back."

I took the small bag I'd packed and went into

the bathroom to change. I looked in the mirror and fluffed my hair. I put on some red lipstick, spritzed myself with perfume, and applied a little extra eye makeup. When I emerged from the bathroom, Luke was lying on the bed naked, holding a glass of champagne. He looked up and his eyes popped. I smiled.

"Jesus Christ."

He was instantly hard, which I must say was rather gratifying. He put the flute of champagne down, never taking his eyes off me as I walked to the bed, hoping like hell I wouldn't trip in the high heels.

"Happy Birthday, honey," I said, crawling across the mattress to him.

"You are so fucking hot." He put his hand behind my head and pulled my lips to his.

We kissed for just a moment, a deep, passionate kiss, and I pulled away so I could look into his brown eyes. I straddled him and wordlessly ran my fingers through his hair.

"I am so glad I married you," he said.

I unsnapped the garters so I could slip off the thong. "Hang on," I said. I stood, shimmied out of the thong, and reattached the garter to the stockings. All the while Luke's eyes ran up and down my body.

"I'm the luckiest man on earth."

For the next two hours, all thoughts of mortgage payments and redecoration and bills and holiday meals were forgotten. Luke kept pulling out so he wouldn't come. "Baby, we've got all night," I assured him.

He shook his head. "Not yet."

When he finally came, he collapsed on the bed beside me. "Damn it."

I lay on the bed with my head resting on my arm, a smile on my face. "I think a more traditional declaration would be something like, 'Oh, God.'"

"Did you come?"

"Four times."

"Four times? You never come four times. Three times maybe."

"I did tonight."

He smiled.

"I'm starving," I said. "We have to order room service. Now."

I picked up the black leather menu from the nightstand and handed it to Luke, who didn't look at it but rather at me.

"What looks good?" I asked. I'd had my fun and now I needed another kind of sustenance.

"You." He kissed my breast.

"I'm serious, Luke, you know how I get when I'm hungry."

He did know, so he sat up and looked at the menu with me. After we'd ordered, I refilled our champagne. Luke took me in his arms and I rested my head on his chest, idly twirling his chest hair with my finger.

"I love you," I said, kissing him.

"I love you, too."

"What made you fall in love with me?"

"Well, you're the most astonishingly beautiful woman I've ever seen."

I gave him a light slap on his chest. "Yeah, right."

"I'm serious. You took my breath away."

Because my cheek was pressed against his chest, he couldn't see me smile.

"Then I talked to you and learned you were smart and fun and kind."

The first months of our relationship had been

otherworldly. We went ice skating, Rollerblading, hiking, biking. We took Lucy and the kids on walks and played endless games of catch, throwing the ball for Lucy to chase and gently lobbing Nerf balls to the kids. We flew kites and went on picnics. Once we even went up in a hot air balloon. But when we started planning the wedding, we had no free time anymore just to have fun. I was looking forward to when the house was done and the holidays were over and we could go back to a life where we knew how to have a good time.

We ordered another bottle of champagne, ate an exquisite meal, and made love again. The night was filled with everything—everything except sleep, that is.

Chapter 9

Amber

Sixteen days before Christmas

All day I stood around in front of the cheese shop, smiling despite my uniform and answering questions about cheese and sausage and what sorts of gift baskets we offered. I spent the entire time thinking longingly of going home and putting on some soothing music.

But when I got to my apartment, instead of being able to relax in the snug warmth of my little home, I opened the door to an arctic chill. I looked at the thermostat. Fifty-eight degrees? I'd be warmer outside sleeping in a refrigerator box.

I trudged back outside my apartment and crossed the hall to my neighbor's place. Diane was a few years younger than me and made her living working for a record company. She earned almost no money, but she got to expense most of her meals and all of her entertainment. Despite the fact that she was broke and worked seventy-hour weeks, she often hung out with megamillionaire music stars.

It was a strange sort of bipolar life—constantly living on the edge of wealth and fame while technically being about as far from wealthy and famous as it was possible to be. I liked Diane, but because she worked so much and was always going to concerts until two in the morning, I didn't see her much, and our friendship hadn't evolved past superficial friendly nods and occasional five-minute conversations as we passed in the hallway.

But I took my chances and knocked on her door and for once she was home—and wearing a winter coat, ski gloves, a hat, and a scarf. She wore her long wheat-colored hair back in a ponytail with a few Bo Derrick cornrow braids dyed blue. With her delicate features and small nose beneath her big fluffy hat, she looked like a little Eskimo child.

"Hi," I said.

She made a facial expression like a snarling lion before it attacked the weakest antelope.

"I take it you don't have heat, either. Any word on when we're getting some?"

"I've already called the super, so you don't need to bother. He said he'd get someone to fix it as soon as possible, but who knows when that's going to be. I was just packing to go crash at a friend's place. I don't think it's very likely that they're going to get it fixed tonight. It's already almost eight."

I sighed. "Yeah. Thanks."

"See you around."

"See ya."

I wrapped my coat tighter around me and walked back over the snow-wet, green-carpeted halls to my apartment. I had several friends who would let me crash on their couch, but the thought of heading back out into the freezing cold to impose on someone and get a crappy night of sleep on their couch was not appealing. It was looking like I was headed for a crappy night of sleep either way, but at least if I stayed here I wouldn't have to go back outside.

I changed into long johns and put on flannel pajamas and wool socks. Over that I put on two sweatshirts, a scarf, gloves, and a knit hat. I pulled my comforter off my bed and wrapped it around me and lay on the couch. Very little of my skin was exposed—just the area around my eyes, really—but it was like an open window that let cold air get through to my entire body. I tried to read a book, but I couldn't concentrate. I felt like I was ice fishing *in* the water along with the fish.

My only hope for getting through the night was to get my mind focused on something other than how cold I was. Maybe there was a captivating movie on TV that would transport me to a tropical spot where I could lose myself in adventure and romance and the scorching sun beating down on hot flesh.

I grabbed the remote off the floor and flipped through the stations, past the cooking channel, past an *E! True Hollywood Story*, past reruns of *MADtv*, finally stopping at a station playing *Paper Moon*, an old black-and-white movie that earned Tatum O'Neil an Academy Award when she was only ten years old.

I was in luck—the movie had just begun. It was the part where they were at Tatum's mother's funeral. As I watched, I thought about how I might be slightly less frigid if I had a little alcohol inside me to warm my insides and dull my mind a bit, but I didn't usually keep alcohol in the house. I didn't keep anything in the house that wasn't immediately necessary for basic survival—there simply wasn't room. Then I remembered the rum Chrissie brought over that night when she came with Scott and the other guys. Still cocooned in my comforter,

I padded over to the cabinet where I kept cans of soup and other emergency items. Eureka! A half-filled bottle of rum stood next to boxes of Tuna Helper.

I'd never gone camping before, but as I attempted to move around while mummified in several layers of clothing and gloves, I suspected that this might be a little of what it was like. Except if I were camping, I'd have a tent, which would at least offer some protection from the elements, unlike this apartment, which seemed to hold in the cold—it was the opposite of the Green House effect, it was the Ice Box effect.

I took a swig of the rum. Though I wasn't a fan of the taste, right away it warmed my throat and stomach.

I returned to the couch trying to remember to be thankful for small favors. Yes, my tiny apartment was turning me into a human frozen dinner, but I also had some rum to warm my chilled bones and a good, funny movie to help me pass the time. I reminded myself that everything happened for a reason, and that sometimes what seems like the worst thing that can happen to you turns out to be the best thing for you. *The universe is looking out for you. Everything is going to be all right.*

Eventually, the combination of rum and laughter helped me push aside thoughts of money and the cold and I passed the night in a suitably contented way.

When I got off work from the Cheese Haus the next day, I came home to a warm apartment that smelled of burning plastic. The noxious fumes were suspiciously toxic in nature.

I was unlocking the door to my apartment when my upstairs neighbor Giselle came clomping down the stairs in enormous furry snow boots. I guessed Giselle to be no more than twenty-three, but she had a grandmotherly quality about her. She was sweet and always smiling, but she spoke quietly and didn't crack jokes. She wore matronly clothes that would be better suited to a plump woman in her fifties than a thin, porcelain-skinned twenty-something.

"Hi," I said.

"Hi. Do you smell that?"

"Yeah. Do you know what it is?"

"Some guy came by today to fix the furnace, but I don't think he knew what he was doing. The furnace isn't supposed to be blasting hot air all the time. You know how you can hear it kicking back on several times a day?"

I nodded.

"Well, the guy said it was just going to be on all the time. I think it might be ready to explode."

"Great."

"I think I'm going to turn it off until we can get someone who knows what he's doing to come take a look at it. I'd rather be cold than have the building explode with me in it."

"I think that's wise."

I opened my apartment door, went inside, and locked the door behind me, feeling grouchy. I was sick of being broke. I was sick of living in a hovel that could explode at any moment. I was sick of life being hard. I knew life was always hard, but there were different sorts of challenges. I wanted the kind of challenges that didn't involve figuring out how I could avoid living in an apartment building that didn't refrigerate me and then threaten to blow up in a fiery blast of flames. I wanted challenges like, "Should I spend my bonus check on a trip to Hawaii or as a down payment on a new luxury car?" or "How can I make my dazzlingly successful and lucrative career even *more* dazzlingly successful and lucrative?" or "Do I want a romantic weekend trip with my smart, kind, sexy husband who is great in bed, or would a romantic dinner at home with candles and wine be even more sensual and exciting?" Challenges like that.

The whir of the furnace suddenly stopped—Giselle had succeeded in her mission. It didn't take long for me to feel the difference in temperature, and then *really* feel how cold it was.

Once again I piled up layers of clothes and entombed myself in my comforter. I lay on the couch like a larva in a cocoon with only my eyes exposed from my blanket. When the phone rang, I looked at the cordless phone lying on the floor in front of me. To get it would mean risking exposing an entire arm to the elements—and thus frostbite. I risked it, shooting my arm out and then bringing the phone back under the comforter with me.

"Hello?"

"Amber, are you okay?" Chrissie asked. "You don't sound like yourself."

"The heat in my apartment went out."

"I'm sorry, hon. You know you can come over to my place. You can sleep on my couch."

"Thanks, Chrissie. Maybe I will. What's up?"

"I was calling you because I have some news."

"Yeah?"

"Do you remember Scott?"

My heart fluttered. "Yeah."

"He hasn't been getting much work lately, so he sold his Range Rover."

"He owns a truck in New York?"

"Right. That's why he sold it. He doesn't need it."

I paused a moment, trying to figure out why she was telling me this. "Yeah? So?"

"So, he sold it on eBay to this guy who lives in LA. Scott's family lives in San Francisco, so his plan was to drive the truck out to LA and then have his brother pick him up and take him home for Christmas, then he'll fly back to New York."

"He's *driving* to California? That's got to be like a fifty-hour drive." I shivered. "Why are you telling me this anyway?"

"Because when I heard what his plans were, I told him about how you were desperate for a ride to Colorado, and he said that it would be great if you could ride with him that far, because then he'd have company and someone to help share the driving."

I sat up, still keeping the blanket wrapped tightly around me. A drive to Colorado with Scott would mean that I'd be trapped in a tiny space with him for at least three days.

Chrissie mistook my silence for hesitance. "I know it's a long drive, but think of it as an adventure," she said.

"It *is* a long drive." I was all casualness and composure. "But that would solve my problem of how to get home for the holidays. Thanks, Chrissie. That was nice of you."

"I told Scott I'd give you his number and that you'd call him."

I wrote down Scott's number on a scrap of notebook paper and hung up the phone, then I spent a good minute or so just staring at the numbers I'd scrawled in blue ink. I wasn't doing anything just now. It couldn't hurt to call him and see what the scoop was. I could always turn down the offer and spend the next week freezing to death in my apartment all alone.

He picked up after four rings.

"Hi, may I please speak to Scott?"

"This is he."

"This is Amber Taylor. I'm a friend of Chrissie Morgan?"

"Yeah. She said you'd be calling."

"She told me you might be able to give me a ride home for Christmas." Of course, that didn't solve the problem of how I'd get back. I could probably get a one-way ticket pretty cheap, and by the time Christmas was over, I would have at least a couple hundred bucks or so of much-needed Christmas cash: Dad could usually be counted on for fifty bucks, as could my grandparents. Mork's siblings usually sent twenty-five bucks. Aunt Lu was the wild card. Sometimes she sent beloved cash and other times she sent gift certificates. Gift certificates were nice in theory, but people didn't understand that when you lived in a microscopic apartment, you really needed to live a minimalist lifestyle and cold, hard cash for paying bills was preferable to a gift certificate that required you to buy things you didn't have room for.

"I'd love it if you could come with me. You wouldn't mind taking turns helping me drive, would you?"

"Of course not." I paused. "I guess I should warn you that I haven't done a lot of driving in the past several years. I moved to New York when I was eighteen and I haven't owned a car since then. I might not be the greatest driver, but I think I'll be good enough to avoid getting us killed in a multicar pileup."

"That's all I ask."

"When were you thinking of leaving?"

"On the eighteenth. Early."

"On the eighteenth? But that's less than a week away."

"I know, but it's going to take three days to get to Colorado, another couple of days to LA, and then another half a day to get to San Francisco. I want to be home in time for Christmas."

"Yeah, I guess that makes sense." I would lose my job at the Cheese Haus for taking off without warning, but I was sure I could find an equally humiliating and low-paying job without too much trouble when I got back. I hadn't bought a single gift and I would have to do laundry and pack. I had things to do and no time to waste.

"Scott, thank you so much. I can't even tell you how much this helps me."

"No, you're the one helping me. And don't worry, all the gas and lodging is on me."

I hadn't even thought of that. "Oh . . . You don't have to do that."

"I was going to have to do it if I went by myself anyway. Trust me, you're the one doing me the favor."

I gave him my phone number and address, and we agreed that he would pick me up at eight on Monday morning.

I hung up the phone and smiled. I *knew* the universe was looking out for me.

Chapter 10

Emily

Fifteen days before Christmas

Love was messy. This morning I woke up to find dog pee on our (brand-new!) carpeting—all the moving and carpet installation must have made Lucy nervous, or maybe this was her little way of saying we were not spending as much time taking her on walks as we used to and she wasn't happy about it. She didn't understand that we were all crazy busy—there was no reasoning with her. I was still in my robe when I discovered the puddle. Luke was already dressed in his hiking boots, gloves, and a hat.

"Snow?" I asked, retrieving the carpet cleaner and a rag from beneath the sink.

Luke nodded. "I'm going to go shovel the drive."

"Thanks, hon."

Not ten seconds after I cleaned up Lucy's pee, I heard Josh crying. "Josh, honey, are you OK?" I sprinted up the stairs to his room. He had puked all over himself. *No, no, I simply don't have time for this today.* "You poor sweetie, come here, we'll get you all cleaned up. It's OK, honey, it's OK."

I kept a smile on my face to let him know that he had done nothing wrong and I wasn't mad at him, but I couldn't help but think about how much easier my life was when I was single, when I only had myself to worry about and clean up after. Of course then I wouldn't have Claire and Josh and Lucy and Luke in my life, and I'd much sooner cut off a limb than trade them in.

I peeled the pukey clothes off Josh and heard Luke come back from outside, his heavy-booted steps stomping around the house.

"Emily?"

"We're up here!" I called.

Luke's thudding footsteps tramped up the stairs. "Woo! It's cold out there."

I looked up at him. He was still wearing his coat and boots and immediately I noticed the wet . . . no, God, no . . . the wet and *muddy* trail he'd tracked through the house. "Look! Look what you've done!"

He cringed. "Sorry."

"Take off your boots!"

I wasn't sure he heard me because he'd just realized that Josh was crying.

"Hey, Josh, buddy, what's the matter?" Luke knelt down so he was nearly eye level with Josh. Josh rubbed his eyes, trying to push the tears away.

"I sick."

"What's wrong? Your tummy doesn't feel good?"

Josh nodded. An unpleasant cable of green snot hung from his nose. I ran to the bathroom, grabbed a tissue, and instructed Josh to blow.

"I'll see if Mom can take him. Otherwise . . ." I cringed at having to take the day off from work. I'd just had to take a day off the other day when the carpet was installed. I didn't want my coworkers to think I was slacking off. "Can you get him dressed? I'm going to call Mom. And take off those boots before you take another step!"

I went to the bedroom, picked up the cordless phone, and fell back on the bed. After speed dialing Mom, I threw my arm across my eyes with childlike theatrics as though if I couldn't see the world, all the hassles in it would disappear.

"Mom, how did you manage to raise two children? This is the hardest thing I've ever done. There is no order to any of this. Nothing is predictable."

"What's wrong, dear?"

"I won the statewide math competition in eighth grade. I graduated with honors in mathematics from a prestigious university. I managed to find true love after thinking it was just an impossible dream, but this, this is too much."

"Is it safe to assume you're having a bad day?"

I sighed. "Josh is sick and I know this is terrible, but I just took a day off of work when the carpet was installed, and I just don't want to deal with this right now. I hate to ask you this, but you wouldn't be able to watch him today, would you?"

"I'm sorry, dear, but I'm meeting with some clients this morning. I could come by after two."

"Thanks, Mom. I'll call you back if we need you. I love you."

"I love you, too."

I hung up the phone and glanced at my watch, which revealed I was going to be seriously late to work. I trudged back to find Luke and Josh. Luke had taken his boots off right where he'd been standing, proving that he did listen to me on occasion. That was something at least. I found him in Josh's room changing Josh into pj's. "Luke, Mom has to work." I buried my face in my hands.

Luke nodded. "I'll stay home with the little guy."

"I not little," Josh protested.

"Of course you're not, buddy. Why don't you pick out a bedtime story?"

"I know you're really slammed at work. I'm sorry," I said.

"Don't worry about it. It'll be nice to have the break. Oh, I cleared the ice off your car so you're good to go."

"You're the best. I'll call you in a couple hours to check up on Josh." I kissed Luke good-bye. His lips were slightly chapped.

"I love you," he said.

I smiled. "I love you." I kissed Josh's too-warm forehead. "Feel better." He nodded sleepily.

I had a brief, evil thought that perhaps Josh would still be sick through the weekend so we wouldn't have to go to Gwen's. Immediately guilt and logic took over, but still, it was one of those moments that made me really glad other people couldn't read my thoughts.

Fortunately, my momentary vile wish didn't jinx the kid. Josh was already feeling better that night by the time I got off of work.

So, with all of us in perfect health, on Sunday afternoon we all bundled up and headed south to Pueblo.

When Amber and I were little, we bickered endlessly on long car trips. For the first time in my life

I could fully appreciate just what sort of hell we put our parents through as Josh and Claire argued for most of the three-hour trip.

"Kids," I said. "I'll give you cupcakes to take to school with you tomorrow if you just stop bickering for five minutes." We hardly ever let them have cupcakes with lunch. They got sandwiches, a piece of fruit, and either peanuts or pretzels, depending. I thought they'd be all over this limited-time offer, but they went right on bickering. "Just five minutes." I rubbed my temples.

My nerves were thoroughly rattled by the time we got to Gwen and Jay's. Gwen and Jay lived in the kind of home meant for entertaining—and showing off. It was large and had a stunning garden with beautiful landscaping. Of course now the garden was in winter mode, but in the spring, summer, and fall it was a spectacular blast of colors. Flowers lined a stone path that wove its way up the front walkway and the theme was continued all around the stone patio in the back that overlooked a small pond with running water and gold fish swimming peacefully.

The interior of the house itself was overly ornate for my taste. I doubted Jay had much say when it came to decorating because the design theme could best be described as Floral Explosion. The couch and love seat were cream-colored with tiny red roses in a tightly crafted pattern. Gwen had embroidered pillows with pink roses. Watercolor paintings of flowers adorned the walls and vase after vase of silk flowers lined all available shelves and tables. In the spring, Gwen cut flowers from her garden and put vases of them all around.

Gwen had a "more is better" attitude toward everything. Seven of her fingers dripped with large, thick gold rings. A clunky gold necklace and two thinner gold necklaces—one with a cross and the other with a diamond-encrusted heart pendant—hung around her neck, and large gold earrings stretched her earlobes down toward her shoulders. Her short, highlighted-blonde hair was teased and hairsprayed into a bouffant as airy as cotton candy. Skeletally thin with long colt legs, Gwen had a prow-of-a-ship mono-bust protruding from her expensive sweater. She wore black pants that showed off her long, thin legs and a pretty cashmere cardigan twin set that accented her frosted hair.

Her home was as overdone as her heavily decorated body. Every inch of shelf not adorned with flowers was heavy with knickknacks.

"How are you, my beautiful grandchildren?" Gwen knelt down and hugged Josh and then Claire. She pulled away from Claire, regarded her carefully, and smiled.

"You're such a beauty, just like your mother."

Claire smiled shyly. She had been a wild, screaming banshee in the car for the last three hours and now she had suddenly transformed into some shy, demure child I barely recognized.

Gwen stood and gave Luke a big hug. I shifted my weight from one foot to the other.

At last she broke away from Luke and gave me a quick, tight hug. "Hi, Emily." She pulled away and gave me an appraising look. "You look stressed."

"I've been busy."

"Too busy to get to the gym, I see." She tittered as if she was just kidding, but we both knew she was right. Then, clapping her hands together and swiveling her head to address the group, she asked, "So, what can I get you to drink?"

"A glass of wine would be wonderful," I said, taking Claire's coat, then Josh's. Jay wordlessly took all of our coats and headed down the hall.

"Luke, I assume you want a Heineken?" Gwen asked.

"Sounds great, Mom."

"And you two, you want Shirley Temples?"

Claire and Josh nodded wordlessly.

"Can I help?" I asked.

"No, no. Have a seat. There are snacks on the coffee table."

The four of us sat on the couch around the coffee table that had an array of cheeses, crackers, nuts, strawberries, and sliced green apples. I helped Josh and Claire make up small plates of food and then served myself. I wasn't particularly hungry, but just now I had the urge to gorge myself.

When Gwen returned with the tray of drinks, I had just attempted to take a bite of a Ritz cracker with a hunk of cheddar on it. The cracker splintered in a cloud of crumbs and in a feeble effort not to get crumbs all over Gwen's pristine couch and carpet, I shoved the entire thing into my mouth. Cracker particles spattered across my lips as I tried to chew. Gwen flashed me a look with her perfectly made-up eyes. I felt like a pig at a trough.

I put down my plate. "Gwen, can I help you in the kitchen?" My tone was overly animated; it was like a cheerleader poltergeist had taken up residence in my body, forcing my eyes to open extra brightly and raising the pitch of my voice a few octaves.

"I've got everything under control."

I turned my attention to Josh. "Careful. Keep the crumbs on your plate, OK?" Josh's Campbell's Soup–kid cheeks were even rounder as he chewed his apple slice with cheese.

Luke gave my hand a reassuring squeeze. "Emily

is doing a great job of decorating the new place. She's never had to paint before, but you'd never know it. She's a natural."

A fissure of worry splintered through me as I wondered again about what Gwen would think of my stab at domesticity. Luke and I had taken a colorful approach to painting our walls, making each room a different color scheme, but we kept decorations to a minimum. Gwen took the opposite approach. Her carpet and all her walls were cream-colored, a cream so light the floor and walls were nearly white. Then she bombarded the place with decorations.

Jay returned from dropping off the coats and he sat next to Gwen on the love seat. Jay was naturally a reserved man, but I suspected he had become even more quiet after being married to talkathon Gwen for the last thirty or so years. He'd never get a word in around her.

"I've always found decorating a home to be such a joy," Gwen said.

Luke picked up his beer and took a sip. "I don't know about that, but we've finished painting and got the new carpeting, which Lucy was kind enough to christen."

I laughed.

Gwen, her sharp features even as a mask, tilted her head and gave me a stern gaze. "Emily, you really shouldn't smile so much. It's giving you crow's feet."

My smile disappeared. There was a faraway part of my mind that knew only a whack job would be against smiling, but a louder voice in my head said, *This is your husband's mother. You must make her like you.* "Gwen, I see you've got all your decorations up."

As with everything Gwen did, her Christmas

decorations were plentiful and pristine. It looked like a ruler had been taken to her enormous Christmas tree to measure the exact distance between the ornaments.

"I find Christmas to be such a fun season."

I nodded. There had been a time in my life when I'd felt the same way. When I was young it had been such a thrill to do something as seemingly insignificant as open the little boxes on the Nativity calendar each December. Mom had always made sure that Christmas was a happy time for Amber and me. Baking cookies, making handmade ornaments, listening to holiday music . . . Back then the season had been magical. After our parents divorced, Christmas got even better because we got two Christmases for every one that other kids got. But somewhere along the way, things had changed.

"So Gwen, how's work going?" I took a sip of wine. As I set down the glass I looked over at Josh. His lips, cheeks, and hair were covered in crumbs. I grabbed a cocktail napkin and reached to clean him up . . . knocking over my glass of red wine in the process. It spilled over the pale cream carpeting in an extravagant gush, making the floor look like Gorbachev's forehead.

Gwen's shriek was so high-pitched all the dogs in the neighborhood must have been driven into high alert. She leapt up and raced to the kitchen as I futilely attempted to absorb the wine with tiny red and green squares of cocktail napkins.

When Gwen returned with some white wine, a spray bottle of carpet cleaner, and a damp rag, she pushed my hands out of the way.

"Gwen, I'm so sorry. What can I do to help?'

"You've done quite enough."

Gwen poured the white wine onto the carpet

and gently blotted the stain out and then used the carpet cleaner to clean up that. I was sure the white wine thing was some trick women who gardened and actually cooked were magically privy to. Around her, the rest of us stood statue-still.

At last Gwen surveyed her work and sighed. "Well, I may need to get the carpets steam cleaned. This is the best we can do for now."

"Gwen, really, I'm so sorry."

"Everyone, why don't we go to the kitchen?"

Two pieces of data immediately sprang to mind: one, she didn't acknowledge my apology and two, she wanted to get us into her dining room where we presumably would do less damage to her home.

Her table settings were impressively adorned with an arrangement of dried blue flowers (I had no idea what kind of flowers they were) and blue candles. Fleur-de-lis gold napkin rings held navy blue linen napkins that rested on china plates with a pale blue flower design. Everyone, even the kids, had crystal glasses. Gwen had made a Thanksgiving-feast worth of food. Garlic mashed potatoes, green beans in mushroom soup topped with French onions, roast chicken, and several dishes whose ingredients I couldn't quite identify.

Gwen asked Luke how lunch with Carol had been. I sat up a little straighter. I focused intensely on cutting up Josh's meat.

"It was fine. She seems to be doing well. She's enjoying her new job."

"What did you talk about?"

"We talked about work. People we used to know from school."

I snuck a glance up at Luke, who was busy chewing a bite of food.

"You're going to see her again, aren't you?" Gwen asked.

He shrugged. "We didn't make any plans."

Gwen pursed her lips and looked down at her plate. She poked at her green beans. "How's work going?"

"It's good. It's stressful but somehow a little boring, too. I've been thinking I need a little more excitement."

I'd been about to take a bite of mashed potato when my hand froze in midair and my eyes snapped over to look at Luke. All I could think was, *Getting married and buying a new house isn't exciting? What kind of excitement are you looking for?*

"Are you thinking of getting a new job?" Gwen asked.

"Actually, I'm thinking about getting a motorcycle."

My fork clattered back down to my plate. "You what?"

"It's something I've been thinking about for a while."

Gwen looked at him with as much shock as I felt. "Luke, honey, those are very dangerous."

"I wouldn't need something super high-powered."

"You don't need something high-powered to get turned into road smear by another driver. At least in a car you have some protection." My voice was shrill.

"You have to get training before you can get a license. I'd be fine."

"Luke"—I laid my hand across his arm—"I had a coworker whose brother is brain damaged and confined to bed for life, and he'd only been going a few miles an hour on his motorcycle. I had an-

other friend of a friend who lost his leg riding one.
I can't even tell you how many horror stories I've
heard."

"Sure, but how many horror stories have you
heard about terrible car accidents? It's dangerous
out there. I've been doing some research on this,
and . . ."

"Whoa, whoa, whoa, whoa." I suddenly felt too
nauseous to eat. "You've been doing research?"

"I've asked around. Looked at some different
brochures."

"Why didn't you ever tell me about this?"

"I'm just looking at stuff."

"Luke, you have two small children," his mother
said. "Do you really think you should be taking up
extreme sports?"

Finally, an issue his mother and I could agree on.

"You know, I'm sorry I brought it up. Let's
change the subject."

Gwen knew how to pretend things were fine,
and she managed to steer the conversation to a
less volatile topic, asking the kids about what they
wanted for Christmas and whether they were excited about Santa coming.

After dinner, Gwen brought out coffee and then
came out with the cake. It had a round bottom
layer and a smaller top layer that were both covered in pale blue frosting that glistened like an ici-
cle. Because Luke worked for a weather laboratory,
Gwen had ingeniously created shapes of the sun
and clouds and a tornado and a crashing wave just
like a chef would create life-size flowers on a wedding cake. It was truly original.

We all oohed and ahhed and declared it too pretty to eat. Luke blew out the candles. I wondered what it was he wished for.

After our plates had been reduced to crumbs and Luke had polished off his second piece, Gwen smiled. "I'll be back in just a second."

When she returned, she was carrying a large, thin, square-shaped present wrapped in shiny silver paper with a giant red bow.

"For me?" Luke smiled.

"For you." Gwen sat down again and looked at Luke expectantly.

Have you ever opened, say, a box of cereal expecting to find something healthy and delicious only to find it oozing with maggots? That was pretty much my reaction when Luke opened his present to reveal an oil painting of a nature scene. The dark brown and orange color scheme wouldn't match any room in our house. I couldn't imagine that it would match any room in any house.

"It's great. Thanks, Mom." Luke hugged her.

"I saw it and I said, 'That's Luke.' You always loved the outdoors."

Luke looked genuinely happy with it. Was he just a good actor, thereby meaning I'd have to forever doubt his sincerity when he thanked me for a gift? Or did he actually like it, thereby meaning he had truly atrocious taste in art?

"We found it at the Ryker Gallery." The sound of Jay's voice was startling. I was fairly certain it was the first thing he'd said all night.

"Oh, yeah?" Luke said. "Emily and I went there for a show a while back."

The four of us adults discussed art until the kids began falling asleep in their chairs. Luke and I thanked Gwen and Jay for dinner and carried the kids out to the car where we buckled them in, their sleeping forms slumped in the backseat.

As we drove, I stared out the window at nothing, my jaw locked. The farther we drove, the more irritated I became with Luke for not noticing that I wasn't talking to him. What good was the silent treatment if he didn't care that I wasn't talking to him?

Finally Luke said, "She wasn't that bad."

"Luke, it's not your mother I'm upset about." I continued looking out the passenger-side window.

"What is it then?"

Now I looked in his direction, but only so I could glare at him. "I didn't realize that you were so terribly bored with your life, that's all. God, Luke, we just got married a few months ago. If you're bored now, what's it going to be like a few years down the road?"

"Emily, don't be ridiculous. It's not you I'm bored with. You, the kids, you guys keep me sane. It's just that I've been working at the same job doing basically the same thing for nine years. I need some new hobbies. It's always been important to me to learn new things."

Annoyingly, that had been one of the things that had made me fall in love with him. He'd been more than willing to take ballroom dance lessons for our wedding. Whenever we went to a museum, he always took care to read every placard beneath every exhibit or painting. He read lots of history and other nonfiction books. He'd taken up guitar lessons after Elizabeth died. But this, this was different. "Why do they have to be hobbies that involve helmets and trips to the emergency room?"

"Emily, you're supposed to support my dreams and goals, remember our vows?"

"That's a cheap shot, Luke, and you know it."

"We never said the dreams and goals needed the prior approval of the other person."

"So you wouldn't mind if I suddenly had a hankering to take up sky diving?"

He paused a moment. "No."

Why wouldn't it bother him if I took up a life-threatening sport? *Ga!* Men were so irritating. "Why didn't you ever talk to me about this? Why did you have to spring this on me in front of your mother?"

"Emily . . ." He shook his head, a put-upon expression on his face.

We didn't discuss motorcycles—or anything else, for that matter—for the rest of the drive home. We carried the kids to their beds, then went to bed ourselves, lying as far away from each other as our king-size bed let us.

Chapter 11

Amber

Eight days before Christmas

Scott promised to pick me up at 8 AM sharp, and I was supposed to be downstairs waiting for him in front of my building, but I was fifteen minutes late getting out of my apartment. I'd packed the night before, which was something of a miracle for me, *and* I'd actually woken up on time. Still, I ran into a few snags that caused the unfortunate delay.

By eight, I was showered and dressed in a T-shirt, jeans, and a long sweater. I even applied a little lipstick and mascara. I studied myself in the mirror: my goddess pendant was wedged between my cleavage. As my fingers traced its contours, I couldn't help but remember when Scott had touched it. I lost myself in the memory for far too long, and by the time I snapped out of it, I was officially running late. I grabbed my bags, locked my door, and bumbled down the stairs carrying my suitcase, backpack, and cooler. I was setting my stuff down on the front steps just as Scott pulled up. There was no place to park so he pulled next to the parked cars and hopped out of his black Range Rover.

"I am so, so sorry, I'm late," he said. He was wearing a tight black sweater and blue jeans. His eyes were more liquid brown than I remembered.

I sighed and affected a look of annoyance. "It *is* really cold out here." I could tell he genuinely felt bad. I smiled. "I'm kidding. I literally sat down a second ago."

"Is this all you have?" He gestured to my stuff as he went to pick it up.

I nodded. "I got small gifts for everyone."

He put my things in the backseat. "You're done Christmas shopping?"

"You're not?"

He shook his head.

"When exactly did you think you'd finish up?"

"I'm sure I can find some things along the way."

"Shot glasses at gas stations?"

"Something like that."

I got into the passenger seat and he got into the driver's seat just as a car behind us started honking for us to move.

"Nice truck."

He put the gear in DRIVE. "Thanks. I bought it in the days when I actually had money."

"I'm sorry you have to sell it."

He shrugged. "It's silly to have a car in New York anyway. I don't know why I bought it. You must have been shocked to find someone who was driving West and could give you a ride to Colorado."

"Not really. I believe the universe is always looking out for you. I believe that sometimes when it seems like things couldn't possibly get worse, you're presented with opportunities you wouldn't have otherwise gotten." His smile made me nervous, so

I kept talking. "I brought some road snack goodies. All the major food groups: Chee-tos, cheese popcorn, Oreos, granola bars, and Pop-Tarts. It's important to get several servings of dairy, oats, and fruit into your diet every day."

He nodded. "It really is."

"I brought water to drink; I wasn't sure what you'd want. I didn't want to buy a whole bunch of soda if it wasn't going to be something you liked, but there's plenty of room in the cooler. We can stop and pick some up along the way."

"You don't drink soda?"

"Not usually."

"I'm a root beer junky; Coke if I need the caffeine."

"I don't like the carbonation. Or the taste, for that matter."

"Haven't you ever heard the expression 'Don't drink the water, fish fuck in it'?"

"I hate to break it to you, sporto, but the soda you like so much is about ninety-five percent water."

"But all those chemicals ensure nothing gross could possibly survive."

"I see you've thought this through carefully."

He stopped at a stoplight, turned to me, and smiled. It was one of those cute and charming smiles I found annoying because it made it difficult for me to think straight.

"You know I'll pay for everything, right? Food, lodging, gas, everything," he said.

"You don't have to do that."

"No, really, I want to. You're doing me a huge favor. By having somebody I can switch turns driving with, I'll be able to get there a lot faster."

"But you're broke."

"I'm not broke-broke." The light changed and

he moved forward, though with traffic at this time in the morning, we weren't getting very far very fast. "I still get residuals and the odd job here and there. My agent has a pretty good lead for me for a modeling job."

"Modeling what?"

"Cars. I'd be in a brochure. I fit in nicely in the role of 'vaguely ethnic but not scarily so.' Anyway, I understand you're struggling on the money front yourself."

"How'd you figure that out? The fact I took a side job looking like a buffoon at a retail establishment so I could sell cheese or the fact that I'm willing to sacrifice three days of my life *driving* to Colorado?"

"Those were pretty much my main clues. I thought massage therapy paid pretty well."

I shrugged. "It would be a lot better if I had a larger client base. Right now between the expense of renting an office and not having enough clients, it's been kind of rough."

"Do you have any corporate clients?"

"What do you mean?"

"Sometimes companies will have masseuses come in once a month or whatever and spend a day or two giving the employees chair massages as a perk."

I considered this. "I never thought of that. It's a great idea. But how would I even go about getting clients like that?"

"The best way is by knowing somebody."

"I don't know anybody in high places at any company. Well, the one I used to work for, but that would be too weird."

"You could contact the HR people—mail fliers or something. My dad is kind of a hotshot CEO, so he knows lots of people in high places. I could ask him to ask them to think about hiring you."

"You'd do that for me?"

"Sure."

"Why?"

"Because you're a cool girl, I guess."

"You barely know me."

"Yeah, but I can tell you're cool."

I turned and looked at the road ahead, trying not to smile. Suddenly my economic forecast seemed a whole lot cheerier. When I got back to New York I would do a better job of promoting myself and I'd make a livable salary running my own business. I'd never have to wear a uniform or sell dairy products again. Everything would be great. I turned to Scott again. "That's really cool of you. Thank you."

"That's what friends are for." He stopped for another light and looked at me in all his actor/model beautifulness. "What's your boyfriend doing for Christmas?"

"I'm currently between boyfriends."

"An attractive girl like you?"

"It's a mystery, I know. What about you? Any girlfriends?"

"I'm currently between girlfriends."

"What about that blonde girl I saw you with at the Cheese Haus?"

"She was just a friend."

"Oh."

He didn't say anything for a minute. "Why don't you have a boyfriend?"

"What do you mean why don't I have a boyfriend? It's not like I can call and order one like I can order up some Chinese takeout."

"You're a pretty girl. I don't see why you wouldn't have a boyfriend. You must get hit on all the time."

"Sometimes I go out on dates. It just never feels right."

"Why not?"

"What do you mean why not? You either connect with someone or you don't."

"What's wrong with these guys?"

"I don't know. I guess I just have a low tolerance for male bullshit."

"What's 'male bullshit'?"

"You know, the usual. The lying, the cheating . . . the putting football, beer, and his friends before his relationship with you."

"Not all guys do that."

"I know." I shrugged. "I just need to find the right guy. Would you mind if I took my shoes off?"

"Go for it."

Without my shoes on, I folded my legs under me and tried to pretend I was at home on the couch watching a very boring television show with a seat belt across my chest.

We drove in silence for several minutes, then Scott punched on the radio. Some thrashing, shrieking noise assaulted my ears. I waited for him to change the station. When he didn't, I asked, "Could we listen to something that doesn't completely suck?"

"This doesn't suck."

"Oh, but I do believe it does."

He hit the dial. A Tori Amos song came on. "How's that?"

"Much better."

"What do you like to listen to?"

"The Indigo Girls, Dar Williams, Norah Jones."

"Hippy music." His grin showed that he was just teasing me, and it bothered me how much I liked it.

"It's not hippy music! What music do you like?"

"I like just about everything. I like the Foo Fighters, Finger Eleven, Incubus."

"Those bands don't suck."

"I'm glad you approve."

"Do you want some Cheetos or cheese popcorn?"

"Cheetos sound great."

"Don't you love foods that turn your fingers orange?"

"You know, I really do."

Was a mutual admiration of processed cheese products enough to base a relationship on? I suspected not, but he was so good-looking I was willing to work with what I could.

We drove for a while listening to music as I watched the city fade into the distance. We drove by run-down warehouses heavily covered in graffiti, playgrounds next to large, gray paved parking lots, and billboards advertising things in Spanish.

"What's the coolest acting job you've ever had?" I asked. Talking with him gave me an excuse to look at him.

He thought a moment. "I was an extra in this shoot-'em-up movie. To be in it, I needed to do all this martial arts training. I really liked it. I keep meaning to take it back up but somehow haven't gotten around to it."

"Have you ever had a fight in real life?"

"One time I was at a bar with a couple of buddies. One of them had long hair, and some idiot started giving him a hard time about it. My buddy made some comment about the idiot's weight or something like that, and the idiot threw the first punch. My friend punched back, and then the idiot's friends got involved, and it turned into this whole bar brawl. I had to help my friend out, of course. The deal with a barroom brawl is that you basically punch anybody you don't know."

"Is that right? I didn't know that. So what happened?"

"We got out of there just before the cops came."

"Were you hurt?"

He shrugged. "Black eye. A couple bruises. No big deal."

"No big deal? I stub my toe and want to be taken to the emergency room and have Vicodin administered intravenously. I could never be a guy."

He smiled. "It's not so bad. What about you? Chrissie told me you're an actress yourself. What's the best role you've ever played?"

"I'm not an actress. I messed around with it a little in high school and college, but I gave it up."

"Why?"

"I wasn't committed enough to it." There was that awful "C" word. Mom and Emily were always accusing me of not being able to commit to a job or a man. "I had fun playing around with acting, but I like almost anything creative. I like to sew and paint and cook. That doesn't mean I want to make a career out of any of these things."

I forced myself to stare at the road so I wouldn't stare at Scott. I held the bag of Cheetos between us. He took a few and I took a few. For a time, the only sounds were our crunching and the crackle of the plastic bag as our fingers reached in for more.

I was the first to break the silence. "It's not an emergency or anything, but if you see a bathroom, I wouldn't mind stopping."

"No problem. I need to pick up some root beer and Coke anyway."

I licked the orange powder off my fingers as best I could. I didn't want him to know just what a Cheetos hog I could be, so I was cutting myself off far sooner than I would have if I'd been alone in the privacy of my apartment.

"The first rule of the road is never to pull off the road unless you see a gas station, restaurant, or hotel. Otherwise you'll be driving for miles," Scott said.

I nodded. "Absolutely."

"What sorts of road trips have you been on?"

"I've driven down to Florida on Spring Break with friends. And when I was—I don't know, eight or something—Mom and Jesse, who is my mom's husband now, took us to Yellowstone. Another year Dad came in from California and took Emily and me to the Grand Canyon."

"Emily's your sister?"

"Yep."

"You two get along?"

"Yeah. I love her."

"You have a lot in common?"

I paused. "In some ways, yes. In other ways, no. Emily has always been this really organized person. I'm *so* not."

"Judging by your apartment, I'd have to agree with you."

I gave him a look. "It's not my fault. I live in a very small space. It's impossible to keep things neat."

I stared at the passing road signs. GAS FOOD LODGING. DON'T DRINK AND DRIVE . . . IN MEMORY OF CAROLINE SUTTY. THINK JESUS. "In some ways my sister and I are a lot alike. We look alike and have the same laugh and tend to enjoy the same movies, but she's always been steady and focused, while I can't keep jobs or boyfriends."

"Why can't you keep boyfriends?"

That was a very good question. The beginnings of relationships were always so great. Your guy was always telling you how pretty you were and how beautiful your eyes were and how good you smelled and how soft your skin was. For a brief moment, you almost believed all the great press about yourself. But then one day you realized that no matter how many nice things he said to you, it was all a crock of shit and the good times wouldn't last.

"I don't know. Just haven't found the right guy, I guess. My sister, on the other hand, found the perfect guy. She's just disgustingly well adjusted. It makes me look bad, you know?"

"I do know. My older brother went right into business with my dad. My brother has a nice house and a wife and a baby on the way. I look like a slacker by comparison."

"My sister, too! Older siblings can be so damn irritating. They set the bar too high."

"Older siblings tend to be overachievers, while younger siblings tend to be performers. I can't even tell you how great it was to land that Verizon commercial. I made more money off those twelve hours of work than my brother made in a year."

"Sweet."

"Exactly."

"And think about this: we artsy types lead more interesting lives than the corporate drones do. We'll be able to cling to those memories when we're homeless and living off welfare. That's something."

"So true."

"You know what was really annoying about having an older sister? She always got to open the Nativity calendar on the first day of the month. And of course you know what that means."

"She got Christmas Day."

"She got Christmas," I agreed in mock bitterness. "By the time I was old enough to figure out her trick, we already knew the scoop about Santa and the jig was up."

"It was the same thing with tic-tac-toe. I could never figure out why my brother always won."

"And when you finally figured it out—"

"He no longer wanted to play."

I nodded understandingly.

We saw a sign for a gas station and pulled off. I got out of the car and did a sort of half-backbend to stretch out my back. My legs felt wobbly as a newborn colt. A potbellied trucker with a belt buckle the size of an avocado smiled at us as we entered the gas station.

Every now and then on the road you get a bathroom bonanza—a clean bathroom with real liquid soap, not the foam-air bullshit, and an actual choice between an air hand-dryer and paper towels. Other times, of course, you get cracked slivers of soap lying soggy and limp as a human tongue in a dish that looks as sanitary as a bumper grill after several hours of highway driving. That, sadly, was where I found myself now. It was a bathroom hell trifecta—the disgusting bar soap, a discolored loop of towel that you were supposed to dry your hands on that had likely been there since the 1950s (as if pulling it around a few inches somehow negated the millions of hands that had been dried on it and made it sanitary), and a toilet with a cracked seat and water pooling around the cement floor. The bathroom reeked of a bubblegum-scented air freshener that had to be worse than the smells it was supposed to mask. Remarkably, there was a small roll of toilet paper, though it wasn't on a dispenser but perched precariously on the top of the toilet.

Scott was already waiting by the truck when I was done.

"Do you want me to drive?" I asked.

"I'm still good, thanks."

As we drove, I closed my eyes but didn't sleep. Scott must have been getting bored or lonely because the moment I reached for my water bottle—showing that I wasn't napping or trying to nap—he said, "Are you looking forward to seeing your family?"

Daylight was in full force now and we drove under the vividly bright sun, which made the road ahead shimmer. "I'll be seeing my mom and stepdad and sister. My dad lives in California with his wife."

"How old were you when your parents separated?"

"Six."

"What was that like for you?"

I took a long sip of water. "It was really hard on my mom. That was the hardest thing—seeing her in so much pain. She's a good lady. She had a really tough childhood but did everything different with my sister and me than her parents had done with her. I met my mom's mom a few times. She didn't die until I was fourteen, but she never sent me so much as a birthday card. She never called to wish us Merry Christmas. And our grandfather was even worse. There were so many kids in Mom's family there wasn't enough money for food. They'd eat powdered milk and powdered eggs and the only produce they ever got came out of a can. Mom and her brothers and sisters were lucky if they got a pair of socks for Christmas. That's partially why Mom is so nutso about the importance of Christmas now. She's a great lady but she can be sort of a pest."

"How?"

"Aren't all mothers pests?"

"I don't think my mom is. She can be a little overly doting. When I have dinner with her, she asks at least twenty times if I've gotten enough to eat as if I'm not a grown man who has been feeding myself and keeping myself alive for years just fine on my own. Speaking of food, are you getting hungry?"

"I could eat."

We waited until we came to a decent-sized town and then stopped at a brew pub for lunch. It was one of those big, airy places with high ceilings and wood floors. A busty young hostess showed us to our table and handed us our menus. As she walked away I said, "You think she's hot?"

He gave her a glance, pretending like it was the first time. "Eh," he said with a shrug.

"See, that's just the sort of thing that makes my male bullshit-o-meter go ding-ding-ding-ding-ding." I opened my menu with a flourish and pretended to look at it.

"What's that supposed to mean?"

I looked up from my menu. "How can you not think she's hot?"

"She's all right."

"She's hot."

"Fine. She's hot."

"See, I knew it. But you wouldn't admit before."

"And why, Dr. Freud, wouldn't I admit that before?"

"Because you think you have a chance of sleeping with me, so you're saying what you think I want to hear."

"Excuse me? What makes you think I want to sleep with you?"

"You said you think I'm attractive. Why wouldn't you want to sleep with me?"

"You think I want to sleep with every attractive woman who crosses my path?"

"Yes. Yes I do."

"You don't think very much of men, do you? We're not complete animals, you know."

"Hmm," I said, dubious.

"You've been burned by a guy, haven't you?"

Before I could answer, the waitress stopped at our table. She looked to be about eighteen years old and her smile was all gums. Her teeth were too small—they were the same size rather than having her front teeth larger than the rest. She wore thick black eyeliner and she ran her fingers through her long processed hair more or less constantly.

Scott gestured for me to go ahead. I asked for a salad (eating all those Cheetos made me feel like I needed to consume something vaguely nutritious); Scott got a cheeseburger with fries.

When the waitress took our menus and walked away, Scott said, "So what's the deal with you and guys? Why don't you trust us?"

"I didn't say I didn't trust guys."

"Not in so many words, but it's obvious you've got some issues."

"You want my dating history or something?"

"Sure. We've got time."

"Let's see," I bit my lip, thinking a moment. "First there was my major college boyfriend. He was a poet and was all emotion and high drama and moody pensiveness. After I broke up with him I said good-bye to artsy types forever. Then there were a spattering of short-term relationships. Most of the time they were *very* short-term. One or two dates at the most. One of the guys was my neighbor in my apartment building. We shared a wall. I broke up with him after six weeks and he acted like we'd been together for six years or something—crying, theatrics, what have you. So of course he had to immediately go out and get another girl to have loud and raucous sex with. For the record, I am all about the enthusiastic murmur in the bedroom to let the guy know he's on the right track." I gestured like an air traffic controller as I said, "Yes, yes, you're going the right way. Don't stop." Scott laughed. "I'm all about the enthusiastic murmur," I repeated, "But *screaming*? That's a little overly theatrical for me. So who does he pick up? A *sca-rea-ma*. I would just lie in bed at night listening to her racket and not sleeping, of course, going, *oh, so this is why you don't sleep with your neighbor*." I mock shot myself in the head with my index finger and thumb. "Lesson learned. I've gone on lots and lots of first dates but I just never seem to feel that spark. What about you, what's your sordid dating history?"

"It's not that sordid. I fell in love with a girl named Rachel when I was nineteen. She was a couple of years older than me and she won a Fulbright scholarship and went over to Holland where she fell in love with someone else. I've dated since then but nothing has really lasted more than a few months."

"Tell me the truth, are you a man slut?"

"No." He paused. "Well, after Rachel dumped me I went through a phase but it was brief." He looked at me, trying to read my expression to see if I believed him or not. "I'd like to find the right woman and settle down. I hate dating."

"Sometimes it's kind of fun, but that lasts about eleven minutes."

"The first few dates can be a rush," he agreed. "But then it turns out you're not as into her as she is with you or vice versa. I hate that part."

"That part is crushing. Really, the only thing I like about it is that it's fun to look into other people's lives. I dated a firefighter once and oh, my *God*, the stories he came home with at the end of the day. Like once he told me this story about some meth-lab bust where these crazed meth addicts were attacking cops and there was gunfire and police officers were shot down and the firefighters were there all night helping the cops secure the place and officers from the Drug Enforcement Agency were there in Hazmat suits—"

"Hazmat?"

"Hazardous materials."

He nodded.

"When I would tell him about *my* day," I continued, "I'd be like, 'well, I massaged a client. He had a really sore lower back. We don't know why it was sore. But it was very sore. Then I went on a walk. Then I ate some yogurt that was very tasty.' The end. It's like, so not interesting." Scott laughed again. "And if you asked me the next day what I did *that* day, I'd be like, 'well, I massaged a client. She had a really sore neck. Boy did she ever store tension in her neck. Then I went on a walk. Then I ate some yogurt that was very tasty.' It's the same thing day after day."

The waitress brought our drinks. A water with lemon for me and a root beer for Scott.

I squeezed the lemon into my drink. "One of the things I hate about dating someone new is that you're always speaking in the conditional tense: you know, '*If* we're still together when such and such concert is going to be, we should go together.' There are so many ifs and unknowns."

"But that's what makes it exciting."

I shrugged.

"Do you think you have a 'type'?" Scott asked, taking the wrapper off his straw and spearing it into his drink.

"Do you mean physically or personality-wise?"

"Both."

"Lately in terms of profession, I've been falling for computer programmers and engineers. They don't have cool stories like cops or firefighters, but their mathematical logic seems to offset my creative flakiness. In terms of looks, I tend to go for taller guys."

"Makes sense. I'm six feet two inches."

"Interesting." I gave him a look, but his expression was blank. "I tend to go for guys with brown or hazel eyes."

"I have brown eyes."

"Yeah." Again I tried to get a read on him and couldn't. "I can see that. And I like guys who are generous and thoughtful and kind. I tend to go for older guys."

He said nothing, just looked at me. "How much older?"

"At least a few years. Not significantly older or anything. I guess I just kind of like guys who are established in their careers—like I said, I'm trying to find someone who can balance me out."

Our food arrived and Scott took the ketchup and smacked a hearty dollop next to his fries and then on his burger. I watched his large hands bring the burger to his mouth, his strong jaw flexing as he chewed. I had to pry my eyes away and focus on my own plate. I felt like a seventh grader with a crush, which I can't say was an entirely bad feeling. If I had to be stuck in a small space with someone for thirty hours, I could have found worse company.

After Scott finished chewing he said, "Tell me a secret about yourself."

"Why?"

"I just want to get to know you."

I had to think for a moment. I took a bite of my salad and then started to speak. Unfortunately, the act of swallowing had encouraged an unseemly amount of saliva to form in my mouth and I watched as the smallest drip of spit wafted from my mouth in a cascading arc and landed on his cheek. Truly, it was a dust-mite size of liquid, but it felt like a tsunami. I may as well have vomited on him. For an endless, pregnant moment, he closed his eyes and smiled. There was nothing to do except laugh and apologize.

"I'm really sorry. Really."

He brushed his fingers across his cheek and smiled. "Don't worry about it."

"I'm really embarrassed."

"Nah. Don't worry about it. You can spit on me all you want."

I laughed out of embarrassment and a deep appreciation that he was laughing, too.

He paid for lunch. We went out to the car and I took the wheel for a while, turning on the radio. The weather forecasted a light snowfall. The sameness and monotony of driving along the highway gave me ample time to daydream about Scott and about life.

Sometimes I felt like I led an imaginary life. For years I'd been taking imaginary Pilates classes—I'd sign up, go twice, and then never actually go again but pretend to myself I was going to go. I imagined having a boyfriend I was deeply in love with. I imagined having a much more successful business and better money-management skills than I actually had. Just now, though, life didn't seem fictional, it seemed real. And strangely enough, I rather liked it.

The first nine hours of the drive weren't too awful, but as we were closing in on twelve hours, my butt was getting sore and my back was starting to ache. I yawned.

"I'm getting tired, too," Scott said.

I'd driven only a couple of hours all day, and he hadn't gotten any sleep. The couple of catnaps I'd taken had had apparently no effect on helping me feel rested.

"We're coming to a town," Scott said. "We'll find a place to stay there."

I nodded dumbly. I was in a zombielike state of exhaustion.

When we finally pulled into town, I scanned the main strip through the city for a name of a hotel I recognized—a Marriott or a Radisson—but all the hotels had names like "Jim's Sleep Inn" or "Mary's Microtel." We randomly pulled into one such place.

The woman behind the counter looked like she must have been born before the Civil War. She was tiny and her upper back was severely hunched. Her white hair and glasses barely came up to my belly button.

"Hi, how much for a room?" I asked.

"Sixty-five dollars for a single, seventy-five dollars for a double."

"Sixty-five dollars *each?*" I said. "We don't want to *buy* the hotel, we just want a room for the night."

She shrugged.

"I told you I'd pay," Scott said, taking his wallet out of the back of his jeans. "Don't worry about it."

"Scott, I won't be able to take the guilt. Let's share a room. If you were by yourself you'd need to get a room anyway. This way I won't have to feel bad."

"You trust me?"

I nodded.

"One room. Double beds," Scott said.

Though the woman had promised us it was a nonsmoking room, the scent of stale cigarette smoke hung thickly in the air. I dumped my bags on the floor and stripped the paper-thin comforter off the bed. The comforter was a dark brown color with orange flowers—you could spill blood, wine, and paint on this thing and it would blend right in.

"What are you doing?" Scott asked.

"I saw on some TV show that the maids almost never clean the comforters, so you have the dead skin particles and grime of hundreds of guests on them. The sheets get cleaned, though."

My mattress looked like the last thing to sleep on it had been a rhinoceros, judging by the cavernous sag in the middle. Lying down on it I felt like a human taco.

"I think we might have had a more comfortable night of sleep in the car," I said. "Can you help me up? I don't have the proper equipment to belay out of here."

Scott gave me a hand and hoisted me out of the sand trap of a mattress.

"Hungry?" he asked.

"Very."

We walked to the diner next door and had a meal of what I believe was gristle with a side of baked sponge. As we waited for our check, Scott rolled his neck and massaged his shoulder.

"Sore?"

"Twelve hours in the car will do that to you."

I nodded. "I can massage that for you."

He looked at me.

"Free of charge."

"You don't have to."

"I want to. It's what I do. Besides, you're hauling my ass to Colorado. It's the least I can do."

When the waitress brought our check, Scott handed her his credit card.

"You don't have to get dinner." I fished through my wallet for some cash.

"Amber, don't worry about it. Seriously, I can handle a seventeen-dollar tab."

"But you're broke."

"Like I told you, you're doing me a favor by driving out to Colorado with me. You're doing *me* the favor, I mean it."

"All right. Thank you. I'm probably going to have to go puke the meal up because it was so revolting, but it's nice of you to pay for it."

"No problem."

We walked back to the room not talking. It felt weird—we were going out for meals and he was paying for everything, and it all felt decidedly date-like. Scott unlocked the hotel-room door and I went into the bathroom and brushed and flossed my teeth, washed my face, and changed into shorts and a T-shirt to sleep in.

I emerged from the bathroom and told Scott to

take off his shirt and lie down. Without a word he took off his shoes and pulled off his shirt to reveal flawless light brown skin and incredibly well-defined pecs and abs.

He lay on his bed on his stomach and I straddled him. I began with my hands on either side of his hips and rubbed my fingers slowly up his back to his shoulder blades. His skin was soft and nearly hairless.

He moaned. "That feels so good."

I swallowed. When was the last time I'd had sex? The exhaustion I'd felt earlier disappeared. I felt suddenly alert and wide-awake, extrasensitive to the sensation of my fingertips against his warm skin.

"You have a serious knot here," I said. I worked on the knot in his shoulder, kneading it down through his muscles. "You're going to need to drink a lot of water after this."

He nodded vaguely.

Normally when I gave massages, there was nothing sexual about it. But as my hands kneaded Scott's flesh, I had an intense urge to lick and suck and kiss his back.

"You must work out a lot," I said.

"Every day."

"Every day?"

He nodded.

I continued rubbing him, sneaking occasional glances to appreciate how his ass and thighs filled out his blue jeans. I didn't know how long I was working on him when he rolled over on his back and looked at me.

"Thank you so much. You are really good at that."

"Thanks."

"I feel so relaxed now." He sat up and his eyes

met mine. The intensity of his gaze made me feel suddenly shy. In his eyes I saw an unquestionable flash of desire. I wasn't sure anyone had ever looked at me that way before—for that instant, I felt beautiful and sexy and confident. It was like looking into a mirror that made me look ten pounds lighter. He leaned in and kissed me. My stomach dropped. His second kiss was deeper, sexier, more exploratory. My nerves exploded like fireworks. I pulled away.

"Well," I said, averting my gaze, "we should probably get some sleep. We want to hit the road early tomorrow."

"Yeah."

I hopped off his bed and went to my own, pulling the covers back and then climbing beneath them.

"Ready for lights out?" I asked.

"Sure."

I turned off the lights and felt more awake than I had all day. Was he just horny and I happened to be the only likely female candidate in the area, or was there a possibility that he was actually attracted to me?

It was the last thing I thought about before drifting into a welcome sleep.

Chapter 12

Emily

Twelve days before Christmas

When Janice asked me again to go to a yoga class with her, my initial thought was, are you nuts? Who has got time for exercise? I don't care if my jeans are about to explode off my body in a cloud of denim dust. My diet plan these days was to eat and eat and miraculously get rich so I could afford liposuction.

But the part of my brain that wasn't fogged in a haze of food addiction and fat consumption knew that I did need to figure out a way to relieve some of my stress and if I could possibly burn off a calorie or two, it certainly wouldn't hurt me any, so I agreed to meet her there.

The class was in Cherry Creek, a swanky neighborhood with big houses, posh boutiques, and a country club. Unlike the rest of Denver, which had metered parking, Cherry Creek had the kind of parking system where you had to walk several blocks to a kiosk, pay by credit card or loose change, get a receipt, walk all the way back to your car, and put the receipt on your dashboard. The machine didn't take dollar bills and I didn't have enough change with me. It did take dollar coins, but I ask you, when was the last time you carried dollar coins with you? I shoved my credit card in, punched the "Add more time" button until I was at two hours, and then hit the "Print receipt now" button. "Take Card Quickly," the machine instructed in urgent, pulsing letters. I tried to pull my card out, but it wouldn't budge. It was like I was in a tug of war with an invisible elf who lived inside the machine. "Take Card Quickly," it flashed.

"Well if you'd fucking let go of it, you fucker, I would."

I finally wrested my card free. No receipt appeared.

"Uh! Print my receipt, you thieving piece of shit! I'm late for yoga! I need to fucking relax and unwind!"

Since it obviously didn't like my credit card, I rifled through my change purse and began feeding the meter quarters. I ran out after five quarters, which only gave me an hour and fifteen minutes. The class was an hour and a half, and if you factored in getting dressed and undressed, I needed an hour and forty five minutes minimum. Nuts. Maybe I had a few more quarters in my car—I tried to keep loose change in the cup holder on the passenger side of the car for just such an occasion. I sprinted back to my car and pawed through the pile of change until I at last retrieved the three precious quarters that I needed, then I raced back to the machine. Just as I was about to feed it additional money, it timed out. Instead of giving me my change back, it printed out a receipt. This receipt would only get me to 10:15. I needed it to go till 11. With these kind of machines, you couldn't explain that you want to add on time starting at 10:15, so unless I wanted to leave in the middle of class to do this whole thing again then, I'd just wasted another buck twenty-five, and I was no closer to being able to leave my car and go to class.

As Amber would say: *I. Am. Not. In. A. Zen. Sort. Of. Place. Right. Now.*

All right. I could deal with this. I'd just have to dash across the street and get change for a dollar. Who needed yoga? It was an aerobic workout just trying to get parked.

I ran across the street to the yoga studio, but there was no person at the front desk to give me change. *Mr. Yogi Person, where are you? I need you.* Why didn't I just stay at home? I could be cleaning, I could be baking, I could be wrapping gifts. Instead, I was working myself up into a frenzy of stress and misery . . . Oh, thank goodness. A lithe, serene-looking young man emerged from the hall.

"Hi, I've been having some issues with the parking meters outside. It's a long story, but do you think I could get a couple dollars' worth of change?"

"Of course."

I got my change, sprinted back out, got a receipt that would keep my car safe for the next two hours, raced to my car, and put the hard-won receipt on my dashboard.

Finally, I could get to the damn relaxation part of this whole stupid thing.

Inside, I put my coat, scarf, gloves, shoes, and socks in a locker, and went to the yoga room wearing only my yoga pants, sports bra, and tank top. I rolled out my mat and began stretching. I stood straight, raised my arms up overhead as I inhaled, then exhaled and bent over, doing my best to bring my nose to my knees.

"Hey, you."

I nearly toppled over when I looked up to see Janice. "Hi."

"How are you?" Janice unrolled her mat. She wore tight black yoga pants and a tight black tank top.

"I just battled with the parking meter outside. It was like a WWF match. I'm trying to find my Zen place."

"Your Zen place?"

"It's something my sister talks about a lot. Ever since she got laid off from her corporate job, she's been into all this yoga, meditation, and self-help stuff."

"I think we could all use a little Zen right now."

The young man who'd helped me out by giving me change began the class. In a soothing voice, he asked us to begin by breathing in and out for six counts. Unfortunately, I was too pathetic to even get the breathing right. I kept running out of air at about count four, thereby either nearly asphyxiating until we could exhale again or having to sneak in a quick breath without getting caught by the teacher—I had to be sure there was no telltale rising and falling of my chest when he was looking in my direction. Fortunately he paced around the room and I could take in the much-needed extra breaths when his back was turned.

He led us through various standing poses and then brought us to Eagle pose, asking us to wrap our right arm under our left and wrap our right leg over our left and sink into it.

I did as he asked and after about ten seconds, the muscles in my legs started to hurt as I strained to keep from falling over. All I was doing was standing on one leg. How could it possibly hurt this much?

"Steady yourself by gazing at one spot on the wall," he said. "Be sure your leg muscles are engaged. Notice if you are standing so all four corners of your foot are pressing into the ground equally . . ."

My standing leg began trembling. How was I supposed to relax and live in the moment when my leg was a fiery burning ember of throbbing muscle?

We ended the class by spending a great deal of time lying on our backs breathing. This was the kind of exercise I was up for.

"Remember," the teacher said as we lay on our backs with our eyes closed, "your attitude is up to you. If you get stuck in traffic on your drive home, you can get angry and upset about it, or you can use your time and energy on the road by choosing to send a prayer out to your loved ones. You can think about what you *do* have rather than what you don't."

I thought about our dog, Lucy, and how eager and cheerful she was when I took her out on a walk each morning and evening. I thought of Josh's smile and bright eyes when we went to the playground or he got some ice cream. Sometimes just looking at the size of his tiny gym shoes gave me a feeling of joy. Thinking about Claire as she talked enthusiastically about what she learned at school each day always brought a smile to my face. Thoughts of Luke smiling at me, laughing with me, making love to me, all made me feel truly blessed.

As I rolled up my mat, I said to Janice, "You were right. I do feel more relaxed."

"See, I told you. What are you up to now?"

"I basically have every single free second of the next couple weeks blocked off with something to do around the house. Last night Luke and I spent hours putting up a new ceiling fan in the kitchen and replacing all the handles on our cabinets with a more updated look. I'm sure we have an equally exciting evening waiting for us tonight. What are you up to?"

"I'm sure it will involve Hank watching *Star Trek* reruns or playing computer games." She slid her mat into her bag. "Are things really okay with you?"

"Yeah. Why?"

"You seem a little down lately."

I exhaled. "Luke and I have been arguing. I never thought being married would be easy, but somehow I didn't expect it to be *this* hard. I thought we would at least get a year or so of newlywed bliss."

"It's the opposite. The first year is the hardest."

"Why?"

"Because you're suddenly living with the person and figuring out things like how you're going to pay bills with your combined salaries. It's especially challenging for you because there are two kids in the picture. And buying a new house is one of the most stressful things you can do, especially when you have to do work on the place."

"I guess." I looked down at my wedding ring. It was a thin band with channel-set diamonds that lay against my engagement ring. When I was single I'd look at married women's rings and be jealous, assuming they must be so happy because they'd found their life partners. I felt like my ring was a fake. It said "I'm happily married" when in fact I was struggling to figure out what the hell I was doing. Wedding rings should be like flags—you should be able to wear them at the equivalent of half-mast when things weren't going well. *There is no reason to be jealous of me, my single girlfriends,* the half-mast ring would say. *Trust me. It ain't easy.*

Or maybe wedding rings could be like mood rings—they could change colors to indicate, "Yes, I have it all, be jealous," or "You get to have sex with whomever you want and I am dying of sexual boredom and would do anything to be free of the bondage of marriage," and everything in between. I didn't think this would catch on with married women, but I could have used such a system when I was single. I still would have married Luke, but I think my expectations might have been a little different.

It was like the first time I had sex. I used to read romance novels in which virgins were always finding rapturous pleasure with hunks the very first time they ever made love. The sex always ended in "waves of carnal delight" that coursed through their bodies. The first time I had sex, I stared at the ceiling the whole time and wondered what the fuss was about. It lasted for what seemed like forever and I just wanted it to be over. Of course, eventually, I figured things out. Now I just needed to figure this marriage thing out.

On my way home, Luke called me.

"Hi, honey," I said.

"Hey, babe. Do you want me to cook dinner? I was thinking I could make chicken marinara and spaghetti."

"That's sweet of you, but there are some dishes I want to practice before Christmas."

"Are you sure? You've been cooking a lot lately."

"And you've been working twelve-hour days.

Don't worry about it." At the beginning of our relationship, Luke and I had always traded off who did the cooking. Neither of us had a particular passion for cooking, but we each had a few dishes we weren't completely ashamed of and we'd each experiment with new things. Whoever didn't make dinner usually ended up doing the dishes. It was a system that worked well for us. Lately I'd been cooking more, not because Luke was working such long hours but because I was trying to figure out what dishes would work well together for Christmas dinner and figure out a system of how I could get everything prepared and cooked so it would all come out of the oven perfectly timed.

"What are we having?" Luke asked suspiciously.

I pretended not to have heard his question—cell phones were very handy for that sort of thing. "I'll be home soon, honey. I love you." I shut off my phone and threw it back into my purse. I suspected that Luke was getting very sick of ham—tonight would be the third time in two weeks that I'd made it—but I needed to perfect my cooking technique before December twenty-fifth. I didn't have time for cooking classes, so I just had to practice.

When I got home, I got started on dinner first thing, running around in a blaze of preparation. When everything was in the oven cooking, I had a blessed few minutes of peace before the kids came down from their rooms and Luke appeared from his office. I went into the living room and fell on the couch, exhausted.

As my body rested on the couch, I glanced around my living room and smiled. The house was really coming together. The freshly painted walls and new carpet gave me a little boost of happiness every time I looked at them. I'd cleaned the house last night, and since the kids had been in school all day unable to mess things up, it was still neat and tidy, which gave me a strange sense of satisfaction. Wasn't the key to happiness to find pleasure in little things? A clean living room with new carpeting and freshly painted walls was all it took to put a smile on my face.

I'd always liked keeping my place clean; I liked things to be orderly, so everything was in its proper place, but I never liked cleaning per se. Now that I owned my own place, however, I got a strange kick out of vacuuming the rug. I'd find myself actually smiling at the gleaming appliances in the kitchen. I cleaned the bathroom mirrors even when they were already sparkling.

I got off the couch to finish off dinner. I paused a moment to look at our new black ceiling fan with four square, art deco–styled lights illuminating our kitchen. I would never admit to anyone just how excited I was over a light fixture, but secretly, I just couldn't get enough of it.

I was so off my rocker these days that I even got a kick out of the distance I had to walk from one room to another. For the last twelve years I'd lived in a tiny one-bedroom apartment. If I walked two steps in any direction I'd find myself in another room. I could never have more than one or two guests over at a time. I'd spent so many years dreaming of the day when I'd have a husband and kids and my own place. (No more needing quarters to do the laundry—yippee!) All of my dreams had come true, except I realized now that I should have been a little more specific in my fantasies—I should have said that my kids would be delightful and well behaved at all times, my husband would never drive me crazy, and I would be able to deal with the stress of having a home and a family in a way that didn't zap me of my sex drive and leave me exhausted from sleep deprivation.

"Ham again?" Claire said when I set the meal in front of her. She rolled her eyes.

Luke wasn't quite so expressive, but I could tell that inside he had the same reaction to the meal as Claire did. They'd be sick to death of every dish well before the holiday ever came.

After dinner Luke put the kids to bed, and I fell into bed myself. Then he came into our bedroom and said, "Hey, you." His eyes had that look that said, *I'm ready for sex now.*

Ugh. I was exhausted, not to mention still slightly sweaty from yoga class since I'd been too tired to shower. I hadn't brushed my teeth, and I was wearing my ugliest cotton workout underwear.

Luke started kissing and pawing at me.

"I'm kind of tired, Luke."

"We haven't had sex in forever, baby."

Hadn't we? "OK, but do it quickly." I pulled off my yoga pants and underwear. He pulled down his jeans and underwear just enough for the necessary equipment to be exposed.

When we started dating, we'd have sex until we were raw and then have it some more. We'd have sex until we could no longer feel a thing. When we'd wake up in the morning, torn condom wrappers would be everywhere and used condoms would have been flung haphazardly aside because there hadn't been any time to throw them into the garbage. But now . . .

Luke and I had only been married for a few

months and already we were having keep-your-socks-and-shirt-on sex. It was the sexual equivalent of stuffing a sandwich from a vending machine down your throat while you were driving—it satiated your hunger but it was far from a gourmet meal.

In the morning, I rushed through showering, then Luke and I played bumper cars with our bodies as we tried to share a bathroom, me drying my hair and him brushing his teeth and shaving.

I was sprinting through the hallway half-dressed, trying to find my white fuzzy sweater (sometimes Claire borrowed my clothes to construct landscapes for her dolls and stuffed animals—the white fuzzy sweater made a good cloud setting and could double as a snowbank, so it was a particular favorite) when I nearly knocked over the kids.

"*Oof!*" I said, stopping myself just in time.

"Emily?" Claire looked up at me with her big brown eyes. Her blonde hair, for the moment, was neat. The second she put on her knit cap, though, something would happen to make her look like a tornado survivor.

"Can you make me a turkey sandwich for lunch? I hate peanut butter."

"Since when?"

"Since yesterday."

"Me, too!" Josh piped in.

I thought of the giant tub of peanut butter I had just bought. This was the mandarin orange incident all over again.

"You want turkey, too?" I asked Josh.

"Cheese."

"OK. One cheese, one turkey, coming up."

After I made them lunch and sent them off with their father, I raced through the living room to finish getting ready for work myself and nearly went headfirst into the wall when I slipped on one of Josh's toys.

When I was single, my house was always perfectly organized. Now the floors were perpetually booby-trapped with toys and trucks and games. I'd straighten things up, have a momentary satisfying glimpse around, walk into another room, and come back moments later to find that Toys "R" Us had exploded in my living room. I'd just cleaned the other night—they must have woken up at the crack of dawn to be able to make such a mess before school. Really, it was almost impressive how much chaos they could create in such a short time. Looking at the mess made my body twitch involuntarily. I was desperate to straighten up, but I had to resist the impulse or I'd be late to the office.

It was actually a relief to get to work. I never thought I'd think that, but today it was how I felt.

"Good morning, Emily," Janice said.

"Hi."

"You look tired."

"Yeah. I didn't sleep much last night."

"The yoga didn't relax you?"

"It did. And then I pulled into stop-and-go traffic and came home to my family and I was wired again."

She smiled and shook her head. "You're going to need to work on that."

"Things will get back to normal soon," I said. At least I hoped they would. I'd thought hosting a wedding with one hundred and fifty guests had been stressful. Now I realized that was nothing compared to preparing to host my first Christmas.

This was a slow time of year at the office. It was something of a ghost town since so many people had taken vacation time. I'd finally be able to get some shopping done—online.

If it were up to me, I would have had everyone's gifts bought and wrapped before Thanksgiving. Two things prevented this: one, this year had been far too crazy for me to be my usual organized self and two, people never seemed to get their lists done until they started Christmas shopping themselves and saw the wondrous array of things available to buy. But I simply couldn't wait any longer. Since I still hadn't gotten lists from anyone except the kids, I decided that I was obviously going to have to write up some ideas myself. I fished out a scrap of paper and a pen from my purse. I thought a moment about what my friends and relatives would want the most, and then began to write.

Gwen: Cyanide so she can poison innocent children and small animals, as I suspect she loves to do.

Jay: Gift basket—chocolate/coffee, etc.

Mork: Sci-fi novel or movie or computer games. But what doesn't he have that he would like? Must ask Mom.

Luke: Tickets to a play. New Neil Gaimon and Christopher Moore novels. Tickets to Avalanche game. DVDs.

Mom: Sweater. Jewelry. Things to relax like bubble bath.

Amber: A million dollars. A new boyfriend. Some focus in her life. Sweater. P.j's. (so she'll stop wearing those awful tatty sweats!) Books on meditation.

Dad: Latest Dan Brown novel.

*Laurie: Gift certificate for a massage (must look
    up spas in CA).*
*Aunt Lu: Gift basket—nuts, dried fruits, cookies,
    etc.*
Charlie & Stu & the Boys: Hell if I know.

Luke and I had a large coterie of friends, but
fortunately we had a rule about not sending presents. A few of my girlfriends might send me a
small trinket but nothing big.

I went to Target.com for the kids. They were
easy to shop for—all I had to do was do a search of
the things they asked for on their lists and add a
few other things that caught my eye. I knew it was
simply a vain attempt to win over their affection
through material goods, but I couldn't help myself. Anyway, it killed me that Santa would get
credit for most of this stuff. I wanted to say everything was from me. (Love me, kids, love me!)

Last year, when Luke and I had been dating,
Luke had bought all the presents for the kids himself. This year, I insisted on doing it myself, just as I
insisted on paying all the bills. I liked being in
charge of things. As a child of divorced parents, I
was always getting shipped back and forth from
house to house, and I hated how out of control life
felt. I'd been trying to make up for that feeling of
instability ever since.

As I searched other sites, I found that for every
gift that looked good for a family member, I
wanted three things for myself. I hadn't bought
any new clothes or shoes in ages. What kind of wife
would I be if I wore the same bras and underwear
for months on end? Didn't I *owe* it to Luke and to
my marriage to get a few things from Victoria's Secret? And surely Luke was getting sick of seeing me

in the same sweaters and pants and pajamas all the time. It was really for his sake that I needed to buy new clothes.

I quickly spent lots of money on loved ones and myself. This was so much easier than battling crowded parking lots and long lines at the mall. How had the world survived before the Internet?

All in all, it had been a highly productive day at the office. I sat smugly at my desk thinking of all that I had accomplished when my cell phone rang.

"Hello?"

"Is this Mrs. Garrett?"

Who the hell was Mrs. Garrett? Oh, man, that was me. "This is she."

"This is Mrs. Crandall at Horizon Montessori. I'm here with Josh and Claire. School closed half an hour ago and I wondered if someone was on their way to pick them up?"

My heart thumped double time . . . Something had happened to Luke. It was his night to pick the kids up. Or was it? Hell, was it my night? What day of the week was it? It was Tuesday . . . no, wait, today was Wednesday. Shit. It *was* my night.

"I'm so sorry. I thought it was my husband's night to pick up the kids. Things have been really hectic lately. I . . . I'll be right there."

I shut off my computer, gathered up my things, and raced out to the car. A thin layer of ice covered all the windows and I attacked the ice with a vengeance, furious with myself. I had once been a woman who was always on top of everything, and now I could no longer even keep straight what day of the week it was.

The second I pulled out of the parking lot I called Luke. Normally I didn't believe in talking on the phone while driving, but this was an emergency.

"Hi, honey," he answered.

"Hi." I exhaled. "I . . . sort of abandoned our children at school. For some reason I thought it was your night to pick them up." Luke didn't say anything so I rushed on. "I'm on my way right now. I'll be there in a few minutes. I'm so sorry."

"Emily, it's all right. It happens."

"Have you ever forgotten your children at school?"

"I've been late a few times."

It didn't make me feel any better. "I thought it was Tuesday. *Tuesday.*"

"Just pick the kids up. Everything will be all right. I should be home in about twenty minutes. Do you want me to pick up some dinner?"

Ooh—dinner. I could get them their favorite meal and smooth things over with a simple trip to McDonalds. The Happy Meal was my Get-Out-of-Jail-Free card. "No, that's OK, I'll take care of it. I'll see you soon."

It was only a fifteen-minute drive to the school, but it felt longer. How many years of therapy would it take for the kids to get over the fact that they had been abandoned, left to wait on a dark, cold night alone with just their teacher in an empty building?

When I pulled up to the school, the hurt looks on their faces broke my heart. They were standing just inside the building behind the glass doors bundled up expectantly in their coats, hot and uncomfortable and irritated. Their teacher stood beside them, wearing an expression that was a cross between pity and condescension.

I put the car in PARK and ran to the kids.

"I'm so, so sorry, you guys. I thought it was your dad's night to pick you up." I hugged them, but they were rag-doll limp. "Mrs. Crandall, I'm so sorry. This will never happen again. It's the holidays. You know how hectic they can be."

She said nothing. Her face said it all. Mrs. Crandall was probably right around my age. An immensely pregnant woman with short, mousy brown hair, she was a sweet, quiet woman who I was certain would never forget *her* children at school.

"Come on, guys. We'll get some McDonald's for dinner. How does that sound?"

Josh looked over at his sister to see how to react. Claire looked at the ground and shrugged. She was frowning; her mouth drooped.

"It's a special treat. Whaddya say?" Nothing. I couldn't even bribe them with fast food. The situation was officially grim.

I buckled them into the car and turned on the kids' SpongeBob SquarePants CD, hoping the music would rouse them, but they remained silent. I pulled into the drive-through and ordered the usual: Happy Meals for the kids, a salad for me, a Big N' Tasty and fries for Luke. The smell of french fries filled the car.

"How about I tell you some more of that story tonight? Remember, the one about the little girl?"

Again Claire shrugged, but Josh seemed to perk up a little.

"Right after dinner."

I slowed for a stoplight, waiting impatiently for it to change, staring at it as if I could will it to turn green. As I stared, the red light became blurry. I became blurry. Before I started dating Luke, I hadn't gone to McDonald's in years and now it was a regular occurrence. SpongeBob sang on happily. Where had my Joss Stone and Jack Johnson gone? Where was Green Day and The Killers?

I came to when the car behind me honked. I drove the rest of the way home feeling dazed. I pushed the button for the garage door opener and as the door slowly rose, I saw that Luke's Insight was already there. "Look. Daddy's home."

Wordlessly, Claire opened the car door and she and Josh slipped out and ran into the house. When I brought the food in behind them, I saw Claire hugging Luke. She was crying. I'd only been half an hour late.

"It's all right, honey, it's all right," Luke soothed. "Let's get some dinner into you. Go wash up, OK?"

Claire nodded, rubbing tear-filled eyes. She ran to the bathroom, avoiding my gaze.

The look of disappointment on Luke's face was almost worse than the look I'd gotten from Claire.

"Luke, I'm really sorry. I feel terrible." I set the bag of food on the table and took off my coat. "It could have happened to anyone. I don't understand why Claire reacted so strongly. I mean it might have been a little scary, sure, but . . ."

"Emily." Luke's tone was grave. "When Elizabeth died in that car crash, she'd been on her way to pick up Claire from preschool. It took an hour for the teacher to track me down at work because I was in an off-site meeting. Claire was stranded at school alone with the teacher for almost an hour and a half."

I pulled a chair out at the table and slunk down into it. Guilt squeezed a tight fist around my heart. "Christ." I buried my head in my hands. How could I mess things up anymore? "The kid must hate me."

"No. It's the opposite. She was scared because she loves you. She was worried that something had happened to you."

"I've scarred her for life."

"She lost her mother in a tragic accident when she was only four years old. The kid is already scarred."

I looked up. "Well, I certainly didn't make things any better, did I?"

"Emily, Claire will be okay. Kids are resilient. She just had a little scare. Give her a couple days. She'll be fine."

I really, really hoped that he was right.

I went upstairs to Claire's room with the bag of McDonald's and knocked gently on the open door. Claire was flipping through the pages of one of her books, doing her best to ignore me. "Would you like me to tell you some more of the story about Clarisse and the magic pebbles and the witch and the three-headed monster?"

She stopped flipping the pages. Without looking at me, she shrugged her shoulders. I took that as a yes and smiled. "Let me get your brother."

I went to Josh's room where he was playing with a toy airplane. "Hey, Josh, whatcha doing?"

"Playing with my airplane. Name ten kinds of airplanes."

I paused. "Well, there are passenger planes and jet planes . . ."

He rolled his eyes. "Cessna. Boeing 747. Boeing 757. Piper Twin Comanche . . ."

"Uh, that's great, Josh. I was thinking I was going to tell some more of the story of the little girl and the magic pebbles." Josh looked up at me blankly. "And the three-headed monster with snot dripping out of its noses."

"Yeah!"

"Come on. We'll go into your sister's room." I took Josh's hand and we went into Claire's room.

Claire moved over on her bed. Again I sat in the middle. Josh snuggled up next to me.

As the kids ate french fries and cheeseburgers, I began where I left off. "So you remember that the witch had just given Clarisse the magic pebbles. Well . . .

Clarisse went home and put the pebbles into her small silk change purse. Her father came home from work that night and made dinner. After dinner, her father whittled a piece of wood into another piece of doll furniture for Clarisse's doll house and Clarisse sat close to him on the couch doing her homework.

"It's time for bed, pumpkin," her father said.

He walked her to her room, tucked her under the covers, and hugged her good night. He smelled like sweat and lumber. Clarisse liked the feel of his soft flannel shirt against her cheek. He told her good night and turned off the lights.

As soon as Clarisse was alone she climbed out of bed and, using the light from the moon to see by, she opened her silk change purse and touched the smooth pebbles. They didn't seem like magic pebbles to her. Clarisse was sure the old lady was as crazy as all the kids at school said she was. Clarisse put the pebbles back into her purse, determined to test them out first thing in the morning. Then she climbed into bed and fell fast asleep.

The next day Clarisse woke up and reached for the pebbles. She took her change purse into the kitchen with her, pulled out one of the pebbles, threw it up in the air, and wished that breakfast would be made for her. The moment the pebble hit the ground, the kitchen table was covered in scrambled eggs, a platter of crisp bacon, toast dripping with butter, a stack of pancakes covered in butter and syrup, and two tall glasses of fresh-squeezed orange juice.

When Clarisse's father came downstairs and saw the incredible feast in front of him, his eyes grew wide.

"What's all this?" he asked.

"I made breakfast," Clarisse said with a smile.

"I guess you did," her father said.

He sat down and helped himself to a heaping plateful of food. At first, Clarisse felt proud of herself for providing her father with such a wonderful meal, but as she watched him eat, she realized that she'd wasted one of the pebbles on something as silly as pancakes, which she could have made on her own. She realized that she hadn't really expected the pebbles to work. But they did, indeed, seem to have magical powers, just like the witch said. What if Clarisse needed them, really needed them for something? Like what if the three-headed monster attacked her, and she'd used up all the pebbles on pancakes? Clarisse decided then and there that she would be more careful the next time she used a pebble.

Clarisse made herself and her father each a sandwich for lunch, then she kissed her father good-bye and walked to school. At school, Clarisse saw her best friend, Susie. Susie told Clarisse that there were rumors that the three-headed monster was on the loose and a whole bunch of kids were going to try and spy on it that afternoon.

"Meet me by the big weeping willow tree at four," Susie said.

Clarisse promised that she would. All through

the day, Clarisse was excited by the prospect of seeing the three-headed monster. Up until today, she'd only heard rumors about it. She was looking forward to seeing the creature with her own eyes. Though she feared it, there was something thrilling about knowing that she could face her fears and if anything went wrong, she had magic pebbles to protect her. At four that afternoon, Clarisse walked to the weeping willow tree and waited for her friend. After several minutes, Susie still hadn't shown. First Clarisse was mad. Had some other kids asked Susie to go to the lake with them? Had she decided to go with them instead? Or had she chickened out completely? Then Clarisse began to worry. Maybe something had happened to Susie. Maybe the three-headed monster had gotten out and . . .

Stealthily, I took my elbow and banged it against Claire's backboard just as I said:

"What was that?" Clarisse said.

Both Claire and Josh jumped, their eyes wide. I smiled: mission accomplished.

Clarisse looked around but she couldn't see what had caused the noise. It was getting dark out, and Clarisse was scared. She picked up her schoolbags and ran home through the dark forest.

When Clarisse got to school the next morning she saw Susie with a group of other kids. Clarisse marched up to Susie and asked her where she'd been last night.

"What do you mean where was I last night? Where were *you*?"

"I waited by the weeping willow tree for hours for you."

"I told you to meet me by the lake. Why would you meet me by the weeping willow? That's not where the monster lives."

"But you said!"

"I did not. You were just too scared to see the monster like the rest of us did."

The other kids laughed at Clarisse; she was outraged.

"I am not scared to see the monster. I *want* to see the monster."

The kids began taunting Clarisse that she was a scaredy-cat.

In a sing-songy voice I said,

"Clarisse is a scaredy-cat, Clarisse is a scaredy-cat."

"Am not!' she protested, but they wouldn't stop.

"Clarisse is a scaredy-cat, Clarisse is a scaredy-cat."

Susie was the loudest of them all. Clarisse felt so angry at Susie, so betrayed, that without thinking of the consequences, Clarisse pulled out another pebble from her pocket, threw it up in the air, and wished Susie would just shut up. Clarisse was as stunned as Susie when Susie's lips were instantly sewn shut.

Claire's eyebrows jumped up as she clapped her hands over her mouth.

The other kids all gathered around Susie. She tried to talk but found that she couldn't. She couldn't even open her mouth. All the children murmured excitedly amongst themselves.

"You're a witch, too, just like that old lady!" one of the boys said to Clarisse.

Soon, everyone was chanting, "Witch. Witch. Witch. Witch."

Clarisse raised one hand to silence them. "I am not a witch. But the witch is my friend."

Quickly all the children fell silent. No one wanted to tease a girl who was friends with the witch. For a moment, Clarisse savored the feeling of being feared and in control, but she realized that if she didn't help Susie with her problem, Clarisse would probably spend the rest of her life in detention. So, she pulled the final pebble out of her pocket, threw it in the air, and wished that Susie could talk again. In an instant, Susie's lips opened, and she let out a blood-curdling scream. Clarisse gave her a cautionary look. When a teacher came running out to see what was the matter, Susie just looked at the ground.

"Sorry, Mr. Horn, I thought I saw a snake, but I just imagined it."

Mr. Horn sighed. "All this talk of that mythic monster is putting everyone on edge. Come inside, kids, it's time for school."

All day long, everyone was extra nice to Clarisse. She didn't mind it one bit. But when she walked out the doors at the end of the day to go home, the kids she normally walked home with weren't there waiting for her as they usually were. She waited for several minutes, but neither Susie, nor Charles, nor Karen ever showed up. Clarisse walked home alone. As she walked through the thick, dark woods, she heard yelling and shouting and screaming in the distance. She could see the flashing lights of an ambulance and a police car. Without thinking, Clarisse ran toward the commotion. As she ran, she wondered if the three-headed monster had struck again for the first time in years, but when she was close enough to see what had happened, she realized it was much worse than that.

Her father was trapped under a huge tree, and no one could get it off of him. Clarisse screamed and began crying. She was furious with herself for having used up all the pebbles on such silly things. Through her veil of tears, Clarisse saw the witch appear and smile at her. The witch floated through the air and disappeared in an instant, making herself completely invisible. It happened so quickly Clarisse wondered if she'd really seen the witch at all or if she'd conjured the image in her mind. But when the huge tree rolled off her father, Clarisse knew it was the witch's doing. Clarisse ran toward her father. She could see that his legs were bloody and mangled, a horrible look of pain twisted his face. Just before Clarisse reached him, his expression changed from pain to confusion. His legs were still bloody, but suddenly they were no longer twisted at strange angles. Clarisse threw her arms around him. He squeezed her right back, and then he tried to stand up.

Around them, paramedics and fellow woodsmen and police officers were all shouting for her father not to move. When he stood up and walked, everyone gasped in shock. Clarisse knew the witch had come to her father's rescue and fixed his legs before anyone knew what happened.

I could see that Josh's eyes were getting heavy; he was fighting to stay awake. Besides, I had no clue what happened next. "That's all for tonight, kids."

"But why is the witch helping Clarisse?" Claire asked. "How did the witch become a witch?"

"Why don't you think about that? We'll talk about it more another night. I'll finish the story then." I gathered up the trash from dinner and tossed it into the garbage. I took Josh in my arms, holding him to my hip. With my free hand I helped tuck Claire under her covers and I gave her a kiss on the forehead. "Good night, Claire. Sleep tight."

"Good night, Emily." Her eyes looked into mine. She no longer looked angry. I didn't know if I was imagining it, but I thought I saw love in her eyes.

I paused a moment in the doorway. She closed her eyes. I smiled and shut off the lights.

Chapter 13

Amber

Seven days before Christmas

I awoke when a ribbon of sunlight hit my eyelids like a laser. Scott was at the window, pulling the curtain back an inch or two. I crawled out of bed and joined him at the window.

Snow was coming down, floating gently, twinkling in the sun like fairies' wings. The earth was covered like icing on a wedding cake.

"It's beautiful." My voice was still husky with sleep.

Scott nodded.

"You're not irritated by it? It might put us off schedule," I said.

He shrugged. "I don't know. It's almost Christmas. Snow feels right."

I showered and changed, then Scott showered. I usually let my hair air dry, but it was so long and thick that today I blew it dry partway to help it along because I didn't want it to freeze when we went outside. I saw Scott in the reflection of the mirror watching me dry my hair. It felt strange to share a room with a man I was sexually attracted to but not having sex with. I'd had about twenty sex fantasies about him this morning as I tossed between slumber and wakefulness, and that made things even weirder. I couldn't stop thinking of the way he'd kissed me last night. I could still feel the sensation of his lips on mine.

"You hungry?" he asked as I made one last check around the hotel room to see if we'd left anything.

"Yeah. But I don't want to go back to that awful diner. Let's take our chances on the road."

He nodded.

We never did find a place to stop for breakfast, so we munched on cheese popcorn and drank gas station coffee until we could stop for lunch. As we drove, fragmented images of our kisses flashed through my mind. Occasionally Scott would look over at me and smile. It was such a knowing and mischievous smile—I wondered if he could read my mind or if my desire for him was just that obvious.

I tried to mask my feelings for him by casually chatting. We'd covered a lot of the getting-to-know-each-other basics the day before, so today we shared random stories about our lives. It was all very stream-of-consciousness and strangely therapeutic.

Ordinarily if I was with a guy as attractive as Scott I would stutter and stumble over my words, but with Scott I felt perfectly comfortable just being myself.

I wondered how old he was. He looked so young; I was hoping it was a trick of Botox and whatever else Hollywood types did to stay looking young until well into their sixties. Even though he was out of my league, I harbored the hope that we might have a chance for something more than friendship and a few kisses.

In the afternoon I took my turn at the wheel. As I drove, I thought about how odd it would be after this trip. I hadn't talked to a guy like this in a long time. Scott was buff and masculine but he also felt comfortable sharing about himself, which I was sure was a product of him being an actor. In every acting class I'd ever taken, all we ever seemed to do was get in touch with our emotions, drawing on past experiences. I found his mix of masculinity and sensitivity incredibly appealing. But I knew that after three days of getting to know each other, we would go back to New York and never see each other again. Maybe we'd go out for coffee a couple of times, but then we'd stop calling and the closeness I felt now would quickly disappear. I hated that. There were just some people you could feel incredibly close to in a short period of time and then in a snap of a finger, that bond would disappear. It had happened to me a few times in my life: in high school I'd sat next to a girl on a field trip to a museum and we'd talked all day. I thought we'd become good friends, but as soon as we got back to school she never spoke to me again. There was the guy I'd gone on a first date with and talked to for eight hours straight who never bothered to call me back like he'd promised.

Dusk fell over the highway. I wasn't a fan of night driving, so I was looking forward to handing over the wheel to Scott.

"Scott, I'm hungry, and if I eat one more Cheeto or Pop-Tart, I'll explode."

"We'll pull into the next town and get something to eat."

"Hey, look up ahead at all those lights."

"What's the first rule of the road? Never get too far off the highway."

"I thought the first rule of the road was to never pull off unless you saw the gas station, restaurant, or hotel you were looking for."

"It's all part of the same rule. You don't pull off unless you can see the place you want to go from the road because otherwise you drive all around Timbuktu and get lost and everything goes to hell."

"We're already here. Why not drive just a few extra miles?"

"If we get lost, I'm blaming you."

"Fine."

I pulled off and we bumped along on a dirt road, rocks popping out from under the tires. As we neared the lights, I could see that there were several little buildings strung with Christmas lights beside a cross-shaped stone church with a steeple. Another mile closer, I realized those weren't little buildings, but wooden booths decorated with evergreen bows, ribbons, and tiny lights.

"It looks like some kind of Christmas festival," I said. "I'm sure we can get something to eat there. And maybe you could finish up your shopping."

Scott nodded.

Several dozen cars and trucks were parked in a field across from the church on a rocky plateau. I had to drive up a slight hill to park. Across the "parking lot" was a life-size Nativity scene. An open "barn" had been decked out with mannequins of the Three Kings, Mary and Joseph, sheep, and, of course, the Baby Jesus in a manger.

I opened the door and climbed out, taking a moment to luxuriate in being able to stretch my scrunched muscles. "Oh, that feels good." The first few moments my legs felt unsteady, like when you return to gym shoes after taking off your Rollerblades.

I inhaled the smells of cinnamon, gingerbread, and fresh pastries. One booth was selling hand-blown ornaments with Christmas scenes painted on them. Another sold spiced wine. I didn't want to get a headache, so I skipped that and opted for the warm cider.

It was cold out but not bitterly so; the fresh air against my face felt good.

I watched the townspeople strolling up and down the stands. It seemed that everyone was part of a family—moms holding their kids' mitten-covered hands, dads carrying little ones on their shoulders, grandparents walking beside their kids and grandkids. It made me ache to get to Colorado so I could see my own family.

As Scott and I took in the sights, I had to fight the urge to take his hand in mine. He hadn't brought up the kisses all day. I wondered if he'd felt rejected by my reaction last night and wasn't going to give me another chance.

"What do you want to eat? Want a brat?" Scott asked.

I nodded.

He walked up to the vendor. "Two brats, please."

We ate our brats and drank our warmed drinks and milled around looking at handcrafted nutcrackers and toys and hand-knit sweaters and lace. Scott bought a couple ornaments as gifts. Just as he was paying for one of them, we heard a horrible crash.

We turned toward the Nativity scene. Scott's Range Rover was rolling down the small hill—and rolling right over the Wise Men! We turned just in time to see the Baby Jesus go flying through the air as the manger was crushed to tinder.

"What the hell?" Scott shouted as the two of us raced to the scene of the accident. Fortunately the truck stopped moving where the ground flattened out.

"I guess I forgot to put the parking brake on," I said, wincing.

"I guess you did." Scott inspected the truck carefully. "I don't see any damage."

I exhaled.

Scott stood there, arms crossed, a grim frown across his face, watching me.

"I told you I was a flake. I didn't get us into a multicar pileup. That's something, isn't it?"

He looked away, wordless.

The accident quickly attracted a crowd of onlookers. A plump older woman introduced herself as the manager of the festival. I wondered how much my mistake was going to cost me.

"I'll pay for any damages," I told her, wincing again.

She took a moment to look around and then picked up the Baby Jesus, whose arms were raised as if he wanted his mother to pick him up. "Jesus doesn't have a scratch on him." She shook her head. "What do you know? Must be a miracle." She smiled.

Why wasn't she screaming at me? I'd nearly smooshed Baby Jesus.

"I'm really, really sorry. I'm from New York. I don't drive much. I forgot to put the parking brake on."

"Don't worry about it, darling. A few Wise Men got knocked down, Baby Jesus went for a joyride, and some hay got thrown around. The only thing damaged is the manger, and my husband can fix that in a jiff."

"Are you sure?"

"I'm sure."

"Let me help straighten up a bit at least."

Scott, the woman, me, and a couple other people did what we could to clean things up. The woman reverently set the Baby Jesus down in a pile of hay, sans manger. We propped the Wise Men and sheep back up, and gathered up the hay that seemed to have exploded everywhere.

When we'd done all we could do, we paused a moment to look at our work.

"There, that doesn't look so bad," the woman said. "I'm Margie Smith, by the way."

"It's nice to meet you. I'm Amber Taylor and this is Scott Cardoza."

"Where are you headed?" Margie asked.

"Denver," Scott said.

"You're going to Denver all the way from New York? That's quite a drive."

"Sure is," I said.

"No wonder you're a little scatterbrained." She smiled kindly.

I was so grateful that she wasn't beating me up over this I wanted to kiss her. If this had happened in New York I probably would have been gunned down or had a hit man sent after me. I was also grateful that she wasn't some sort of religious fanatic who would treat a plastic stand-in for Jesus as if he were the real thing.

"Merry Christmas," the woman said. "Have a good drive."

"Thank you. And again, I'm really sorry."

"Mistakes happen. At least nobody got hurt."

Scott took the driver's seat and I took the passenger's seat. I felt the eyes of every last festival-goer on me as we drove back to the highway.

Scott and I went several minutes in silence when I heard a strange noise coming from him. I turned to see him attempting to suppress a laugh, but it was no good, he started roaring. I giggled, thinking about the way the plastic Baby Jesus had gone hurtling through the air like a football. There was no doubt I was going to hell for laughing at such a sight, but I couldn't help myself.

"I can't believe you nearly crushed Jesus."

"I didn't intentionally do it. We've been on the road for several hours. I was tired and hungry and I made a simple mistake."

"Did you see him flying?" he wiped at the tears in his eyes. "I was raised in a religious household and I should not be laughing at that, but damn, it was funny."

"Thank goodness that lady was nice about the whole thing. The damage could have been a whole lot worse and I'd never get out of debt. And at least you were able to buy a few Christmas presents."

"I left them behind."

"You did?"

"I dropped the bag when I saw my truck rolling into the barn. Presents were the last thing on my mind."

"That's too bad. I'll buy some more for you."

"Don't worry about it. It was just a few ornaments. No biggie. We should find some place to stay for the night," he said.

"Yeah. Sure. Good idea."

We stopped at another cheap hotel. The carpeting in our room was dark brown and the television looked like it was about twenty years old. After I pulled the comforter off the bed, I sat down on it. Scott sat on his bed and flipped through the channels. We went through every station at least twice and there was nothing either of us wanted to see.

"You know what?" Scott shut off the TV. "Let's get out of here. I saw a bar across the street. Let's get a drink."

I nodded. "That sounds like fun. Give me just a sec." In the bathroom, I put on a little lipstick and eye makeup. I brushed my hair, reapplied my deodorant, and spritzed on some light perfume. I traded the hiking boots I'd been wearing for a pair of black leather boots. I had on jeans and exchanged my sweatshirt for a navy blue lace halter top that gave me the illusion of cleavage. Over the lace halter I put on a thin navy blue sweater.

When I came out of the bathroom, Scott looked me over and nodded. "Damn, girl, you look good."

"Thanks." I smiled, feeling shy.

The bar was a country-and-western place with cracked peanut shells on the wood floor, which was sticky with spilled beer that had long since dried.

"Do you know how to two-step?" Scott asked me.

I shook my head. "You do?"

He nodded. "I was in the chorus of *Annie Get Your Gun* in high school. I can teach you. But first we need drinks. What's your poison?"

I thought a moment. "How about a margarita? Salt. On the rocks."

He nodded. "I'll be right back."

There were no available tables, but along the wall there was a shelf to set drinks on, so I stood against the wall and watched the dancers—men in their cowboy hats, cowboy boots, and mustaches;

women in jeans and heavily hair-sprayed hair. I tapped my feet along to the music.

When Scott returned, not only had he bought two large margaritas, he had two shot glasses of tequila as well.

Uh-oh. Tequila shots. This wasn't going to be pretty.

Whatever you do, do not get drunk and sleep with Scott. You have many more hours of driving with him and it would be awkward beyond belief. Besides, you're too old for one-night stands.

"Cheers!" he said with a smile.

"Cheers." We downed the shots. I winced as the liquid burned its way down my throat, warming my stomach. I quickly took a large gulp of my margarita to dilute the taste of the straight tequila.

"Ready to dance?" he asked.

I nodded and took his hand as he pulled me out to the dance floor. He showed me the basic moves and we practiced slowly at first.

"Step back with your right," he instructed as he stepped forward with his left. "Step back with your left. Step back with your right. Hold. Step back with your left. Hold. Good. That's it. Let's try the same thing again."

I kept my eyes closed and concentrated on the count, only stepping on his toes a couple times. Then we tried it faster, and for the first minute or so he had to repeat the instructions: *step back with your right, step back with your left, step back with your right, hold*. After a couple of minutes of me being able to go through the steps without closing my eyes or stepping on his toes he asked, "Ready to try it with the beat?"

"No."

"Let's just give it a shot. You don't have to do it perfectly the first time."

He put one hand on my back and took my hand with his free hand. I rested my other hand on his shoulder. He was wearing a cream-colored cable-knit sweater, but even through the thick sweater I could feel his broad chest and muscular arms.

We flew around the dance floor, spinning in circles. I didn't come anywhere close to getting the foot pattern right, though I miraculously managed not to step on Scott's feet. He was exactly five inches taller than me, which was the ideal height difference for dancing. When he stepped back and I stepped forward our strides were evenly matched. For part of the song I felt like I was basically just running after Scott trying to keep up, but I couldn't stop laughing—it was so much fun.

After a song, Scott asked me to stop so he could take off his sweater. We went back to where our drinks were and he pulled the sweater over his head.

"That was really good for your first time."

"Oh, please. I was pathetic. I was like the Inspector Clouseau of two-stepping."

He laughed. "I love Inspector Clouseau. Besides, imperfection is endearing. Let's practice at our own pace a little more before we go out there again." He took a long sip of his margarita and, for courage, I did the same.

We resumed the proper stance. Beneath the sweater he was wearing a black T-shirt, and when I put my hand back on his shoulder, I could feel how unusually soft the fabric was. It was a curious juxtaposition—his hard, muscular shoulder beneath the soft material.

Scott was a patient teacher. For several minutes we practiced by the wall off the main dance floor. Then he upped the speed and I nearly went flying into a nearby table. Scott caught me just in time, pulling me close to him. The feeling of his strong arms around me was intoxicating.

We practiced some more and then returned to the dance floor. After a few songs I was vaguely getting the hang of things.

"You're a natural," he shouted over the din of the music.

I rolled my eyes, but I couldn't suppress my smile.

When the song ended, Scott said, "I'm hot. Let's take a break. There's a table that just opened up over there. Why don't you hold it and I'll get us some more drinks?"

I sat at the table, which was sticky from spilled drinks. Two mostly finished beers and a stinky ashtray cluttered the table.

When Scott returned, he didn't just have two more margaritas, he had two more shots as well.

"I can't do any more shots," I protested. "I don't want to be hung over tomorrow."

"Come on, live a little." He handed me a shot. This one didn't burn quite so much because I was already a little numb. I licked the pad of my middle finger and pressed it up against a few grains of salt on the edge of my margarita glass, then licked my finger clean.

"Ouch, what happened to you?" Scott lightly touched the blister I had on my knuckle. The touch shot a jolt of excitement through me; I didn't want him to take his hand away.

"An unfortunate pizza injury. You should never drink alcohol while cooking."

"Ain't that the truth."

He took another sip of his drink and smiled at me. His lips were perfect. Soft. Not too thin or too thick. Recalling the kisses he'd given me last night, I felt tremors of lust I hadn't felt in a long time.

Scott said something, but over the roar of the music, I couldn't hear him. "What?"

He said something again.

I shook my head. "I can't hear you."

Scott took his chair and did an awkward crab walk over to me, pulling the chair beneath him. He leaned in close to me. "I said, I'd like to kiss you."

He'd seen me staring at his lips. Damn. "I don't think that's a good idea."

"Why not?"

"We have to go back and sleep in the same hotel room. If we start kissing here, I'm going to want to sleep with you." Damn it. Already the alcohol was acting like truth serum, getting me to tell him things I didn't want to tell him.

He smiled. "Then I definitely think we should kiss."

He was so close to me I could feel his breath on my neck. "Scott, just how old are you anyway?"

"Twenty-five."

Ouch. It was worse than I thought. The boy was a mere pup.

"Why? How old are you?"

"Thirty-two."

"Wow. You look good. I thought twenty-seven, tops."

"Just how old do you think thirty-two is?"

"It's not old. Not old at all. I'm just saying you don't look it."

I told him I needed to use the bathroom and wove

my way through the crowd, going into the room marked "Cowgirls," and locked myself in a stall. The toilet seat was smokers'-teeth yellow and nearly coming off its hinges. It wasn't the ideal place to meditate and seek guidance from a Higher Power, but I didn't have much choice. I did some deep breathing exercises and sent brief prayers up to the heavens asking what to do. Should I sleep with him? Not sleep with him?

Of *course* I shouldn't sleep with him. It was a ridiculous idea. A one-night stand would never work. If we slept together and he never called me again, I would be crushed.

I returned to the table and Scott smiled at me. "There will be no kissing," I said.

"Why's that?"

"I don't believe in one-night stands."

"Who said anything about a one-night stand? We'll both be going back to New York. I definitely want to see you after this trip is over."

"I'm sorry, Scott, but I think it's time we go to bed. Each of us to our own."

Chapter 14

Emily

Seven days before Christmas

I woke up with a start, breathing heavily, panicked, scared. In the dream I was in a murky brown lake trying to reach the surface. Some horrible, shark-like creatures were trying to eat me and I couldn't reach the surface. (I knew that sharks don't live in lakes, but this was a dream, after all.)

I glanced at the clock—4:45 AM. The alarm was set for five so we would have time to shower, drive to the airport, and catch our eight o'clock flight. I always woke before the alarm when I had a flight to catch. In fact, I usually woke every hour on the hour before the alarm went off. But this time it was the dream that jarred me from slumber. It didn't take a dream specialist to figure out what this was about. I knew I was being attacked but I couldn't see what was trying to get me because I couldn't see anything around me. I was trying to get away from it all, but just couldn't make it.

This holiday was going to be the death of me.

I didn't want to leave the comfort of my warm bed—the soft indigo sheets and down comforter, Luke's body radiating heat inches away from my body. I wrapped my arms around him and kissed the warm flesh of his chest. He stirred in his sleep. I'd let him catch a few more minutes of rest before I woke him.

I sat up and went to the bathroom to shower, my eyes stinging. We had a painfully early flight this morning, and then we'd return just as quickly tomorrow afternoon. I felt terrible about spending such a short time with Dad, but I didn't know how else to fit everything in. I didn't want to feel like a visit with Dad and Laurie was a chore I needed to check off my to-do list, but I was afraid that was sort of how it felt. Next year maybe we'd go visit them in January, when life was back to normal or we'd go out there for a week in August. This year, we were just going to have to make the most of the time we had.

I'd helped the kids pack the night before. They'd never been to California before, and the idea of getting to see the ocean thrilled them. Ever since they'd seen the pictures from our honeymoon in Puerto Rico, they'd been dying to see the ocean for themselves.

Happily the plane was on time, and I thought about how strange it was that the kids were going to meet Laurie, who was technically my stepmother, though I'd never called her that. You might say it was a double standard that I had a secret wish for my kids to call me "Mom" when I called my own stepparents Laurie and Jesse (that's what I called Mork to his face, anyway), but my rationale went like this: I never lived with Laurie and Dad. Mom didn't marry Mork until I was a senior in high school, and while Mork did dadlike things for me occasionally (like when I'd been single he'd helped me with plumbing problems and car troubles), he'd never been around to raise me, so he'd never felt like a dad. (Of course, by those standards, my own father shouldn't have felt like a dad, either, but what are you going to do?) Anyway, I had a mother and father, I didn't need more. On the other hand, Claire and Josh had been incredibly little when their mother died. I'd be the main woman in their lives for much longer than she had been. Besides, since they no longer had a mom, who better to fill the role? Everyone needed a mom, after all.

My father's wife, Laurie, was an attractive fifty-something blonde. Dad had married her about eleven minutes after the divorce papers were signed—he wasn't good at being a bachelor. I was glad he had found her. She was a nice woman and a great cook. She kept a beautiful home and ensured my father didn't die of scurvy as he surely would have if it had been up to him to feed and care for himself.

Dad picked us up at the John Wayne Airport when our plane arrived early that afternoon. The kids had been mercifully well behaved on the flight. The reason wasn't a result of mere luck, however. No, it had more to do with Luke and my perpetual threats that Santa wouldn't come if they didn't behave. I remembered how that threat had worked like a charm on Amber and me as kids, and I felt no compunction using the same scare tactics now that I was a parent. I figured Luke and I only had one or two more years using this warning on Claire, but I was going to milk it for all it was worth while I still could. It was so effective it almost made me wish Christmas came a few more times a year. Then I remembered how I was ready to hurl myself off a very high bridge and decided well-behaved children weren't worth the hassle and expense of the holidays after all.

Dad, a tall, thin man with a thick swatch of silver hair, worked as a corporate trainer, a job that involved a lot of travel.

Because Dad had been gone so much when Amber and I were little, I couldn't say we were exactly close, but he was a nice guy who was fun to be with. When we were kids, he would take Amber and me to baseball games and—when we were a little older—concerts. He was a big fan of all kinds of music, good music that Amber and I liked, too, and I'd always thought it was cool that I had a dad who would actually take me to rock concerts. The one thing that bothered me about him I felt guilty about disliking: he had an artificial jocularity about him. He always had a smile on his face, even if the world was imploding around him. You might think this was a good quality, but in fact the false walls he put up kept anyone from getting close to him. We always had a cordial relationship, but nothing that felt deeply genuine.

"Dad, hi."

"It's so good to see you!" he said. Dad ended many of his sentences in exclamation points.

"Gwampa!" Josh said as Dad lofted him into his arms.

"Howya doing, big guy?"

"Santa's coming."

"Pretty soon, huh?"

Josh nodded.

"And how are you, little lady?"

Claire smiled and turned from side to side, shyly averting her gaze.

"Do you have a hug for your grandpa?"

She nodded.

He knelt down, set Josh on the floor, and gave Claire a squeeze.

Dad stood again and gave Luke a hearty, manly handshake. "Luke."

"Steve. How are things?"

"Good. Good. Well, shall we blow this pop stand?" Dad had been using that same catchphrase for as long as I could remember.

Dad grabbed two large pieces of our luggage and headed toward the door. I'd tried to buy small gifts for Dad and Laurie but even so, it seemed like we needed a ton of storage space for everything, so traveling light just wasn't an option.

I held Claire's hand with one hand and rolled my suitcase behind me with the other. Claire had her own adorable little bright purple suitcase that she insisted on pulling on her own.

"It's too bad Amber couldn't be with us," Dad said. "She'll be in Colorado next week, right?"

"That's the plan," I said as the sliding glass doors whooshed open and we were greeted by sunny skies and mild weather.

"Have you ever been to California?" Dad asked the kids, who shook their heads. "You're in for a treat."

I let the kids take the window seats and insisted that Luke ride shotgun. I'd visited Dad in California many times and figured they deserved the better view. "See that?" I asked the kids as I pointed out the window. "That's the ocean. Pretty cool, huh? We'll get to see the ocean right up close pretty soon. Would you like that?"

The kids nodded eagerly.

Dad's house was an obscenely expensive two-story with a Spanish clay-tile roof, elegantly land-scaped walk, and a swimming pool and Jacuzzi in the back. In this neighborhood, a two-bedroom condo could easily go for nearly a million bucks.

Laurie was waiting to greet us with a smile on her face. After giving us organ-crushing hugs, she took the kids' luggage to the guest bedroom down-stairs. There were two single beds in there, both of which were covered with stuffed animals Laurie's children left behind when they'd moved out.

"I assume Luke and I are upstairs?"

"You assume right," Dad said.

Luke and I dropped off our luggage and came back down the winding stairs.

"What can we do to help you with dinner?" I asked Laurie.

"Actually, dinner is going to be pretty simple. Why don't you take the kids to the ocean? You have to see the ocean before you leave."

"I'll take you," Dad said.

Claire started hopping around with excitement. Moments later Josh began mimicking her.

I smiled. "I take it that sounds like fun."

"Ocean! Ocean! Ocean!" Claire cried, and after a moment Josh joined the chorus.

"You're going to have to stop hopping and come out to the car or we'll never see it," Luke said.

Claire dashed to the door, and Josh quickly fol-lowed behind her. We drove the ten minutes down to the shore and parked the car. The kids bolted out the doors and started running in the sand along the beach. Dad ran after them while Luke and I walked slowly behind them hand in hand. It felt like the first moment of peace we'd had in months.

Claire came running up to us. "We saw a sea snail!"

"You did? Where?" Luke asked.

"Here. Come see."

We followed her back to where Dad was. All I could see at first was what appeared to be a puddle, but my eyes followed Claire's pointed finger, and I saw that the puddle was teeming with life. Little crabs inched along the sand, mollusks clung to the rocks' edges, algae waved like flags in a breeze. It was a kick to see these animals going about their daily business in their natural habitat. Back in Colorado, I saw squirrels, the occasional bird, and house cats, and the only other animals I ever saw were the ones at the zoo, far from their natural environment, on display like paintings at a museum. But here, in this small little puddle of water, a brown-spotted sea slug inched along the sandy bottom, living its life without regard to us. Two little tentacles poked out from its head.

"What are these?" Claire asked.

"Those are mollusks, sweetie," I explained.

"Mock-ups?"

"Mollusks. A mollusk is an animal with a shell, like a snail or a clam. I think this is a clam." I hoped I wasn't lying to the kid. I took a biology class about a trillion years ago. It was embarrassing that I wasn't quite sure what was what. I felt that as a mother I should know all about this sort of thing.

"They are all so close," she said.

"They sure are."

"How do they get food?"

"Well, I think how it works is that when the tide comes in, they absorb the nutrients and little creatures in the water." That *sounded* right anyway.

"Look," Luke said, "it's a sea anemone."

He took a small stick and lightly poked the bright blue animal; immediately its tentacles closed in as it wrapped itself into a strange-looking ball. The children clapped their hands. I thought it was pretty cool myself, but it was even more fun watching it through their eyes.

As soon as the sea anemone unfurled its tentacles so it looked like a flower with many thin petals, Claire and Josh insisted that Luke, "Do it again! Do it again!"

Luke smiled and did it again. And again. And again.

This was one of the many fascinating things about children: you could spend hundreds of dollars taking them to some place like Disneyland and they'd get bored within minutes. Then you could poke a stick at a sea anemone thousands of times in a row and it thrilled them every single time.

As for me, on the other hand, the thrill wore off after the first, oh, twenty or so times.

Finally, Luke said, "That's it, kids. We'd better be heading back for dinner."

Josh and Claire pleaded to stay just a little longer, and with all the negotiations, it took another fifteen minutes to corral them into the car.

We came home to find our "simple" dinner included prime rib, twice-baked potatoes, and grilled asparagus lightly coated in olive oil and toasted sesame seeds.

Laurie called everyone to the table as Luke poured the wine and I helped serve the plates on the beautiful marble table. Beneath it was a beautiful and obviously wildly expensive Oriental rug that covered part of their wood floor.

"How are the renovations on the house coming?" Laurie asked me.

"We're just about done. It feels really good to look around the place and see how far it's come," I said. "I never used to notice things like people's lighting fixtures or faucets, and now I'm obsessed with every doorknob and light switch."

"Welcome to home ownership," Dad said.

"This is a wonderful meal, Laurie," Luke said.

"It is delicious. I *love* these potatoes." I took another bite of the twice-baked potato. Oh, how I loved carbohydrates.

"I can give you the recipe," she said.

"That would be great." Yeah, right. As if I'd ever have time to make twice-baked potatoes. Getting Tater Tots heated was a major accomplishment.

"It is excellent," Dad chorused. "Although I think the prime rib might be a little overcooked."

I wanted to kick Dad in the shins. Why did he have to zero in on the one part of the meal that was slightly off? Luke always thanked me for cooking, even when I burnt half the meal and didn't cook the other half quite enough. But I said nothing.

I took a glance at the kids' plates to see how they were doing on their dinners. "Claire, please eat a little of your asparagus," I said.

"I don't wanna. I don't like 'spargus."

"Laurie went to a lot of trouble making dinner. You want to be polite, don't you? Just a few bites."

"No!"

"Claire, you have to take just a few bites or you don't get any dessert."

"I don't have to listen to you. You're not my mom." She crossed her arms over her chest.

I swallowed. My cheeks flushed with embarrassment and hurt. Luke's eyebrows furrowed. "Hey, don't talk to Emily that way. She's your stepmom and you'll do as she says. And I'm your father, and I say eat some of your asparagus."

"I won't." She took a handful of the asparagus and threw it on Laurie's beautiful Oriental rug.

"Oh!" I leapt out of my chair and scooped up the offending vegetables.

Laurie pursed her lips. "Don't worry about it."

The grease from the olive oil left a dark spot on the hexagonal slate blue and red patterned rug.

"I'm so sorry," I said.

Laurie bit her lip and shook her head. "Oil. I'm not sure how to get that out."

Behind us I heard Luke scolding Claire and ordering her to her room as she burst into tears. "I hate you!" she screamed at me. Luke swooped her up and gave her a light and totally ineffectual spanking.

"I'm really sorry," I repeated in a whisper to Laurie as we knelt above the greasy spot and inspected the damage. "She thinks I'm trying to take her mother's place. There are just some anger management issues that we need to work out." The renegade tears came in a flash storm, though I was able to keep from making any noise. I didn't want Claire to see me crying.

Laurie wrapped me in her arms. "I know, sweetheart. It's so hard. It's hard being a mom even when you give birth to them. I can imagine what you're going through. Just give it a little time."

I cleared my throat and forced myself to stop crying, affecting a look of calm and control. "I know. Things will be fine. Uh, the Internet . . . I'm sure we can get some tips on getting the stain out on the Internet. Is the computer in the office already online?"

Laurie nodded. "Just click the Explorer icon and you're ready to go."

"I'll be right back."

Laurie nodded kindly.

In their office, I did a Google search, wrote down some notes, and came back downstairs. Dad was clearing the table while Laurie was in the kitchen preparing a tray of cookies for dessert.

"I need paper towels, corn starch, a vacuum, and Dawn dishwashing soap," I said.

"Don't worry about it sweetie. I'll take care of it."

"No, no. I'll clean it up. You're working on dessert."

She fetched the things I needed while Luke did the dishes.

"Who wants tea and who wants coffee?" Laurie asked.

The stain did come out, thank goodness. Laurie brought a tray of cookies and small cakes into the living room, offering a cup of tea or coffee to the adults and a mug of hot chocolate for Josh. Eventually Luke put Josh to bed and the rest of us spent the next couple of hours talking and pretending Claire's outburst never happened. When my yawns became more and more frequent, I excused myself and went to bed.

Even though I was exhausted, I couldn't fall asleep. I could never quite get comfortable—Dad and Laurie had pillows that put my head and neck at a 90-degree angle to my body, they were so high. Even if the pillows weren't inducing head trauma, I wouldn't have been able to sleep. My mind was whirling. I had enough girlfriends with kids to know that Claire's outbursts were normal, but none of my friends were stepmothers. I didn't know anyone who had gone through what I was going through.

Just as I was finally about to doze off, Luke came to bed. The movements of his body rolling around beneath the comforter as he tried to get comfortable snapped me back from the brink of slumber. Moments after his head hit the pillow he began snoring, thereby *keeping* me awake. I punched him. He moaned, stopped snoring for a split second, and then started right back up again. I huffed, punched my pillow, and reveled in a feeling of ill will. I wished we were back home so I could go sleep in our guest bedroom. Here at Dad's house, I had no place to go; I was trapped with Luke's roaring nostrils. Over the next few hours, I managed a little light and unsatisfactory sleep.

When Laurie's clattering around the kitchen woke me that morning, I knew that I wouldn't be able to nod off again. Luke was still sound asleep. I padded downstairs to where Laurie was slicing strawberries and preparing batter to make waffles.

"Good morning!" she said cheerily.

"Good morning." I mustered a smile as I pulled an oversized mug from the cupboard and poured myself a cup of coffee.

"How'd you sleep?"

"Great," I lied.

Luke shuffled into the kitchen with mad-scientist hair. "Coffee?" he croaked, hopeful and bleary-eyed.

Laurie poured him a mug. "Here."

He took one sip and spit it into the sink. "No, no, that's a travesty. Coffee shouldn't be flavored. The only flavor for coffee is coffee flavored. That stuff is a crime against humanity," he joked.

Laurie laughed. "Sorry. Emily, do you mind vanilla coffee?"

"No problem."

"We'll give the rest to Emily and make a fresh pot of the regular boring stuff."

"Thank you," Luke said.

I took my mug of coffee to the dining room table and glanced at the copy of the *LA Times*. One of the top stories was an article about whether this was going to be a good year for retail. *Will last-minute consumer gift buyers give retailers the lift they need?* the headline read, as if consumers were foot soldiers fighting an all-important war for capitalism.

After waffles with strawberries and powdered sugar for breakfast, it was time to open presents. Dozens of gifts surrounded the Christmas tree, most which were for the kids. I loved watching their excitement as they ripped through the wrapping paper.

I opened my first gift from Dad and Laurie. It was a beautiful turtleneck sweater that I would absolutely never wear. I had a passionate aversion to sweaters and shirts that went around my neck—it made me feel like I was wearing a neck brace. It was a confining, uncomfortable feeling. But Dad and Laurie only saw me once or maybe twice a year, so they had no way of knowing that I was a V-neck sweater sort of girl.

The next gift from them to me was a very pretty, very expensive gold watch that I would never wear. It was much too ornate for my taste, and all my jewelry was either silver or platinum.

"Thank you," I said, wondering how many homeless people I could feed on Christmas Day by returning the watch for a refund. Laurie and Dad hadn't included the receipt, so I'd probably have to just bring it to a pawn shop. Actually, Mom would probably like the watch, but she'd know it wasn't from me because I was maniacal about always including gift receipts when I gave presents.

I bought Laurie a silk scarf in a pale pastel floral pattern and a pair of classic gold earrings. She thanked Luke and me graciously for the presents. Dad was always a much bigger challenge. He was obsessed with golf and that was about it. After I'd gotten wolf-themed presents for years and years after confessing that I thought wolves were neat animals who didn't deserve extinction (red wolves were the first predators brought back after being officially declared extinct in the early eighties), I was hesitant to give gifts based on one of the few hobbies or passions a person had. After all, did Dad really need more personalized golf balls or golf club covers or golf tees or golf shirts? I didn't think so. So I always ended up getting him books.

"Have you read that one?" I asked when he opened the gift.

"I haven't. It looks good," he said. For all I knew, he'd never read a single book I'd gotten him.

"Oh!" Laurie said. "I've been wanting to read this."

Good, at least somebody would get some use out of it.

Claire opened another gift. It was another American Girl doll. Those dolls went for a hundred bucks a pop, and she already had four of them. Claire's eyes lit up and she squealed. "Thanks Grandpa and Laurie!"

As I watched the smile on Claire's face as she squeezed Laurie in a tight hug, I sighed and slunk down in my seat. Just then, I heard my cell phone ring. It was in my purse, which I'd left on the end table of the family room.

"I'll be right back," I said. I walked through the kitchen into the dining room to get to the family room, where I fished my phone out of my purse and saw that it was Amber. "Hey, babe," I answered.

"Merry Christmas. Have you gone to Dad's yet?"

"We're here right now. Do you want to talk to him?"

"Does he know who you're on the phone with?"

"No."

"Then no. I'll wait till he calls me on Christmas."

I thought it was sad that I was out here visiting Dad mostly out of a feeling of guilt and obligation just like Amber talked to him on the phone as little as possible, and when she did, it was only out of a feeling of guilt and obligation. Every child, every person, had her own way of dealing with pain and loss. When Dad left us, I dealt with it by shutting down and not feeling anything and Amber dealt with it by going to the opposite extreme—she was very emotional about it, shedding countless tears and getting so angry with him she never completely got over it.

"Are you on the road?"

"Yep."

"How's it going with the sexy movie star?"

"Actually, if you have to be trapped in a small space for long stretches of time, having a handsome actor as company is the way to go."

I laughed.

"Actually . . ." she began.

"What?"

"Nothing."

"Don't 'nothing' me. What is it?"

"It's no big deal."

"He kissed you."

"How did you know?"

"I just guessed. So? How was it?"

"It was nice."

"And?"

"And nothing. It could never go anywhere between us. He's too good-looking."

"Amber, you're gorgeous. Why would he kiss you if he didn't think so?"

"Because I was there. Anyway, you know I don't do one-night stands."

"I didn't say you had to sleep with the guy. But you should be open to seeing if this could go anywhere."

Amber sighed the sigh of someone who had already given up.

"I don't understand how you can always think the universe is going to look out for you in every other area of your life except romance," I said. "You're Ms. Optimism when it comes to everything else and Ms. Gloom-and-Doom when it comes to love."

"I guess. If he calls me when we get back to New York, then I'll see. Anyway, he's way too young for me—he's only twenty-five."

"Is he a mature twenty-five or an immature twenty-five?"

"Mature," she admitted.

"Then what's the problem? Once you're an adult paying your own way and living on your own, age isn't the important thing, attitude is. Remember when I briefly dated Roy? He was that guy who was twelve years older than me, but he was always bragging about how he was just a kid at heart? What he really meant was that he was an irresponsible, pot-smoking slacker. He was almost gleeful about how he spent all his free time playing video games or hanging out with his friends smoking pot and drinking beer. I don't know why some guys have such a major Peter Pan complex, but trust me, just because they might technically be in their forties, they might still mentally be fourteen. You need to take it on a case-by-case basis."

Amber sighed. "I guess you're right. Are you having fun out there?"

"Mostly." I told her about what had happened with Claire and the carpet and the asparagus. "I'm trying so hard to be a good mom, but it seems like the harder I try to get close to her, the more she pushes me away."

"Emily, Claire is a person, not a problem to be solved. You can't force things with her. They have to evolve naturally."

"I guess."

By the time I got off the phone with Amber, it was time for Luke, me, and the kids to head back to the airport. We packed up our things and Dad and Laurie drove us to John Wayne Airport where we hugged and said our good-byes and wished each other Merry Christmas.

On the flight home, Luke was as antsy as the kids. The kids wanted to play with each and every one of their new toys before we got home. I'd fish one of the toys out of our carry-on bag, they'd play with it for maybe five minutes, and then they'd ask for a different toy. I gave Claire her Kaya American Girl doll. I approved of the American Girl dolls because they looked like actual little girls. Unlike Barbie, Kaya wouldn't need to have all of her ribs and internal organs removed to maintain her figure.

"Claire, we'll be home soon. I'm not getting any more toys out. When you get home you can play with all your toys at once if you want." I turned to Luke, who seemed stressed, which was unusual for him. "What's wrong? You seem tense," I said.

He gave me a tired smile. "That phone call I got just before we left your dad's place was from Terry. The application we went live with a few days ago has some bugs in it. There could be some major winter storms coming up and we need to make sure the kinks are out of it. I'm going to need to go into the office as soon as we get home."

"Today?"

He nodded.

"But it's almost Christmas."

"The weather doesn't care whether it's a holiday. We'll get the bugs worked out before the twenty-fifth, don't worry."

It was so unfair. He'd been putting in crazy hours to get this release finished. I'd thought that since the project had finally been put to bed, he'd be able to start working civilized hours again.

I pulled out my Palm Pilot and checked my calendar. If Luke really could finish the project by the twenty-fifth, our schedules were wide open after that. I noticed that we didn't have any plans for the thirty-first. That seemed odd.

"Do we have any plans for New Year's Eve?" I asked.

"Not that I know of."

If I'd been in my twenties, I would have felt like a social pariah if I didn't have plans for New Year's. Since the age of sixteen, I wasn't sure I'd ever welcomed a New Year without staggering around acting like someone who'd recently suffered a brain injury while bathing in a distillery. I could think of no better plans for New Year's Eve this year than watching TV and being in bed by ten. Yippee!

It was true: I was officially old. And I absolutely loved it.

When we got home, Luke left for the office.

I was bringing my luggage upstairs when I swallowed and recognized that familiar you're-about-to-get-a-sore-throat ache. Just what I needed: getting sick just before the holidays when I had guests to feed and presents to wrap and sanity to keep.

"Come on," I said to the kids, "let's get our coats on. We have to make a quick run to the grocery store,"

"I don't want to go to the grocery store," Claire said.

"I'm sorry, but your daddy is working so you have to come with me."

"But I don't wanna."

"Claire, I'm too tired to fight with you. To be honest, I don't want to go to the grocery store, either. Sometimes we have to do things we'd rather not do."

"I don't wanna. I wanna watch a movie."

"The movie will still be here when we get back." If this were an old Western, this would be the part where the good guy and the bad guy faced each other down, walking toward each other, their boots kicking up a cloud of dust, their hands millimeters from their holstered guns, waiting to see who would shoot first. Sometimes I thought that Claire was hesitant to let herself get close to me because in many ways we were so much alike. We both had a lot of pride—we liked being right, hated being wrong, and liked getting our own way. When my way happened to not be her way, we were two stubborn females trying to assert our control.

We were at an impasse—then inspiration struck. "When we're at the grocery store we can get the ingredients to make Christmas cookies. Would you like to make cookies?"

Josh's expression became suddenly animated, and even Claire showed begrudging interest. "Tonight?" she asked.

Ugh. The last thing I felt up for doing was making cookies. Maybe Luke would be home soon and he could help. "Sure. Tonight."

The prospect of making Christmas cookies spurred them to action and I finally managed to start the arduous process of encasing Claire and Josh in winter coats and gloves and scarves.

The entire drive to the store, Claire asked me what kind of cookies we were going to make.

"With red sprinkles?"

"Sure."

"Can we make reindeers?"

"Sure."

"Christmas trees?"

"Sure."

"Green frosting?"

"Sure."

I parked the car and the kids raced through the chilly parking lot into the brightly lit grocery store. "Kids! Hang on. I need to buy some cold medicine first, and then we can get the ingredients for the cookies."

"I want to get the sprinkles," Claire insisted.

"We'll get the sprinkles in just a second." How could there possibly be mothers who had seven or eight or ten kids? I could barely control these two.

I stood in front of the vast array of cold medicines trying to figure out what I needed. I was vaguely aware of Claire and Josh running around me, playing a sort of hide-and-seek game. What kind of medicine did I need? I was stuffy and I had a sore throat. Did I want to be able to sleep tonight or feel good this evening and tomorrow day?

"Ahh!" Claire shrieked. "I got you."

She streaked past my legs. "Claire, don't run," I said, trying to effect a tone that was neither too critical nor too wishy-washy.

I was picking out a daytime and a nighttime cold medicine when Claire decided to use my legs as her hiding spot. When she tried to go through my legs and nearly knocked me down, I lost it. "Claire! Calm down!" She stood still and tears formed like clouds gathering before a storm.

I took a quick glance around and saw the scornful gazes of two women pushing shopping carts. One was a grandmotherly woman who I could easily picture working as a waitress in a truck-stop diner and the other was a slim, attractive redheaded woman in her early forties. The older woman would have raised her children with an iron fist so they would inevitably be well behaved at all times. The redhead's kids would have been mostly raised by a nanny and were probably now in college playing tennis and learning to become successful businesspeople, bringing her nothing but pride and joy.

"Claire, come on now. I'm not feeling well. I'm sorry I snapped at you, but you have to behave or we won't get the ingredients to make cookies. Can you be good for just a few minutes?"

Claire sniffed a few times and then nodded. I grabbed a daytime cold medicine and a nighttime one and threw them in my little red basket. "All right, we can get the cookie stuff now. This way." I went to the refrigerated case where they kept the Pillsbury cookie dough and took the tube of sugar-cookie mix and tossed it into the red handbasket with the cold medicine.

"What's that for?" Claire's big brown eyes looked up at me expectantly.

"That's the cookie dough."

"No. You mix the dough in a bowl."

"We don't have time for that tonight. This way we can decorate them and eat them ten minutes later." I snapped my fingers. "It's as easy as that."

"That's not how Grandma does it."

Under my breath I muttered, "No, I'm sure it's not." Aloud I said, "Let's get the sprinkles."

In the baking aisle there was yet another dizzying array of choices. Claire began picking up bottle after bottle of sprinkles.

"Claire, we couldn't possibly use all of these. We'd have to make twelve dozen cookies. Look, here's a combo pack. It's got it all."

She inspected it. "There are no chocolate sprinkles."

"We'll get this and the chocolate sprinkles." I sighed and grabbed red and green dye for the icing. "All right gang, let's pay for this and get out of here and start baking some cookies."

On the short drive home, the kids were so amped up at the *prospect* of making cookies I realized that if they actually *ate* them they would be bouncing off the walls and I'd never get them to sleep. Why had I gotten myself into this mess? Why couldn't I just tell them they had to come to the store with me because I said so? I was really going to have to get a backbone one of these days.

The moment we were in the warmth of our home, I attacked my cold medicine with the fervor of a junkie.

Properly medicated, I took out the cutting board

and flour and started preheating the oven. I got the kids stools so they could reach the counter, and then I began the cookie-cutter hunt.

I searched all the likely spots, rifling through the junk drawer and the silverware drawer, then trying every other drawer we had. All I could come up with was one circular cookie cutter. Did I even *own* cookie cutters? Why would I? When was the last time I baked cookies, when I was twelve? Until two months ago I'd lived alone. I never baked because I'd eat the entire batch of cookies or the entire cake or the whole tray of brownies myself in about two days, and since I was always pretending to myself that I was watching my weight, this simply wouldn't work at all. Luke should have had cookie cutters, though. He'd had kids for seven years, after all. Maybe in all the hubbub of the move, they were still packed away somewhere.

I turned and faced my chubby-cheeked firing squad.

"We seem to be experiencing a slight setback. I can't seem to find the cookie cutters. Let me call your dad and see if he can pick some up on his way home." I took the cordless phone off the wall and dialed Luke's cell.

"Hey, babe," he answered after several rings.

"Hi, hon. What time do you think you'll be coming home?"

"Are you all right? Your voice sounds weird."

"I'm coming down with a cold."

"I'm sorry."

"I got some medicine and I'm downing Echinacea tea and vitamin C like crazy. I'll be fine. What time will you be coming home?"

"It's going to be another hour or two at least."

"An hour or *two*?" I exhaled.

"I'm sorry."

"It's OK. The kids and I are baking some Christmas cookies."

"That sounds like fun."

Yeah, right. "Don't work too hard. I love you."

"I love you, too. I'll see you soon."

I hung up the phone and turned to the kids. There was no way I was going through the production of bundling them up and hauling them back to the grocery store. "It looks like we don't have any cookie cutters, but this will be even more fun. We'll get to be creative."

I took the cookie dough out of its package and sprinkled some flour on the cutting board. "Who wants to roll it out?" I was assaulted by a chorus of "me, me, me."

"One of you gets to roll it out and the other one gets to help me with the frosting. Dyeing the frosting red and green sounds like fun, doesn't it?"

Claire rolled out the dough and Josh helped me get the proper sugar-to-water ratio necessary for icing, which we split into two Tupperware containers. "Put just a drop of dye in. We can always add more," I instructed. "Good job! That looks good, doesn't it?" He nodded.

"Now we can cut out the cookies. We can use this circular one to make snowmen!"

Claire made one snowman and Josh did another.

"You said we could have reindeers. And Christmas trees," Claire said, pouting.

"Uh, sure. I'll just cut them out by hand, no problem."

I attempted to cut out a reindeer, which ended up looking like some sort of abstract piece of art. It looked vaguely reminiscent of a cave painting of a buffalo. My Christmas tree was completely lop-sided. I continued attempting to cut the cookie dough into Christmasy shapes until the dough was gone, then I placed the cookies on the tray and slipped the tray in the oven.

As the smell of fresh-baked cookies filled the air, I heated water in the teakettle to make us sugar-free hot cocoa. I set three mugs on the counter and tore a packet of Swiss Miss into each one. By the time the kettle was shrieking and I'd stirred in the water, the cookies were done.

Unfortunately, since it had been so long since I'd baked, I hadn't counted on the fact that the cookies would spread out when they cooked. When I pulled out the cookie sheet, what I had was essentially a solid rectangle of cookie.

How could I be such a success at work and such an abysmal failure when it came to making Christmas cookies from already-made dough?

"Where did the reindeer go?" Claire asked, peering from her stool onto the cookie sheet.

"No problem. I'll just cut the cookies apart."

Using a knife I attempted to dissect the cookies based on the loose shapes that remained, which gave the snowmen rough edges rather than smooth circles. The reindeers were giant blobs. The trees bore no resemblance to actual pines. It was the most pathetic batch of Christmas cookies ever made. Even Josh skewered his eyebrows.

"Great! Now we can decorate them!" I hoped my enthusiasm would confuse them.

Spreading newspaper onto the kitchen table, I gave each of the kids a cutting board and put out the two bowls of icing and set all the various sprinkles in the center of the table.

Josh and Claire sat on their knees in the chairs

so they were high enough to reach everything. I laughed watching Josh take his spatula and coat a tree in such a thick layer of green icing it reminded me of my fifth-grade teacher's makeup, which was so heavy it was like a clay mask—if you poked your finger against her cheek you'd leave a dent.

The kids coated the cookies so heavily in icing the cookies could have served as paper weights. And they spared no expense when it came to toppings, either. The end result was red and green blobs coated in sprinkles of all colors. I hadn't thought about saving any icing without dye for the snowmen, so even the snowmen were blood red or emerald green.

"It doesn't look like a reindeer," Claire said.

"The important thing is how they taste."

We each took a cookie. You needed to be a weight-lifter to lift one of these things from the table to your mouth.

I took a bite of mine. It was like eating a fistful of sugar cubes. "So? What do you think?"

Claire shrugged. Neither she nor Josh could eat a whole cookie. It would have been like trying to consume an elephant in a single sitting.

"Brush your teeth!" I called after them as they clambered up the stairs.

Even straight sugar wasn't appealing to them delivered via such a wretched medium. I'd never have thought it possible if I hadn't seen it with my own eyes.

I looked at the cookies and began giggling. Maybe I was high on cold medicine or maybe it was a lack of sleep, but I couldn't help but laugh. What kind of idiot couldn't bake Christmas cookies, especially when the dough was premade!

I helped myself to another cookie and then another. Each cookie was the size of two regular ones, and with all the frosting and sprinkles on them, it was essentially like Hoovering up a bag of sugar. I didn't stop eating until I was nauseous. I staggered to the couch and watched a little TV. After about half a sitcom I started feeling drugged—I was coming down from my sugar high. I could barely crawl up the stairs to the bedroom. I had all the same symptoms as if I had a hangover from drinking too many vodka sours.

I put myself to bed and lay there waiting for death by sugar. I felt so ill I was practically hoping for death at this point.

When Luke finally got home just after ten, I closed my eyes and pretended to be asleep.

Chapter 15

Amber

Six days before Christmas

When I woke up the next morning, the digital clock said it was 11:13 AM.

"Coffee," I said. It wasn't a desire but an order. I'd gotten enough sleep to avoid a hangover, but I was in a foggy place and needed caffeine with something approaching desperation.

Scott awoke and looked at me. "What time is it?" I told him and he bolted upright. "We have to hit the road."

"And we will, as soon as I get some coffee and a greasy breakfast."

"We don't have time."

"We can't just not eat."

"Can't you just have another granola bar?"

"I'd rather eat my own eyeballs than have another stinking granola bar." Sometimes, men could be such *boys*.

"All right, all right. I guess it won't kill us if we don't make it to Colorado today."

Oh, God. Another night in a hotel room with Scott. Danger! Danger! Danger!

"You know, why don't we just go through a drive-through somewhere," I said. "I can get some fries and that'll help me recover from last night."

We packed up the car, stopped at Burger King, and ate in the car.

Scott looked at me and smiled.

"What?" I asked.

"You look really good today."

"Are you making fun of me?"

"No, I'm serious."

"I'm not wearing any makeup and I'm in sweats."

"I know. You're a naturally beautiful woman. You don't need makeup. It doesn't matter what you're wearing."

"Uh . . . thanks." I shoved a french fry in my mouth. "Hey, hey," I said as we were heading out of town onto the highway.

"What?"

"Stop." I pointed to a guy who was attempting to push his car off the road into a parking lot. Scott pulled in behind him.

"Want some help?" I asked the man, who looked to be in his midthirties. Sweating, he nodded gratefully.

With Scott and me helping to push, the car moved much more quickly, and we got it off the road and into a Wal-Mart parking lot.

"Thanks," the man said, breathing heavily.

"Do you need us to call for a tow?" Scott asked.

The man shook his head. "I already did, thanks. I just wanted to get the car out of the way so I wouldn't block traffic—or get hit. Anyway, thanks again. That was cool of you."

"No problem," I said. "Are you sure you don't need anything?"

"I'm fine. My wife is already on her way to pick me up. Merry Christmas."

"Merry Christmas!" Scott and I said in unison, waving our good-byes.

We got back into the car and put on our seat belts. Scott pulled into traffic and quickly got on the ramp to enter the highway.

"That was cool of you," he said.

"What?"

"You stopped to help him reflexively, without thinking. I didn't even see him. I haven't met many women like you."

I paused. "Is that a good thing or a bad thing?"

"I've met some beautiful women who were maybe even a little interesting. I've met women who were sexy and talented. But it's really rare to find a woman like you who is incredibly beautiful and astonishingly sexy and amazingly intelligent and hugely talented *and* hilariously funny."

I blinked, mute. It took me several moments to digest what he just said. "Wow. The words 'thank you' don't seem like nearly enough for a compliment of that magnitude."

"So what do you think?"

"About what?"

"About us."

"What about us?"

"Do you want to date?"

"Each other?"

He rolled his eyes. "Right."

"You mean actually date, not just sleep together?"

"Right, actually date-date."

This couldn't be happening. I was nowhere near

his league. I was pretty, yes, but he deserved to be dating a model or a movie star. Eventually he'd figure this out. We might date for a short time and then he would dump me for somebody better. He would cheat on me at the first opportunity. He'd look at the stretch marks on my stomach and thighs—they were faint but they were there—and he'd think of his young girlfriends who hadn't yet started the battle with gravity and age. Yes, I was still young, but I wasn't in my twenties anymore and I knew it. "You're way too young for me."

He looked at me for too long a moment. It unnerved me.

"Hey, you're driving. Watch the road."

He turned back to look where he was going. "I can't believe you're serious. Seven years? You're going to let seven years stop us? Look at Demi Moore and what's his face."

"I am not Demi Moore. When I look like Demi Moore I can date gorgeous twenty-five-year-old famous actors."

"Wait a second, are you telling me you don't think you're attractive enough to date me?" He laughed. "Man, you have no idea how beautiful you are."

"Anyway, twenty-five would be too young no matter how gorgeous I was. Twenty-five is like, fourteen in girl years."

"What do you mean?"

"I mean that girls mature faster than boys. That's why women tend to go for older men."

"Do I seem immature to you?"

"Well, no, but I don't know you that well."

He shook his head, frowning. We didn't say anything to each other for a long stretch of highway. I had to suppress a smile, despite myself, but my smile faded when I realized that he was saying all this stuff to me because he knew it was what I wanted to hear. He was probably just desperate for sex and I was readily available. He'd have his fun with me at the hotel room tonight and we'd never see each other again after he dropped me off in Denver.

It's really rare to find a woman who is incredibly beautiful and astonishingly sexy and amazingly intelligent and hugely talented and hilariously funny. Could there be even a little truth in his comment? Lots of guys had told me I was beautiful and attractive before, but they were usually guys at a bar who wanted a night of sex. Still, a little external validation, whether legitimate or not, felt pretty good.

We did seem to hit it off. When you talked to someone for twelve hours straight for three days in a row, you could get to know that person pretty damn well. Really, it was like the equivalent of several dates.

"Anyway, you're not my type," I said after a long silence. "Remember? I gave up on creative types when I was about twenty. I'm on to left-brained people now. You're completely not my type."

"Has it ever occurred to you that none of your past relationships have worked out? Maybe your type isn't your type. You can't give up on all creative people just because of one bad experience when you were twenty years old."

I had no reply to that. Why hadn't my past relationships worked out? As my eyes glazed over in the trance-inducing rush of gray pavement, passing billboards and trucks whizzing by in the opposite direction, I took inventory:

Peter. *Background:* College boyfriend. Poet. We were together three months; it had been the longest three months of my life. He was the moodiest person I'd ever known. He'd be tender and loving one minute and sullen and withdrawn the next for no apparent reason. *Conclusion:* I broke up with him.

Gary. *Background:* Engineer. One date. Not disastrous. Just not *right*. He smiled at my jokes but never laughed. He never even got me to crack a smile. *Conclusion:* At the end of the night he said he'd had a wonderful night and wanted to see me again. Not having the guts to say no outright, I said I was sort of seeing someone and wasn't sure I felt right about dating anyone else. BAD PLAN. With men, you simply couldn't let them down easy. Gary kept calling and e-mailing me every couple of months to see if my fictional boyfriend and I had broken up yet. I still didn't have the heart to tell Gary it was him I wasn't interested in, nor could I find it within myself just not to write back. Finally I told him that "Alan" and I were getting married and the e-mails stopped at last.

What's-his-face. *Background:* Successful computer programmer. Three dates. The first date didn't make my heart go pitter-patter, but—and this is terrible—he said he had tickets to this Broadway play I wanted to see, would I join him next week? I went on the second date telling myself I was just giving myself a chance to get to know him better. I went on the third date to ease my guilt about going on the second date to see the play. *Conclusion:* When he asked me out for a fourth date, I said I was moving back to Colorado. I'd lived in terror of running into him ever since.

Neighbor. *Background:* Entry-level public relations guy. Six weeks. He made me laugh but proved to be a total stalker. He called constantly. Wanted to see me every night. He was exhausting. *Conclusion:*

I finally mustered up the courage to tell him I didn't want to see him anymore and he acted as if I'd broken up with him on the eve of our wedding, as if we'd been planning to spend the rest of our lives together.

Sven. *Background:* Highly successful businessman. Two months. He was charming and he had lots of money. He showered me with gifts and fancy dinners and plays. But there was something about him I didn't quite trust. When he went out of town for business, I knew he was cheating on me. *Conclusion:* I broke up with him. He looked furious, told me it was my loss, and charged out of my apartment.

What's-his-face-number-two. *Background:* Copyright lawyer. Three months. Funny guy. When we were together, things were great, but he often had to work late, going out with clients. I knew he was going to strip clubs every night. *Conclusion:* I confronted him about it. He denied it. I told him he was a slave to his work and I wanted someone who could be around more. We broke up. I took it hard for a few weeks but ultimately managed to convince myself it was for the best.

Charlie. *Background:* Software engineer. Three dates. Most negative guy I'd ever dated. Hated his job. Hated his parents. Bitter childhood issues that even years of therapy couldn't erase. *Conclusion:* How I even made it through three dates I'll never know. A person had to keep a positive outlook on life. Otherwise, what was the point?

And of course, who could forget—

Jake. *Background:* Guy in marketing department at company where I worked as an event planner. Never dated, but crush lasted from roughly the third hour I was employed with the company until two years later when a large portion of the office staff was given pink slips. He was ten years older than me, though he didn't look it. He was divorced, with two kids: a girl who was twelve and a boy who was ten. He would stop by my cube and tell me funny stories about things his kids did. Occasionally we'd commiserate about the bad dates we'd been on. He was smart and successful, athletic and fun. He told me that since his divorce he'd been trying different forms of yoga, so we'd talk about the benefits of vinyasa versus ashtanga, Birkram versus restorative, yoga for strength versus yoga for relaxation. He made the time at work bearable. The idea that I might see him encouraged me to put a little effort into my appearance each morning. When the rumors about the layoffs began, we'd chat about that, too. He asked me once for my number—he said there was going to be a pre-layoff happy hour next week and he'd call to let me know about it. The happy hour never happened because that Monday morning the rumors came true and half the staff was laid off. The next day Jake called me. He'd also been let go. He'd said, "The one good thing about you and I not working together anymore is that I can finally ask you out on a date. How's tomorrow night sound?" Of course I agreed. For the next twenty-four hours, I didn't care that I was unemployed and headed for more debt than ever. I couldn't stop smiling. I loved the idea that he'd been waiting two years for the chance to ask me out. We ate at a small, dimly lit Italian place. He ordered a bottle of Chianti. Over salads and antipasto, we talked and laughed about work, about who got laid off and who didn't, about what we thought we'd do next. Over our main courses, we talked about his kids, and then about yoga and how nice it would be now that we had more time for it. By the time dessert came, we had absolutely nothing else to talk about. I'd thought we'd had so much in common, but it turned out we really only had enough conversation for brief cubicle-side chats a few times a week. He accompanied me home after dinner and asked if he could walk me to the door. He asked if he could kiss me and I nodded, hoping that I'd been wrong, that there really was something between us. But the kiss told me everything I already knew: my crush was a product of my imagination, something I'd conjured up to make the long, boring days at the office more bearable. *Conclusion:* When he called and asked me for a second date, I said no.

"Pass me a root beer, will ya?"

Scott's comment startled me. I reached into the back, opened the cooler, and grabbed a can of root beer for him and a bottle of water for me.

Dusk was quickly being overtaken by night. I looked out the passenger-side window and, using the darkness for cover, I allowed myself a smile. *It's really rare to find a woman who is beautiful, intelligent, and funny.* I couldn't help it, it felt good to hear those words describe me.

At some point I began to nod off.

"Amber?"

"Huh?"

"I need you to talk to me."

"I want to sleep."

"No. You can't sleep. I need you to help keep me awake. We're only nine hours away."

"Nine hours is a lot of hours. We need to stop or we'll get in an accident. My friend's mother-in-law fell asleep at the wheel and her car turned over. She has brain damage now."

"Was she wearing a seat belt?"

"I don't think so. What's your point? Would you *like* to fall asleep at the wheel and see what happens?"

"Of course not. I was just wondering."

"I think we need to pull over and find some place to sleep."

"But we're so close."

"There's an exit. Are you going to get off?"

He exhaled. "Fine."

We pulled off the highway. I could see three hotels right away—a Motel 6, a Ramada, and a Comfort Inn. The Comfort Inn was first. Scott pulled into the parking lot, stopping just in front of the door. "I'll be right back."

Scott left the car running so I wouldn't freeze to death. I watched him walk inside, then I closed my eyes.

When Scott opened the door and climbed in the driver's seat in less than a minute, I looked at him with eyebrows raised. "That was fast."

"There aren't any rooms."

"Oh. Boo."

He shrugged. "We'll try the Ramada."

Scott pulled out and we drove the quarter mile to the Ramada. We did the same thing again, with Scott going inside and me waiting in the running car resting my eyes. This time it took Scott much longer, which I took as a good sign until he came out and I saw his expression.

"What's wrong?" I asked when he got back in the car.

"They're sold out, too. I asked the woman at the front desk to call around to find a place that has a room. Every hotel in town is booked."

"You're kidding. But why? This is Nebraska. It's not like a hotbed of tourism."

"Nebraska is in the middle of the country. It's apparently where everyone stops to get some sleep. The woman said things have just been really busy with all the holiday travelers. Don't worry, we'll just drive to the next town. We'll be okay."

I looked at the clock: we had just wasted twenty minutes getting nowhere. We were still several hours away from home, but now it was twenty minutes later at night and we were more tired than ever.

Scott yawned. "Tell me something to keep me awake."

"Like what?"

"When did your dad move to California?"

"He got a job transfer there a few years ago."

"Where in California does your dad live?"

"Southern."

"Are you close to your dad?"

I shook my head. "We get along all right, but close? Not really." Dad had dated several women the first year after he and Mom separated while all Mom had done was cry and stress out over money. He met Laurie during that time, and they were married right after the divorce was finalized. He'd been talking about the wedding before the divorce was official, promising Emily and me that we'd get to wear pretty dresses and stand up in the wedding. Then one night a couple weeks after the divorce was official, Mom, Emily, and I came home to a blinking light on the answering machine. The message was from Dad, who said, "Well, girls! Guess what! We couldn't wait any longer! We eloped this afternoon! Talk soon." All three of us just stared at the answering machine for a full minute. Mom was the first one to excuse herself. She locked herself in her bedroom. We could hear that she was trying to mute the sound of her sobs with her pillow. I was the next to run into my room and burst into tears. As far as I know, Emily never cried.

I wasn't even sure what bothered me most, whether it was the fact that Emily and I had been left out of such a huge event in Dad's life or that he broke his promise about the dress. I'd really been looking forward to wearing that dress.

"So you're not going to see him this year?" Scott asked.

"I just saw him at the wedding."

"I think it would be hard not seeing my dad at Christmas."

I shrugged. "To be honest, sometimes the hardest thing about my parents' divorce was getting schlepped back and forth from Mom's place to Dad's place. I remember one Christmas in particular that was really crazy because we had Christmas Eve night with my mom's parents, then we spent the morning with Mom, the afternoon with Dad and Laurie and Laurie's parents, and then that night we went over to Mork's parents' place. We must have eaten about thirteen desserts in those two days. It was nuts. I remember that Christmas really well. Emily had spent weeks trying to cross-stitch a picture that had a little house on it and the words 'Home Is Where the Heart Is.' The message had so much meaning to her—it was her way of telling Dad that it was OK that we were always being shuttled back and forth between Mom's place and Dad's place like we were in a traveling circus, never being able to get comfortable in any one place. We were always forgetting homework assignments and favorite sweaters at the other house; it was a maddeningly nomadic way to live. Emily worked so hard on that little plaque. She'd stabbed herself with a needle so many times her fingers looked like pin cushions. She framed it and wrapped it and when Dad opened it he said, 'How nice,' in this really fake way. And then he looked at it a little more closely and said, 'What happened here?' He pointed to this spot where she'd messed up a little. She apologized and you could see she was embarrassed—it was like, the tiniest little mess up ever. You'd need a magnifying glass to see it. Anyway, the point was that his daughter had lovingly made him this picture and all he could see was the flaws, not the love that had gone into it. He never put it up. Emily never said anything, but I knew she was crushed. After that Emily decided that she had no artistic talent and that I was the artist in the family. She became a crossword-puzzle fanatic and never did artsy craftsy things ever again."

Scott and I saw the exit at the same time. Wordlessly, Scott pulled off. The only hotel we saw was frighteningly reminiscent of the Bates Motel.

"Um, maybe we should wait until we get to a bigger town," I suggested.

"Yeah . . . maybe. But since we're here, I'll just see if they have any vacancies."

Scott parked the car and I watched him ring the doorbell. The office was dark and looked closed, but after a minute or two, the door swung open and I saw a fat man with a ponytail and a goatee open the door and stick out his head—he looked exactly like the comic-book salesman from *The Simpsons*. He and Scott spoke for a minute or two, and then Scott walked back to the car and got back in.

"Nothing?"

"Nothing. We're just like Mary and Joseph," Scott said.

"Except for the part about me not carrying Jesus inside me."

"Except for that."

The snow was starting to pick up. It would not be fun to get stranded in the middle of nowhere in the cold and snow, even if I was sharing the car with a cute guy. "How are we doing on gas?"

Scott looked as he pulled out of the parking lot and back onto the highway. "We're fine. Check on the map for when we're going to hit the next town."

I opened the map. "What was the last town we were in?"

"I have no idea."

"Well how am I supposed to tell you when we're going to hit another town when I don't have any idea where we are now?"

"There's no need to snap."

"Sorry. I'm just tired." I turned on the radio. "I want to hear what the snow is going to do."

He nodded. The snow looked beautiful, but it was definitely impacting visibility. I could only find one station that would come through, and it insisted on playing terrible music, the kind of truly painful eighties stuff that signaled the decline of civilization.

"I thought you said the universe was always looking out for you," Scott said. "If that's true, why can't we find a place to get some sleep?"

"The universe *is* looking out for you. But that doesn't always mean it's going to give you what you think you want. Sometimes the things that seem like the worst thing that can happen to you can turn out to be the best. Sometimes there are lessons in life that you have to learn."

We came to another small town, but there wasn't a hotel in sight. Just to be on the safe side, Scott filled up the tank at one of those tiny gas stations that still had pumps from the 1950s. I watched the car's digital clock go from one in the morning to two in the morning to three in the morning.

"Hey, hey, hey," I said. "There's a sign for Sterling, Colorado."

Scott pulled off and drove up to the hotel. We were only a couple of hours away from Denver, but we were both punchy from a lack of sleep. Another car pulled up just as we did. I knew without a doubt that they were plotting to take the last room. "You pull up to the door. I'll run in. I need a credit card," I said. He tossed me his wallet and I bolted inside, slapping his credit card on the counter just in front of the other couple.

"I need a room," I said.

"We have one single left."

"Yeah, great, sure, whatever." I didn't ask how much the room was going to cost. At this point I didn't care; I would have paid anything, I was so delirious with sleep. Scott walked inside and I turned to him with a deranged smile on my face. "I got us a room. It's a single, but I don't care."

"Fine by me. I'd sleep in a garbage Dumpster at this point."

We took our bags to the room and I did my usual ritual of stripping the comforter off the bed. "I don't have the energy to brush my teeth or go into the bathroom to change," I announced, "so you're just going to have to deal with my bad breath and turn around so I can put some shorts on."

"Sure." Scott sounded exhausted, too.

He turned around and as he pulled off his sweater, I pulled off mine—I was wearing a T-shirt underneath. I pulled off my jeans and slipped on some heather gray shorts that I would theoretically wear if I ever worked out. Then I collapsed into bed. Moments later, Scott did the same. I was so tired, I barely noticed how close we were, how near his flesh was to my own.

Chapter 16

Emily

Six days before Christmas

Thanks to the cold medicine and lots of vitamin C, I was feeling better in the morning. I'd taken the rest of the week off from work to get ready for the big day. I'd wanted to sleep in till a wild-and-crazy eight AM, as opposed to my usual six or six-thirty AM, but Mom took care of that by calling just before seven.

"Huh?" I answered.

"Are you sleeping?"

"Not anymore." I looked over to see Luke still fast asleep. I hated people capable of sleeping through ringing phones and beeping alarms. I swear if a mouse farted three cities over I was jolted from slumber. I closed my eyes and rested the right side of my head against my pillow as I held the receiver to my left ear. Unfortunately, I was the type of person who found it impossible to fall back to sleep once I'd been woken up.

"I thought you were usually up by six."

"I took this week off. I was up late last night."

"Oh. Well, how are you?"

I noticed she didn't offer an *I'm sorry.* "I'm *tired.*"

"I finally thought of some things I'd like for Christmas."

"Mom, I'm already done shopping." Why weren't people more *organized?* Why couldn't they *plan ahead?*

"Oh. Well, should I tell you anyway?"

I rolled my eyes. "I guess."

"Well, I'd love a gift certificate to Starbucks. I love their Chai Lattes but they're so expensive, you know?"

"Hmmm."

"And I'd like some Bobbi Brown eye cream."

"How much is that?"

"Thirty-five bucks."

I sat up. "What's wrong with Ponds?"

My mother tsked. "And I'd really like a new purse."

"What kind of purse?"

"Black. Medium sized."

"Mom, I have trouble enough picking out a purse that I like for myself. There's no way I could pick one out for you. It would be like Gwen picking out that awful painting for Luke."

"What painting?"

"I didn't tell you? For Luke's birthday she got him this god-awful brown and orange landscape painting. It looks like the artist spent about twelve minutes on it. It's technically original art but it's right off the assembly line. I'm sure the artist must have painted about a thousand of the exact same scene."

My mother didn't say anything for a moment. She wasn't the type to say bad things about people.

As diplomatically as possible she said, "Gwen does have a unique sense of taste."

"Are you kidding me? She gets her accessorizing ideas from Mr. T."

Mom snickered. "She really does like her gold jewelry."

"I'm surprised her earlobes don't reach her shoulders like certain tribes in Africa, her earrings are so huge."

Mom laughed again.

"All right, Mom, I should get going. I'll see what I can do on the presents front. I'll talk to you soon."

"Love you, honey."

"Love you, Mom."

I hung up the phone, slipped on my sweatshirt, and padded downstairs where the kids were watching cartoons.

"Emily?" Claire asked.

"Uh-huh," I said, covering my yawn with my hand as I headed to the kitchen to make a pot of coffee.

"Santa knows everything we want for Christmas, right? Kind of like God knows everything?"

I stopped in my tracks and turned to look at her. "You and Josh already sent your letters to Santa asking for what you wanted."

"I know, but I just wanted to see if he knew what we *really* wanted."

"Without telling him?"

She nodded.

"Well, uh, I'm sure Santa knows everything, but he's a busy guy. He has to go all over the world in just one night. He's got a lot of elf administrative assistants helping him keep everything straight. I think it's best if they have a clear list to work from. What gift didn't you tell Santa about?"

"Baby Anna," Josh said, rolling his eyes. He was wearing thermal pajamas with smiling whales on them. I was fairly certain there was nothing cuter on earth than a skinny four-year-old boy wearing thermal pajamas with whales on them.

"All my friends have them," Claire explained calmly.

"What's Baby Anna?" I had planned on cleaning and grocery shopping today, but suddenly it was looking like I had a new quest on my hands. I would be like one of the Knights of the Round Table in search of the Holy Grail until I found this thing. (And there was no way Santa was getting the credit for this! I'd find the precious doll and Claire would have no choice but to love me forever. Or at least not totally hate me for an hour or two.)

"It's just a dumb *doll*," Josh said.

"It is not a dumb doll. It cries and farts and laughs and everything," Claire said.

"It *farts*?"

"Or maybe it burps. I can't remember."

"I see. Well, Santa is really up to the wire here, but I'll shoot the North Pole an e-mail and we'll see what they can do."

"You can e-mail the North Pole?" Claire asked.

"'Course. Santa has Internet access. You kidding me? I'll send an e-mail as soon as I get some coffee."

Claire smiled as my heart sunk.

I went into the kitchen, made a pot of coffee, and went to the study where Luke and I kept the computer. I tried not to work from home but when I did I used my laptop, so the study was typically Luke's domain. My plan was to check online for Baby Anna and have it rush delivered. The first thing that popped up was Luke's e-mail. Before I could minimize the e-mail browser, my eyes immediately zeroed in on one of the few e-mails that weren't bold, indicating that it had already been read. I would have thought nothing of it, except the name on the FROM line was Carol Travers. My heart thumped painfully. I'd been so busy lately I hadn't had time to worry about his old grade-school pal.

OK, think this through logically. There are many "Carols" in the world. And even if this is his childhood friend, so what? He's just being friendly.

Every part of me ached to open that e-mail and read what it said, but I knew that would be an incredible breach of trust. I had to think about how violated I would feel if Luke did the same thing to me.

Be a better person, a trusting person, a good . . .

I opened the e-mail.

Luke!
It was so good to catch up with you! I know you've gone through so much these past few years, but it sounds like you've found a wonderful woman. I'm sure Claire and Emily will work things out soon. I feel for Emily—it can't be easy for a woman to suddenly get used to becoming a new mom overnight! She'll figure things out.

I have to admit I'm a little jealous that you were able to find someone new. Since the divorce, I've gone on a few dull dates but that's it. It's hard to be in a new town. Friday nights are lonely. Let me know if you ever have a chance to join me for a cocktail or two after work. I could use the company!

Carol

He was telling strange women about how my stepdaughter hated my guts and I didn't know what I was doing in the motherhood department? And what was this "get a cocktail or two" shit? Everyone knew that cocktails reduced people's inhibitions so that they could then go have sex. It was a simple equation: Cocktails = Sex. *Ga!*

But I couldn't confront him about it because then I'd have to admit I was a jealous, untrusting, conniving bitch who was reduced to reading his e-mails. I checked the date on the e-mail. It was two weeks ago. Had Luke seemed unusual lately? Had he seemed unusually busy?

My eyes sprang open—that night when I'd made cookies with the kids! Luke had said he had to work late! Work late, my ass.

I exhaled. OK, I couldn't let myself get worked up about this. So what if he did go out and meet her again? He wouldn't mind if I went out with a male friend. I trusted him.

Anyway, I didn't have time to worry about this now. I'd worry about it later. I opened Internet Explorer with trembling hands and went to www.toyrus.com and searched for Baby Anna. The web site shot me over to amazon.com where I was told in bold, enthusiastic letters that they were OUT OF STOCK and MORE ON THE WAY! The estimated shipping wait was three weeks. Fat lot of good that did me.

I tried target.com, walmart.com, eBaby.com—anything I could think of, and all I got were messages that no Baby Annas were in stock. She looked like a pretty average doll to me except the manufacturers wanted to charge ninety bucks for her. She wet her diapers and cried real tears and came with a whole bag of baby accessories.

Next I picked up the phone and began dialing

local stores I thought might carry Baby Anna. One after the other told me they'd been sold out for weeks but they expected another shipment in two or three weeks. I dialed the last number futilely, glaring at my cup of coffee because it was doing absolutely nothing to jar me from my groggy state.

"Hi, yes, can you please tell me if you have any Baby Annas left in stock?"

I waited for the young male clerk to laugh at me as most of the others had done, so I thought maybe I'd fallen asleep and was dreaming when he said, "Actually, we just had one returned this morning. Apparently both the mother and the father had purchased one for their daughter and they returned one of them."

"Oh, my God! This is wonderful! Can you please put it aside? My name is Emily Taylor-Garrett."

"I'm sorry, ma'am, but we sell them on a first-come, first-served basis."

"You don't understand. I just married a widower and his daughter can't stand me. If I could get her this doll, she might just open up to me a little. It could mean breaking down barriers in our familial dynamics."

"Ma'am, I'm really sorry . . ."

"All right, all right, but do you think you could maybe, I don't know, sort of semihide it under another toy so it would be hard for someone to find?"

He paused. "Uh . . . I guess I could do that."

"Wonderful! Thank you! Tell me what toy so I can head straight to it."

"Uh, it'll be near the Rockin' Puppy."

"The Rockin' Puppy?"

"Just come into the store, go right, and you'll find a whole row of Rockin' Puppys at the end."

"Great. Thank you. Thank you so much." I threw

down the phone and raced into the bedroom where I took Luke by the arm and shook him like a martini.

"Huh? What?"

"I need you to watch the kids. I'm going out shopping for a few last-minute Christmas gifts and I don't have time to talk."

I threw on some jeans and some hiking shoes and bolted out to the garage. At stoplights, I tried to make myself look somewhat presentable by pulling a comb through my greasy hair and applying a little eye makeup and lip gloss. Even so, in the sweatshirt and coat I was wearing I could have been eight months pregnant and no one would be any the wiser.

I got to the store, a specialty toy store I never shopped at because the prices were exorbitant, parked the car, and raced inside. I turned to my right just as the clerk had instructed and immediately I saw a woman lifting up a Rockin' Puppy box and pulling out what I recognized as Baby Anna. The doll itself was rather ugly, not nearly as cute as a real baby, but that wasn't the point. The point was that Claire wanted it and therefore I had to have it.

"Excuse me, ma'am," I said. "Can I please have that?"

She looked at me as though I'd just escaped from a mental institution. "No. I'm buying it."

"The clerk guy hid it under there especially for me."

"If he put it away for you, why is it out here where I can buy it?"

I couldn't think of a response, so I tried a new tack. "See, the thing is, I really need that doll. I just got married to a man who is a widower and he has two kids and one of them is a seven-year-old girl and she thinks that I'm trying to replace her mother or something even though I'm not trying . . ."

"What does this have to do with me?" the woman asked, giving me the chance to catch my breath.

"Well, uh, technically nothing. My point in sharing this story with you was to see if maybe I could draw on your good will and Christmas spirit. The thing is, Claire's mother died in a tragic accident when Claire was too young to really understand what was going on. She has all this pent-up anger that she doesn't know how to deal with. I know that as soon as she opens up, things can be great between us. That's not to say I'm the perfect mom or anything, I've made my mistakes, but I'm trying, you know? Really trying. Anyway, she really wants this doll and I feel like if I can get it for her maybe she'll give me a chance and she can be happy and then I'll be happy and then her father can be happy."

"Look, lady, I'm sorry you've got a bratty kid on your hands, but I hate to break it to you, so do all of the rest of us. I'm buying this doll."

The woman charged past me toward the cash register. She was in her late thirties and had a too-large nose and a lumpy body and hair that needed a serious makeover. I plastered a smile on my face. "Look, miss," I said making my voice as sweet as I could, "Poor Claire's mother died when Claire was only four years old. Claire really wants the chance to be a mother to this doll because her own mother died so young."

The woman glared at me and slapped the doll on the counter. "Lady, if you don't get away from me, I'm calling the cops." She whipped out her credit card as the clerk rang up the purchase. I lingered for a moment, wondering if I might be able to steal the doll from her when she got outside. If I left my car door open and got the car running before she got there, maybe I could get away before . . .

Before the cops came and carted me off to jail over a stupid doll. I had to gain some perspective here. I wasn't thinking straight. If I was going to be able to think clearly, I needed to be much more heavily caffeinated. Mom had said she'd like a gift certificate to Starbucks, so I could buy her an easy stocking stuffer while obtaining my much-needed caffeine at the same time.

I drove to the nearest store and walked in, rooting through my purse looking for my wallet. I got in line, looked up, and saw my neighbor Judy. I'd chatted with her briefly a few times. Every time I talked to her she told me about her boob job. I barely knew the woman, but I had intimate knowledge of her breasts—how much they cost (ten thousand dollars), when she had them done (last year), how painful the surgery was (very), and the fact that after a year they should have begun to sag a little to give them a more natural look, but her breasts simply weren't going down. This was a big problem for her; she simply didn't know what to do. I also knew she had two small boys and she was married to a sweet guy named Stan, but the only reason I knew that was because I'd run into Stan and seen the boys—Judy didn't talk about her family because she was always too busy talking about her boobs.

"Judy, hi."

"Emily, hi. How are you?"

"Oh. You know. I'm crazed with getting ready for the holidays. I'll be happy when it's over and things get back to normal. How are you?"

"Well, I told you about my issue with my boob job."

"Yeah." My voice was flat, but there were just some people in this world who refused to notice nonverbal cues. "You did."

"Well, nothing's changed. They still won't sag at all. I don't know what to do. I really don't want to have another surgery."

"I can understand that."

"But they are simply too high. I want them to look more natural."

Judy's fake boobs were not of the understated variety. They were very much of the "please notice me, I'm desperate for attention" sort. I'd learned from Judy that she would prefer that her breasts weren't perched up nearly to her collarbone, but even if they weren't so astonishingly perky, they were still undeniably gravity-defyingly enormous. I'd known a couple women who were busty but not chubby in other areas, but it was a rare combination. And those women I knew were all soft curves. Judy was skinny and lean, with a distance-runner's long, ropey muscles. As far as I knew, it was unheard of for a woman as skeletal as Judy to have been born with enormous breasts, so it was a little hard for me to sympathize with her plight. She'd zoomed right past subtle several cup sizes ago.

"I'm really sorry to hear that. How are the boys doing?"

"Hmmm? Oh, they're fine. My doctor says that I should just give my breasts more time, but I don't know, I'm a little worried to tell you the truth."

"Uh-huh. And Stan, how's he doing?"

"This is his busy season, but I guess he's okay. So what do *you* think I should do?"

It took me a second to figure out what she was asking me about. "If the doctor says they'll come down eventually, I'd just try not to worry about it. Just see what happens. Let nature take its course." It occurred to me that "nature" had very little to do with her saline-fake breasts, but she didn't seem to notice.

Thankfully, I got to the head of the line and had to order, which cut her off from her endless tit talk for at least a moment.

I got the gift certificate and waited for my drink. As I waited, my cell phone rang. The caller ID let me know it was Luke. "Hey, babe," I said. "What's up?"

"Uh . . ." Uh-oh. No good news ever began with a sheepish "uh." "Mom just called."

"Yes?"

"She sort of told Charlie that she and Stuart and the kids could come for Christmas."

"Charlie" was Charlene, Luke's stepsister from his mother's second marriage to Jay. Charlie was about our age and I really liked her. At Thanksgiving she told me that she and her family were going to be spending Christmas with her husband's family in Florida. I would have been happy to invite her if I'd had time to plan for the extra people, but as it was, I was freaking out over entertaining the nine people I'd known about. I had less than a week left until Christmas. Increasing the size of the party by fifty percent at the last minute seemed daunting to say the least.

"Excuse me, what? Do you mean to say that your mother said she would *ask me* if it was okay to add more people? Because surely she wouldn't invite people to *my* party without asking if it was okay with me."

"Well, it's really *our* party."

"Oh, really. And tell me exactly what you've done to get ready for it. Have you planned all the food? Bought and wrapped all the gifts? Decorated the entire house? Do you plan on doing all the cooking and the cleaning?"

"I helped get the house painted."

"Luke, we had to paint the house anyway. We just had to get it done sooner than later because of Christmas, that's all."

"I don't want to argue with you. You like Charlie. I like Charlie. I just don't see what the big deal is."

"I *do* like Charlie. And I guess it won't kill me to figure out how to expand the menu by fifty percent and plan and buy all the additional ingredients and how to increase the recipes. But that's not the issue. The issue is that your mother invited them without even consulting with me first."

"Well, she did tell me."

"After she'd already invited Charlie! It doesn't count."

"Take a deep breath. Everything will be all right."

I exhaled. He was right. I was overreacting. "I'm sorry. I'm just going on too little sleep these days. I'm a little tightly wound lately."

"There's one other thing."

I rolled my eyes just as the barista announced that my skinny Latte Grande was ready. I took my cup and walked toward the door. That's when I realized I'd been arguing on my cell phone in a public place. Ordinarily if I had to talk on a cell phone in public, I tried to find a secluded corner someplace so I could talk in private and spare strangers the intimate details of my personal life. But Luke had caught me off guard. I opened the door and walked into the frigid winter air. "What?" I asked.

"Charlie and the gang need somewhere to stay. They can't afford a hotel because Stu lost a big contract. That's why they couldn't fly to Florida to see his mom. They were just going to drive here."

"What are you saying?" Then it hit me like an anvil to the gut. "Wait a second, you're not suggesting that they stay with *us*, are you? There isn't even going to be enough room for Amber, let alone a family of four."

"I said that to Mom. She suggested that Amber take the couch and Charlie and Stu take Claire's room. The boys can stay with Claire and Josh in Josh's room. It'll be like a big slumber party."

My blood raced and I hadn't even taken a sip of coffee yet. Was it possible to have a heart attack at the age of thirty-four? Because I imagined this was how your body felt at the onset of an attack. "How long were they planning to stay?"

"Just four or five days."

"*Just* four or five days?"

"They're going to get in on the twenty-third and leave on the twenty-seventh."

"The twenty-third? Do you know how many things I have to get done between now and Christmas? How am I supposed to get it all done if I have a family of four to feed and entertain?"

"I'm sure they can keep themselves busy. They'll stay out of your way. Besides, you have the next few days off."

"Right, and I was planning to use that time to clean and shop and get ready. Now I suddenly need to plan how to feed a family of four three meals a day for five or six days. And if you haven't noticed, our home is a disaster. It still reeks of paint fumes and there are tools and paint cans everywhere. We haven't even finished unpacking."

"I'm sorry, babe, I really am. But the more the merrier, right?"

"The more the merrier? I'm glad I'm talking to you on the phone and you're not standing right in front of me, because if you were standing in front of me, I think I might just have to punch you in the nose. Look, I have to get going. I suddenly just got a whole lot busier."

Chapter 17

Amber

Five days before Christmas

When I awoke, Scott was lying just inches away from me. He was watching me and smiling. I suddenly became aware of just how long it had been since I'd brushed my teeth or ran a comb through my hair. All I could think about were the onions on the burger I'd had yesterday.

"You looked like you needed the sleep," Scott said.

"How long have you been awake?"

"Not long. Twenty minutes."

He'd been staring at me for the last twenty minutes? Had I snored? Drooled? Talked in my sleep? I did vaguely remember having a sex dream about Scott the night before. What if I'd moaned or shouted his name?

"What time is it?"

"About ten. Checkout is at eleven."

"Just enough time to shower. You want to go first?"

"Your hair is longer. Have at it."

"Why are you smiling at me like that?"

"I was just thinking about what you said last night, about the universe looking out for us. We were so tired and just wanted a place to sleep, but as fate would have it, there was no other room except one with a single queen-size bed. Now that's fate, don't you think?"

I looked at him for a moment and sat up. I didn't know how to answer him so I decided to ignore his question. "I'm just going to call my sister and let her know we're almost there before I hit the shower."

He nodded.

"Can I use your cell phone?"

"'Course."

I dialed Emily's cell. "Merry Christmas," I said.

"I want to kill myself!"

"Things are going well I take it."

"Gwen invited Charlie and her entire family to stay with us. I found out about it *yesterday*."

I flinched. "Ooh. Sorry, sis. I was calling to say we're here in Colorado. I'll be at your place in, I don't know, three hours maybe."

"I can't wait to see you."

"I can't wait to see you. I'll be able to help you get stuff ready. Cook. Clean. Watch the kids. Help you plot Gwen's untimely death. Whatever you need."

She laughed. "Great. I'll see you soon."

After I showered, I gave Scott the bathroom and did my best to dry my hair at the desk in the main room. I felt a thousand times better with some sleep, clean teeth, and a shower.

* * *

The last stretch of driving seemed to fly by. I didn't want to say good-bye to Scott. Even being scrunched up in a car for hours on end was fun with him around. There was a part of me that wanted the snow to become a raging blizzard so we'd be forced to pull over and spend more time together, but it just continued falling in light flakes.

Neither of us said anything for the last hour until we started getting close to Denver and I needed to give him directions for how to get to Emily's.

We pulled up her driveway and before we could even get out of the car, Emily ran out to greet us wearing jeans, slippers, and a wraparound sweater she pulled tight around her.

I opened the door, screamed, and ran up to her, nearly knocking her over with the force of my hug. "God, I missed you. It's so good to see you!" I kissed her cheek.

"It's good to see you, too. You look great."

I pulled away. "You're kidding, right? I've spent the last three days cooped up in a car. I'm not wearing any makeup and my clothes reek of the greasy diners we've been eating at."

Behind me I could hear Scott's door open and close. Emily leaned in and said quietly, "There is just a glow about you. You seem really happy. Anything happen on the road that I should know about?"

I smiled. "Emily, I'd like you to meet Scott Cardoza." I gestured toward Scott, who was lingering by the car several feet back.

He walked forward and extended his hand. "It's nice to meet you."

"It's nice to meet you, too."

Scott pulled my bags from the trunk and brought them to the door.

"Would you like to come inside for something to eat? Something to drink?" Emily asked him.

"Thanks, but I have to drop this car off. My brother is expecting me."

She nodded. There was an awkward moment as the three of us stood there not saying anything. I could see the flash of recognition cross her face when she realized Scott and I needed a moment to say our good-byes.

"Amber, I'll bring your bags inside. Again, it was nice meeting you, Scott."

He waved. "Merry Christmas."

"Merry Christmas to you."

With Emily gone, I turned to Scott.

"So . . ."

"I have your number," he said.

I nodded. "Thanks for the ride."

"I get back on the twenty-ninth. I'm flying back, obviously. I'm going to a party for New Year's. Would you like to come with me?"

I smiled and shrugged. "Maybe. Thanks for . . . everything."

"No, thank *you.*"

I stepped forward and hugged him.

"I'll call you when we're both back in New York," he said.

"I'd like that."

"So, I guess this is good-bye for now."

"Merry Christmas."

"Yeah. Same to you. Merry Christmas."

I watched him get back into his truck and drive away, then I turned and walked inside Emily's.

"He was cute as *hell,*" was the first thing she said to me.

I nodded. "This place is adorable." I set my bags near the door and looked around.

"Thanks. So is he single?"

"He's single."

"And?"

"And what? He's a gorgeous young actor who is seven years younger than me. Nothing can ever happen."

"Why not?"

"I just said. He's young. He's gorgeous. He's been on TV and in movies." I started showing myself around since Emily was apparently too busy grilling me about Scott to do it herself.

"But the way he looked at you. He seemed to really like you."

"We had fun driving together, sure. He said he thought I was pretty and fun. But he's way too good-looking. He's out of my league. We might have some fun together for a while, but then he'd just leave me for a younger woman."

"Not every guy in this world is Dad."

I stopped in my tracks, frozen. I felt like I'd just gotten the wind knocked out of me. It amazed me how much Dad's infidelity still hurt. Of course, it wasn't even Emily and me that he'd cheated on, it was Mom, but the betrayal still felt personal. All those nights he'd been on the road when Emily and I were kids . . . the night he decided he no longer wanted to go on pretending. Mom had known. Emily had known. I had known. Even so, the truth was too painful to bear. He left Mom for another woman and then ended up leaving *her* a few months later. There were a few other women that Emily and I knew about, and then came Laurie.

The crazy thing was that Dad actually came

across as a really nice guy. If an apparently nice guy could cheat on his wife and leave her for another woman, any guy could.

"Look, Amber," Emily said. "Mom and Dad didn't work out. Dad's a good guy who cheated on his wife, but his cheating was a symptom of the problems in their relationship."

"Actually, Emily, I believe his cheating pretty much *caused* their problems."

"People don't cheat if their relationship is going well."

"All relationships go through hard times. We're just supposed to ignore our spouse cheating when challenges come up?"

"Aunt Amber!" Claire ran up to me and gave me a hug. I couldn't say I was sorry to have my conversation with Emily cut short.

"Claire, look at you, you pretty girl."

"Wanna see my room?"

"Yeah, of course I do."

I took Claire's hand and followed her up the stairs. Emily followed behind us. "I really love what you've done with the place," I told Emily. She smiled tightly. I knew she wanted to finish our conversation. I got along with Dad all right, but it was excruciating to remember back to the divorce, to when Mom became a single mother scrambling to make ends meet. Dad had no trouble finding women to date, while Mom as a single mother found it considerably harder.

Claire pushed open the door to her room. It was a pink-and-glitter explosion. I smiled. "This is great, Claire."

"Dad and Emily let me decorate myself. Look, this is my pillow." She held up a pink pillow with a glitter rainbow on it.

"That is the coolest. That looks just like something I'd have when I was a little girl."

Claire went around her room and showed me a glitter Raggedy Ann picture on her wall, various toys and stuffed animals, and the pièce de résistance: a trunk covered in shag carpet. "Dad made it for me. I put all my secret stuff in here. Wanna see?"

"'Course."

Claire gave Emily a pointed look. Emily raised her eyebrows, understanding that she wasn't included in this. "I've got some appetizers to work on for Christmas. I'll leave you two alone."

The trunk had a simple lock on it. Claire twisted the numbers, unlatched the lock, and opened the trunk. "Here's my memory book." She opened a pretty green book that had photos in it. "This is my mom."

"She's beautiful."

Claire nodded and pointed to a picture of herself in a pale purple dress. "This is me at Easter when I was a little girl."

I smiled. I loved the idea that she thought her days of being a "little girl" were long gone. "Look at those blonde curls!"

She flipped the page and showed me a picture of her holding Josh. "This is Josh when he was just a baby."

"He's such a cutie."

She went through the rest of the pictures, then she showed me her journal. She'd barely written anything in it, but her handwriting was so large, a few paragraphs took up several pages. She showed me a couple ribbons she'd won in first grade for penmanship in school and a badge she'd earned during her brief foray being a Brownie. Beneath all that, she had a few loose photographs. She frowned and handed them over to me.

"This is Dad and Emily's wedding. Look, you're here."

I flipped through the pictures. Though her dress was simple, Emily looked stunning. Luke was handsome as hell. I didn't look so bad myself. Emily and Luke had had a low-key wedding. I'd been the only bridesmaid, so I'd gotten to wear whatever I felt like. I'd worn a pale green dress, and I have to say the coloring was perfect for my hair and eyes. "What does Emily think of your secret box?"

"I've never shown her."

"Why not?"

Claire shrugged again. She took the stack of pictures, put them back in the trunk, and locked it. I'd met Claire maybe three times ever, and I was already privy to her secret trunk, but Emily, who lived with Claire, had never gotten a single peek. I was beginning to suspect that despite her cute house, gorgeous husband, adorable stepkids, and precious dog, maybe my sister wasn't living the easy life like I'd thought.

"We should go downstairs and help your mom with dinner," I said.

"She's NOT my mom."

"Your stepmom, I mean."

We went downstairs and Claire went off to play with Josh as I joined Emily in the kitchen.

"What are you making?" I asked.

She gave me a conspiratorial look. "Fried chicken, mac and cheese, and mashed potatoes. I'm making salad, too, so I don't have to feel completely guilty about getting dinner from KFC."

"KFC? You? But you're such a health nut."

"Not anymore. Now I'm an as-fast-as-I-can-have-someone-else-make-it-for-me nut."

"Scott and I feel the same way. We share a mutual adoration for processed cheese products."

"Hmmm," she smiled.

"What's with that grin?"

"Nothing. Tell me more about this guy."

I smiled. "Well, he's supermasculine, but he doesn't mind talking about emotions or feelings. I think it's because he's an actor. Anyway, I kind of like it. It's like having the best of both worlds. The strong-sexy-manly type who isn't a Neanderthal."

"I want to hear about the kiss. The trip. Everything."

"The kisses were nice. They were more friendly than anything," I lied. I could tell by the incredulous look on her face that she didn't buy it for a second. "The trip actually wasn't so bad," I continued on quickly. "I feel ill from all the crappy food I ate and it got pretty cramped in the car after a while, but Scott's really easy to talk to. It was actually kind of fun."

"You said he said he thought you were cute."

"Yeah, but I was female and I was there."

"He just wanted a one-night stand?"

"Well, he said he wanted to see me back in New York, but . . . It could just never work. And don't give me that crap about how I can't commit to a guy because Dad couldn't commit to Mom when I was a little girl."

"Dad's been committed to Laurie for years."

"As far as we know. He's out in California. He still travels a lot. We don't really know what he's up to."

"Not all men cheat."

"That's exactly what Scott said."

"You talked about this?"

"Scott thinks I have issues with men."

Emily laughed.

"What?"

"Nothing, nothing. You get the paper plates. I'll get the napkins. We've got people to feed."

Josh, Claire, Luke, Emily, and I sat around the table fishing chicken out of enormous paper vats, our fingers sticky with grease.

"How was your trip?" Luke asked me.

"It was good. I got a ride with a guy who has been in a commercial and a couple independent films. He's a really nice guy, so he was easy to talk to. The time went pretty fast."

"I can't believe you drove from New York," Luke said. "I'd be ready to commit hari-kari."

I smiled and told them about not being able to find a place to stay in Nebraska. I almost told them about smashing into the Nativity scene, but they already considered me a flake. I needed to get out of the habit of getting laughs out of making fun of myself because it just reinforced this image of me as a space cadet. I could be spacey and in my own world, but I was also an intelligent woman and it would be nice if my family could remember that sometimes.

"How's the massage therapy going?" Luke asked.

"Good. I'm still trying to build my client base. It's all still pretty new. Scott had a great idea for me to try to get corporate clients who would sponsor chair-massage days for their employees as a perk. As soon as I get back to New York I'm going to put some brochures together and do a better job of promoting myself."

"I still get a pain in my forearm every now and

then from an accident when I was a kid," he said. "I go to a massage therapist and she just works wonders on it."

"What happened to your arm?"

Luke told a story of how he had broken his wrist when he was about nine. He had been playing Army with a friend of his and went diving to cover a hand grenade and save the rest of his platoon. Unfortunately, he overshot his mark and his wrist went careening into a thick tree trunk. It made me think of a story Scott had told me about something he and his older brother had done when they were kids. They'd taken dozens and dozens of sparklers, tied them together, and lit them. The sparklers flew up into the air like a rocket ship . . . but then they started coming right back down to earth where Scott and his brother were. Scott had cracked me up imitating how he and his brother had screamed and ran away and then later had to go around acting like they'd never been worried at all so they could pretend they were tough guys.

"Did I tell you that the guy I drove out here with has been in TV and movies?" I asked.

"A few times." Emily smiled knowingly.

I finished off the rest of my mashed potatoes as if I were in some sort of contest.

When everyone was done eating, I helped Emily with the very easy task of cleaning up, which primarily meant doing mass destruction to the environment by throwing away an obscene amount of paper products.

"You sure seem to talk a lot about a guy who you don't think you have any future with," she said.

"I . . ." I began to protest. "I mean, I like him. I just spent three days with him. He's on my mind, that's all. I'll get over it before I even get back to

New York. I really hope Dad and Aunt Lu and all the other usual suspects send me enough cash that I'll have a way to fly back to New York." I hoped she didn't notice that I was trying to change the subject. She was right, I couldn't stop thinking about Scott. Would he be to California by now? Was he thinking about me? Would he really call me when we got back to New York? What sort of spell had he put over me that he had taken over my every waking thought?

Chapter 18

Emily

Two days before Christmas

I'd spent the last few days in a blur of preparation and cleaning. Life was a marathon of laundry and dusting and scrubbing. By the time Charlie, Stu, and the boys arrived, the beds were made, the kids' rooms were momentarily neat, the appliances gleamed, and the only thing lying on the floor was our dog, Lucy.

"They're here! They're here!" Claire shouted when she heard their SUV pull into our driveway.

I tucked my hair behind my ears, opened the door, and went out to greet them.

Claire ran out to hug her aunt and uncle and greet her cousins. Josh lingered by my legs, wrapping his hand around one of them.

Charlie's husband, Stu, was a tall, skinny man who didn't say much. Charlie was thin with short dark hair. She was one of those women who was completely transformed when wearing makeup. I didn't know if these women had some magical knowledge about the art of makeup that could change them from being faded and drab to sexy and bold, or if it was just something to do with their natural coloring that made them appear exhausted and plain without a little Clinique or L'Oreal.

Today Charlie was in her fully made-up face. She wore jeans and a blue cable-knit sweater with white snowflakes, and she looked like a Lands End model with a healthy glow and cheerfulness that infused her entire being.

Her two boys, ages eight and ten, were thin and dark like their parents. They were so skinny they looked like stick figures that belonged in a game of hangman. The oldest boy's name was Tim. His younger brother was Bobby.

"Thank you so much for having us," Charlie said, hugging me. "It was really nice of you to let us come at the last minute like this. We'd been waiting for Stu's contract to come through so we could buy plane tickets to Florida, but the deal fell through. We were going to just stay home for Christmas, but then I thought about how much more fun it would be to see all of you. Plus I wanted a sneak peek at your new house."

"Don't worry about it," Luke said, kissing her cheek. "The more the merrier."

There he was with that "more the merrier" crap.

Amber had only met Charlie and her family once at the wedding, but she, too, took a moment to shake Stu's hand and hug Charlie and the boys.

Luke and I helped them with their bags and showed Stu and Charlie to their room while the kids ran off to play.

"The house is adorable!" Charlie said as we crossed through the kitchen and living room and went up the stairs.

I smiled. It was the validation I'd so craved. "Thanks. I'll show you the 'Before' pictures. It was quite a project to transform this place."

"I bet you got a lot of great tips from the Home & Garden Network. Don't you just love those shows?"

Charlie was a stay-at-home mom, so she had time to watch that sort of thing. Though Luke and I had sprung for cable, I hadn't watched anything but cartoons with the kids since we'd moved in.

"I haven't had much time to watch TV lately," I said, setting down their luggage. "This is Claire's room. This is where you and Stu will be staying. I know the full-size bed will be a little cramped . . ."

"Don't worry about it," Charlie said, wrapping one arm around Stu's waist. "It'll be good for us."

"I know the room is a little pink. It was Claire's choice."

"It'll be fun for me," Charlie said. "There's too much testosterone where I live. A little pink will do me some good."

"She's in a glitter stage, I'm afraid," Luke said, picking up one of the shiny pillows that held up her zoo of stuffed animals. "We're hoping she'll outgrow it soon when she moves into the rebellious, smoking-and-sneaking-out-past-curfew phase, which, frankly I think we're looking forward to."

Charlie laughed. Stu smiled, the first gesture since he'd arrived that suggested he wasn't a statue. He worked as a sound-engineering consultant, which meant he went where concert halls and theaters were being built and gave construction advice. He was a brilliant man, and he was friendly when you asked him a direct question. I couldn't ask him how work was going—obviously not very well if they couldn't fly to Florida as planned. Besides work and the boys, I had no earthly clue what to talk to him about.

"Do you need anything to drink?" I asked.

"The kids have had about twelve juice boxes this morning and Stu and I have each drunk an ocean or two of water a-piece, thanks though." Charlie pushed her short hair behind her ear.

"Do you need a bathroom, then?"

She laughed. "We took care of that a couple cities ago, thanks."

"What did you want to do today?" I silently prayed that she would say something that included the phrase "keep out of your hair." Maybe they could go to a museum all day or a movie marathon—anything to keep them occupied for a few hours while I frantically finished up my epic to-do list.

"We would love to go for a hike. It's so beautiful out today."

She was right, it was. Sunny and a balmy fifty degrees, it really would be criminal to spend the entire day indoors.

"We don't have mountains in Nebraska," she added. "We would love to go with you and Luke. It's so important to spend time with your family when you can. Life is just too short."

"That would be a lot of fun," Luke said.

"Uh, yeah, sure. Of course. That'd be great," I said, though the thought of spending two hours in the car to get to the mountains with four young, screaming children sounded about as much fun as getting a cliterodectomy. On the other hand, it wouldn't cost anything more than a few bucks in gas, and that made the activity sound like a winner. "I'll pack us a picnic and then we'll head for the hills."

Charlie followed me down to the kitchen. In the

background I could hear Claire and Josh talking to the boys. The boys were bragging about having gone go-karting a few days earlier.

"Have you ever gone go-karting?" one of the boys asked. "I bet not cuz you're too little."

"Yeah? Well you live in Nebraska," was Claire's retort. "Emily says there is nothing in Nebraska but cows."

Oh, Christ. I was really going to have to learn how to censor myself in front of the kids. They were like parrots revealing all the secrets I didn't want anyone else to know. The good news was that if Charlie overheard she didn't say anything.

Amber walked into the kitchen as I pulled out luncheon meat and mayo from the fridge. "Charlie, Stu, me, and the kids—are going to go on a hike. You want to come?"

"Sure."

Together, Charlie, Amber, and I made bologna sandwiches on white for the kids and turkey on wheat for the adults. I put the sandwiches into a cooler along with granola bars, bottled water, and juice boxes. Luke and Stu took Josh and Bobby in Luke's car. Charlie gave me the keys to her SUV and asked me to drive, but I said I found mountain driving treacherous enough in my nimble little eight-year-old Saturn, I didn't need to drive an SUV for the first time up steep, windy terrain.

"All right, I'll drive and you navigate," Charlie said.

On the drive there, Charlie, Amber, and I chatted about my home redecoration projects. Charlie talked about her own experience when she and Stu moved into their current home. As we talked, the kids played some sort of game that involved kings and queens and the slayings of dragons.

Claire and Tim were the king and queen and they held hands regally; it was too adorable for words.

With coats and gloves and hats, it was a perfect day for a hike. The sun was out and it was the sort of day that really needed to be enjoyed.

"You must go hiking all the time," Charlie said as we wove our way up the winding roads. "It's so beautiful here."

"Hmmm," I said noncommittally. The truth was that I never went hiking unless I had an out-of-town guest who wanted to go. Colorado was a spectacularly beautiful place, but I'd lived here my entire life. It was easy to take it for granted. Whenever I was dragged out to enjoy its beauty, I remembered how lucky I was to live here and told myself I really should get out into nature more often, but then I promptly went right back to taking it for granted.

We paid our entrance fees to Rocky Mountain National Park and I looked on the map the ranger had given us for an easy trailhead.

"Here," I said. "This looks promising. Keep driving. It's just ahead." Charlie nodded and drove forward until I said, "Oh, my God!"—which forced her to hit the brakes.

"What?" Charlie asked.

"Look."

Everyone looked outside to where the elk loomed. A large, majestic creature, it seemed as interested in us as we were in him. He had an enormous rack of horns with six points on each of them.

Charlie stopped the car and Tim slid open the door. Unthinkingly, we all piled out to get a closer look. For a couple of minutes, we all just stared at the creature in mute awe. Tim took a few steps toward it, and the elk started to look defensive, then downright angry.

Holy shit! He was going to charge us!

"Ahhh!" we collectively screamed as we hurled ourselves back into the truck, sitting on each other's laps, pressed up against the windows, our noses smooshed flat.

"Go! Go! Go!" I screamed to Charlie.

The elk began racing toward us just as Charlie turned on the ignition. He stopped dead just across the road from us. Charlie floored it.

"Well, at least we won't need any caffeine to wake us up today," I said. "I think my heart will be racing for, oh, I don't know, another couple years or so."

"That was awesome!" Tim said.

We got to the trailhead and parked. Luke parked a few spaces away. It was already 1:30 so we had lunch first and then took the trail by foot. The woods were beautiful even at this time of year. We clomped along the path through the thick forest, snow crunching beneath our feet. We walked fairly slowly, but the kids kept stopping every few feet to inspect a bug or chipmunk or weed. Stu and Luke stuck with the kids who trailed behind, which gave Charlie, Amber, and me a chance to talk.

"How are things going?" Charlie asked.

"It's been an adjustment," I admitted.

"I bet." She laughed. "Did you always want children?"

I walked several steps before answering. "To be honest, I wasn't sure. Sometimes I thought I did and sometimes I thought I didn't."

She nodded. "That's how I felt. Then I got pregnant with Tim. The whole time I was pregnant with him I wasn't sure I wanted him. Then he was born and I have to say I've never known that I could feel this happy. I didn't know joy like this existed in the world. Of course, sometimes I think I made a mistake and want to trade the kids in and return to my old job and old life, but for the most part, I've been pretty amazingly happy."

I was surprised to hear that Charlie had ever had doubts about having kids. She struck me as the kind of woman who had been planning to become a mother since she was a toddler.

"What work did you do before you had kids?" I asked.

"I was in sales. I sold time-shares for vacation spots. I've worked in Portugal, the Canary Islands, and Mexico. That's where I met Stu. He was vacationing in Puerto Vallarta and I tried to sell him a time-share."

"Did he buy it?"

"No." She laughed again. "He was there for a week and we went out every night. We kept in touch after he left and between projects he'd fly back to visit."

"That's romantic," I said.

"You gave up Puerto Vallarta for Nebraska?" Amber said. God, she was as bad as the kids. Didn't anyone learn about white lies and selective honesty these days? I mean *really*.

Fortunately, Charlie just chuckled. "I was actually very ready to get out of the tourist scene. Plus, in the business I was working in, partying, drinking, cocaine—you name it—it was every-where. That's never been my scene."

"Mom!" Charlie's older son, Tim, called. "I'm hungry."

"Again?"

He nodded.

"I have granola bars," I said.

"Um," he said with a shrug. Clearly he had no desire for a granola bar but was too polite to say so.

"We'll be headed home soon and we'll have dinner right away. Think you can make it?" Charlie asked.

Tim nodded.

The thing about women like Charlie was that they made doing this whole mother deal look effortless. Her sons were astonishingly polite and well behaved. It was embarrassing to reveal that being a mother didn't feel natural to me. Would it have been different if I'd been there from the start? If I'd gotten pregnant and fed them from my own breast? If I'd changed their diapers and heard their first words and seen their first steps?

We hiked for maybe an hour or so and then headed home. By the time we got there, it wasn't just the kids who were dying to eat. I heated the lasagna I'd made the day before and made garlic bread and Caesar salad. Even though the meal was simple, I wasn't used to having such a staggering amount of dishes to do, and it all seemed a little overwhelming. I felt ridiculous for feeling done in by what apparently were easy tasks for everyone else. Entertain a few people. Be a mom. Paint a house. Why did these things seem to come so easily to other women?

After dinner, the kids went up to Josh's room, Stu went up to Claire's room, and Luke went downstairs to his study. I threw my dish towel on the counter and joined Charlie and Amber in the living room. They were on the couch peering out the shades. I slumped down next to them.

"Do you hear that?" I asked.

"What?" Charlie didn't avert her gaze.

"Silence. I'd forgotten what it was like."

She looked up and smiled at me. "Do you know something?"

"What?"

"It's still snowing."

I took my middle and index fingers to part the shades of the window on my side of the couch. Sure enough, snowflakes were floating down.

"Maybe it'll turn into a storm and Gwen and Jay won't be able to get here." The moment the words slipped out of my mouth, my eyes popped open. "Oh, God, I didn't just say that out loud, did I?"

Charlie and Amber laughed.

"Gwen's a handful, I know." Charlie said.

"You get along with her?"

"She and Jay got married when I was just about to leave for college, so I've never really had to live with her. She's always been nice to me. She knows I'm the apple of Dad's eye."

I nodded, and at some point, I must have fallen asleep, because the next thing I knew, I heard four screaming children running down the stairs and my eyes were assaulted by the sunshine sneaking its way in through the thin crack between the shades and the wall.

Chapter 19

Amber

Christmas Eve, Eve

After Emily's comments, I did my best not to talk about Scott, but that didn't mean I didn't think about him.

The night before Christmas Eve, I was tired, but I couldn't sleep. I couldn't stop thinking about Scott. I had his cell phone number. In California it was only about ten o'clock, which was a perfectly respectable time to call someone. But since I had no idea what I'd say to him, I just daydreamed about the time I spent with him. Conversations we'd had, smiles he'd flashed my way, the kisses we'd shared. I was certain that when I did finally fall asleep, there was a smile on my face.

Chapter 20

Emily

Christmas Eve

Mercifully, there was no room for Gwen and Jay at our place so they had to stay at a hotel.

Unfortunately, my hopes for a blizzard to keep my in-laws away didn't come to pass. In the morning the sun was shining and the snow had stopped. I asked Amber to take the kids outside to play in the snow and spent the morning cleaning yet again.

When Gwen and Jay pulled up in their silver Lexus, my heart dropped. All the frantic painting, cleaning, and preparations came down to this moment.

Gwen strode up the walk. She looked glamorous as always, wearing a black leather coat, black leather gloves, and sunglasses. As ever, her blonde highlights looked like they'd been touched up that morning.

"Gwen, hi." I hugged her. "Jay, it's good to see you. I'll give you two a quick tour."

Gwen's eyes scanned the kitchen and I held my breath.

"This is the kitchen," I said, stating the obvious. "This is the dining room. And here is the living room." I paused.

Gwen nodded. "It's cute."

Excuse me? Where was the snide remark? The biting commentary? The sarcasm?

"Thanks. I'll show you the Before pictures. You'll be amazed." Charlie, Stu, the boys, Luke, Claire, and Josh all took turns hugging Gwen and Jay, and then I finished showing them around. Afterward I showed them the Before pictures.

When I showed her what the bathroom had once looked like, Gwen winced. "What was the former owner thinking?"

"Tell me about it." The previous owner, an older woman, had used white wainscoting around the bottom half of the walls. Wainscoting was nice by itself, but she had teamed the vertical lines of the wainscoting with wallpaper designed with wild blue flowers with long green leaves that looked like arms threatening to capture you. On the floor were squares of parquet. And the pièce de résistance was the ceiling—she'd used a trowel to create grooved half moons the size of my husband's hands. The mix of squares, the long vertical lines, the circular half moons, and the sprawling flowers created such a mess of textures the room made me feel like I was lost in a mental ward. We couldn't afford to install new flooring and getting the wainscoting off would be a nightmare, so we kept that, but we removed the wallpaper and repainted the ceiling, making both the ceiling and the walls a nice neutral color.

"Well, you've certainly made the most with what you had to work with."

I smiled. All the work and stress had been worth it. "Thanks."

"Where is Luke going to hang the painting I gave him for his birthday?"

Her question caught me off guard. "Uh, well, we haven't finished decorating. Maybe in the study, what do you think?"

"Maybe. Or the living room. Your living room needs a little more pizzazz."

Ah. There was the Gwen who made the hairs on the back of my neck stand on end.

I brought them to the master bedroom. "It's very colorful," Gwen said.

Since Gwen's home was decorated to look like vanilla ice cream in a snowstorm, I wasn't sure "thank you" was an appropriate response—she may have been making a disparaging remark as far as I knew—so instead I said, "Charlie still has a little Christmas shopping to do. Would you mind watching the kids while I take her to the mall?"

"Of course. I'd love to. I'm going to take the kids out for ice cream," Gwen said.

I looked at my watch. It was early enough in the day that ice cream wouldn't interfere with their dinner. "Sure. That would be fine," I said, as if she'd asked my permission.

Claire came down the stairs just then and smiled at her grandmother.

"Hi, you, oh, it's so good to see you. You are such a beauty, just like your mother. We're going to get some ice cream. Would you like that?"

Claire nodded.

"Go grab your coat. Where's your brother and cousins?"

"They're upstairs playing."

"I'll go get them," Charlie said.

Claire got her coat and stood in front of Gwen, who sat on the couch. When Gwen tried to button Claire's coat, the top button came off and fell between the couch cushions. Gwen lifted one of the cushions. "My God!" Her sharp tone caught my attention, and my gaze looked in the direction she was staring. "That's disgusting!"

She was right. It was. Beneath my couch cushions was an appalling amount of dirt. There was a fossilized half-eaten pizza crust, what looked like two or three fingernail shavings, loose change, two pens, and other miscellaneous grime of unknown origin.

"Wow," I said. "When we moved that couch in just two months ago, I vacuumed it thoroughly."

"This is highly unsanitary. Children should not be living in such a filthy environment. It's unhealthy!"

"Gwen, I'm sorry. I had no idea there was all that dirt lurking under there."

"You should be cleaning under the couch cushions every time you vacuum."

"You clean under your couch cushions every time you vacuum?"

The woman probably pulled her refrigerator out every other day so she could be sure it was spotless behind there. Frankly, I was so busy these days I thought it was pretty remarkable that I kept myself and the kids clean, let alone most of the house. Were all other women on the planet vacuuming beneath couch cushions several times a week? If so, how the hell did they have the time?

"Where is your vacuum? I cannot sit on this couch knowing what's under the cushions."

"I'll take care of it."

Well, so much for impressing Gwen with my domesticity. As Gwen got the kids ready to go out for ice cream, I vacuumed the couch.

"We'll be back shortly," Gwen said. Along with Jay, she and the kids headed out. She'd only been there a few minutes and already I was glad to see her go.

Amber joined Charlie and me at the mall. The mall was so crowded it reminded me of a movie where the earth was being destroyed and people were running for their lives, not caring about anyone but themselves as they charged over fallen bodies and elbowed one another in their stampede to safety.

I told Amber and Charlie about the incident with Gwen and they made all the appropriate comforting comments about how nobody cleaned under their couch every time she vacuumed.

"I don't vacuum *at all*," Amber said. I knew she was trying to be helpful, but Amber had long been known as a slob, so she wasn't exactly the yardstick I wanted to be measured by.

"Really, Emily, don't worry about it. Only obsessive compulsives do that." Charlie's comment, on the other hand, did make me feel better. If supermom Charlie wasn't a vacuum avenger, surely I wasn't the freak Gwen wanted to make me out to be.

We waited in hideously long lines as Charlie bought bicycle accessories for Stu and computer games for the boys.

To make the best of being forced to shop on

Christmas Eve, I asked at every possible store whether they had a Baby Anna, only to be told they'd sold out weeks ago.

"Don't look so bummed out," Amber said. "Claire will live if she doesn't get this doll. She already has a million dolls."

"I know, she's just been through so much lately," I said. "The wedding, the move, it's all been a big adjustment. I just want her Christmas to be perfect."

"You're so tense. Christmas is supposed to be fun," Amber said.

She was right. I was way too tense. I felt like a guitar string that had been pulled so tight it could break at any second. I wanted so desperately for this holiday to be perfect and for everyone to be happy and have a good time. I wanted all their dreams to come true.

"I have the worst headache," Charlie said.

"Malls on December twenty-fourth can do that to you. I've got some Advil at home," I said.

When we got home, Gwen had the kids around the table making Christmas ornaments—Popsicle-stick reindeers with glued-on eyes.

"Looks like you had fun while we were gone," I said.

"Look," Claire said, holding up one of the ornaments she'd made.

"That looks great. Do you want to put it on the tree?"

She nodded.

"Go for it." I turned to Charlie. "I'll be right back with the Advil. Do you want two or three?"

"Four."

"Gotcha." I went upstairs to the linen closet

where we kept the towels and miscellaneous first aid- and beauty-type stuff—sunscreen, Band-Aids, allergy medicine, tampons, hair care products I'd had for years and felt too guilty to throw away. When I opened the door, I blinked in confusion—the entire closet had been rearranged. All the hair care products had been put in a wire basket. The sunscreen, insect repellant, and Band-Aids were in another. My nail polish remover, clippers, nail files, and nail polish were in another. And there were new towels in there, too. Our bathroom was white, with a silver shower curtain and metal waste-basket, so I'd bought towels that were mauve. Suddenly my linen closet hosted a fleet of blue towels.

I searched for the bottle of Advil and couldn't find it anywhere. Usually I kept it right at the front of the shelf for easy access. The old hairsprays and conditioners and various hair tonics were kept in the back, since they were only there so I could pretend that I hadn't wasted all that money on products I'd used once and then forgotten. But now they were all in a basket at the front and center of my closet.

After a lengthy scavenger hunt, I finally found the bottle of Advil. I grabbed four and bounded down the stairs.

I handed Charlie the Advil and turned to Gwen. "Ah, Gwen, did you rearrange my linen closet?"

"Yes, it was such a mess."

I'd thought it had been exceptionally neat. Regardless, the way I'd had it I could actually find what I needed. "And you bought new towels?"

"I made a quick trip to Target. Your whole bathroom is blue; it didn't make any sense to have mauve towels."

"It's not actually blue, it's silver and white. And the baskets?"

"Baskets keep everything in order."

I couldn't believe it. No one had ever accused me of not being organized enough. It was true that I wasn't a great cook, I had a lot to learn about being a wife and mother, and sometimes I was too short-tempered, but organization was something I knew all about. In fact, all I ever heard was that I was borderline obsessive compulsive when it came to neatness. I had no idea what to say to her. *Take a deep breath. Remain calm. You just need to get through the next twenty-four hours. People have survived wars, famines, and floods, you can survive twenty-four hours of Gwen.* "I'm going to do the lunch dishes," I said.

In the kitchen, I went to reach for my dish soap, only to find it wasn't by the sink where I always left it. I opened the doors beneath the sink and discovered that she'd rearranged all of my cleaning supplies into baskets. It took me a good thirty seconds to track down the dish soap.

I washed the dishes from lunch. (If Gwen had really wanted to help out, she could have done them for me, but she had been too busy rearranging everything I owned.) I finished the dishes, dried my hands, and went to get the hand lotion, which I usually kept on the end table in the living room because I put on lotion about twenty times a day and that was the most convenient spot to access it. Except it wasn't there. I checked the closet where I kept the linens, medicines, and hair supplies, thinking that was the most logical place for it, but it wasn't there, either.

"Have you seen my hand lotion? I usually keep it on the table by the couch," I asked Gwen.

"I moved it. The table needed dusting."

"Where did you move it to?"

She paused, looking down at the floor a moment as she thought about it. "I can't quite remember right now. It'll come to me."

Gee, thanks. "What time are our reservations?" I asked her.

"Seven."

"Maybe we should play a game until it's time to get ready," Charlie said.

"Let's play Scattergories," Amber said.

"I'm up for it," Charlie said, "except I don't know how to play."

"I'll teach you," Amber said.

I went and found Stu and Luke, who were cruising the Internet looking at motorcycles. Why couldn't they be gawking over something safe, like pornography? "We're playing Scattergories."

Luke quickly minimized the browser. "Why do I think this is an order rather than an option?" he asked Stu, who just smiled.

Stu, Charlie, Gwen, Jay, and Amber sat around the kitchen table. I went to the closet to get the game; the first thing I saw was my hand lotion. Who would put hand lotion in the front hall closet with the tennis rackets, board games, and coats?

Shaking my head, I grabbed the game and joined the others. Amber explained the rules.

"So this is how it works. I'm going to roll this die and whatever letter comes up, you have to think of words that fit the categories on your card that start with this letter. Like if it comes up an 'R' and the category is 'ice cream,' you might write down 'Rocky Road.' If you can do two words that each begin with 'R' like that, you'll get two points. *But*, if someone else writes down Rocky Road, you cancel each other out and nobody gets any points, so originality is important. Got it? We'll start with list one."

Amber rolled the die and the letter was "S." She set the timer and we were off. I filled in the categories with words starting with the letter "S" and then I came to a category that asked for a household chore. The first thing that came to mind was "sex." Normally I wrote down the first thing that came into my mind because otherwise I'd run out of time, but I didn't write down "sex" because it said more about how Luke and I were struggling than I wanted to admit. It just didn't paint the picture of newlywed bliss that I wanted to project.

When the timer buzzed, we went around reading off what we'd come up with and tallying up our points. When it was Amber's turn, she read what she'd come up with for a household chore. "Skipping rope."

"Skipping rope?" I said. "That's not a household chore."

"Sure it is. It's exercise, something you have to do every day."

I laughed. "Exercise might be a chore, but it's not a *household* chore."

"Sorry, Amber, Emily's right," Luke said.

Amber frowned.

We spent the next forty-five minutes playing and laughing. I was glad we weren't playing Trivial Pursuit. Jay and Stu both had photographic memories and knew the answers to the most obscure questions, whereas I spent most of the game slapping my forehead and saying, "I *know* I learned that in college."

We stopped playing when Mom and Mork arrived, carrying large department-store bags brimming over with gifts. Mork still wore his hair shaggy and he was, of course, wearing his trademark suspenders beneath his sports coat. Unlike Gwen, who always looked striking even if she did go heavy on the makeup and jewelry, Mom was not one of those women who embraced her size and wore well-fitting, high-quality clothes that could forgive an extra fold of flesh here and there. Mom had a severe case of sartorial denial, as if wearing clothes a size too small made her that size. She wasn't a huge woman and she didn't look terrible, but the unforgiving, too-tight fabrics revealed the pouch of back fat she had beneath her shoulder blades and the fact that her curved belly extended out farther than her small, round breasts.

Amber leapt up and squeezed Mom tight, then gave Mork a hug. "You look beautiful as ever, darling," Mom said. "How was the drive?"

"It was long, but I had good company."

"You were with that actor boy?" Mom asked.

"He's gorgeous," I said.

"Hey," Luke said, pretending to be jealous. I stuck my tongue out at him.

"He is gorgeous," Amber confirmed, "but he was also a really nice guy."

"I guess we should get ready," I said, cleaning up the game.

After I got Claire into a dress and helped Josh into his sports coat, I put on a sexy black sweater, gray wool trousers, and black boots with stiletto heels. Luke whistled when he saw me. "You look gorgeous, babe."

I smiled. Luke was wearing khaki pants, chocolate brown Timberland boots, and a white shirt that contrasted with his dark hair and eyes. "You don't look so bad yourself." Luke pulled on his dark brown leather coat and I wore my fitted black pea coat.

Gwen took us to a steak house I'd never heard of. We got there a little early and our table wasn't quite ready, so we waited at the bar. A pianist and cellist played Christmas music in the corner of the elegant, dimly lit restaurant. We sat around a wood coffee table on leather couches and chairs. Within moments our waitress arrived. She wore a black ball gown and couldn't have been more than twenty years old. Scanning the rest of the bar, I saw that all of the waitresses were also dressed up in fancy black dresses or black sequined tops with black dress pants and high heels. None of them was older than their early twenties and they were all thin and attractive.

We ordered a round of cocktails; the kids got Shirley Temples. Gwen raised her glass of white wine. "Merry Christmas."

"Merry Christmas," we chorused.

"We made Christmas cookies the other day," Claire announced.

"You did?" Gwen said. "Should we have some when we get home?"

"They were starting to get stale so we threw them away," I said quickly. I took a sip of my drink: vodka that had been infused with pineapple. It was delicious. It tasted nothing like vodka and was sweet but not too sweet.

"They were kind of funny looking," Claire said.

I laughed. "We didn't really have cookie cutters so we had to get creative."

Mork asked Amber, "How are things in New York?" I wanted to kiss him for changing the subject.

"Good. The father of the guy who drove me out here has lots of connections with CEOs of major companies, and I'm going to try to get some corporate clients to sponsor employee-appreciation days where the staff can sign up for in-house chair massages. It could be really lucrative."

"That would be great. That's so exciting," Mom said.

"That's wonderful," Gwen said. "Being your own boss is so rewarding." Gwen turned to Mom. "You must be so proud of her."

Mom paused just a moment. "Oh, of course."

One of the twenty-year-old model/waitresses told us our table was ready and to follow her. We walked into the dining room and sat around a large, round table covered in a white linen tablecloth. I took the white linen napkin and unfolded it across my lap.

When I opened my menu my jaw dropped. Nothing was less expensive than thirty-five dollars. And whether you got the prime rib or lobster tail or filet mignon, that was all you got. All the sides were extra. A side salad to start was seven bucks. I knew Gwen and Jay had money, but I didn't realize they could afford to take thirteen people out for a meal that was going to cost a minimum of fifty or sixty dollars a person.

We ordered our steaks and a variety of sides—potatoes au gratin, a vegetable medley, marinated mushrooms, a spinach concoction with bacon and cheese. I shared my steak with Josh, keeping the scallops all to myself. Amber shared her steak with Claire.

We sat boy–girl, boy–girl, each couple next to each other. As happened with large groups, little clots of conversation sprang up, depending on who we were close enough to talk to without shouting. Gwen, Mom, and Charlie discussed Charlie's boys and their ice hockey lessons. Luke and Mork talked about their respective jobs. The kids talked about all the presents they'd asked Santa for. Stu and Jay talked about Jay's new Lamborghini. Amber had me laughing with stories about her heating going out and the performance-art piece her friend Nadia had recently put on.

When the waiter passed out the dessert menus and asked who would like coffee or cappuccinos, I scanned everyone's plates. None of the other women had finished their thirty-five- dollar steaks. I figured it came to two or three dollars a bite. When you were paying that much for a hunk of beef, I thought you should force every last morsel down your throat.

I was painfully full but we ordered six desserts for us to share as well as decaf cappuccinos.

The slices of chocolate cake and carrot cake were each the size of two bricks stacked on top of each other. We had crème brûleé, chocolate-chip bread pudding, strawberry cheesecake, and tiramisu. Despite the fact I was stuffed, each time one of the desserts was passed to me I indulged myself. Desserts were passed so quickly, two or three would get backlogged in front of me.

"Hey, slow down," I said. "You're passing stuff too fast."

"Look, missy, there is no time for savoring here," Luke teased. "Stuff your face and move it along."

It was eleven by the time Gwen paid the bill and we headed home.

"Mom, Jay, did you want to come back to our place for an after-dinner drink?" Luke asked. I could've slugged him. I wanted the kids to go to sleep as fast as possible so we could stage Santa's visit and get to bed ourselves.

"That would be lovely," Gwen said.

We caravanned home, with Mom and Mork following behind us; Charlie, Stu, and the boys behind them; and Jay and Gwen behind them.

Luke unlocked the doors and Claire and Josh walked in. Their expressions curdled.

"Uh!" said Claire.

"Ew," said Josh.

I followed behind them. My nostrils were assailed by a vile odor. "Oh, God. What is that?"

"Smells like sewage," Luke said.

Everyone had similar reactions as they followed us inside.

"What is that ungodly odor?" Charlie asked.

"I think it's sewage. I'm going to go downstairs and check things out." Luke took off his coat and headed downstairs.

When Gwen and Jay walked in and I saw the puckered expression on Gwen's face, my heart sunk. "Luke thinks we have a sewage problem."

I followed Luke downstairs. As he'd predicted, our basement was steeped in sewage.

"Our pipes must have burst," Luke said.

Jay and Mork and Stu came downstairs behind us. "Tree roots might have grown into your sewer pipes," Mork said.

I couldn't believe it. After killing myself to make sure we had a beautiful home with new carpeting and freshly painted walls, a house where every pillow had been lovingly fluffed and each cabinet doorknob had been carefully replaced, my home now smelled like a port-a-pottie.

"Could you excuse me for just one second?" I

asked. It took everything I had to maintain my composure as I quickly walked to the bathroom and locked the door behind me. I kept the lights off and slunk down to the floor, burying my face in my hands. I wanted to sob and rant and rave, but my eyes just pooled with a few small tears.

I'd tried so hard. I wanted so badly to have a nice home and a nice Christmas. After so many years of living a life of limbo, being carted back and forth from Mom's place to Dad's place, having multiple Christmases with multiple stepfamilies and stepparents, all the years of custody squabbles and broken promises, I just wanted one family, all together in one house, neat and orderly and happy.

I took several deep breaths, wiped the tears from my eyes, and returned to the living room with the others.

Luke was on the phone and attempting to find a plumber, but on Christmas Eve it was impossible.

"You can all come to our house," Mom offered. "We have a couple extra bedrooms and the couch downstairs folds out into a bed."

"I guess we're going to have to," I said. "We can't stay in a house that smells like an outhouse."

"But how will Santa find us?" Josh asked.

"I'll just call up the North Pole," I said.

Josh's eyes brightened. "You have the number?"

"Sure I do."

"Call now."

I got my cell phone out of my purse and dialed my office. My voice mail picked up. "Hello, is this the North Pole? Hi. This is Emily Taylor-Garrett of Denver, Colorado. We live at 1208 Shermer Road but we'll be spending the night at 3627 Lowell. We just wanted to be sure that Santa knew where to find Josh and Claire Garrett. So it's no problem?

Great. Thanks so much. Merry Christmas to you, too." I shut off the phone and turned to the kids. "It's all been arranged. Santa will swing by Grandma Moss's tonight. We have to get going so you can get to sleep so Santa can come."

"I'm going to stay up all night waiting for him," Josh said.

"Me, too," Claire said.

"Well, we have to at least get you to bed so you can pretend you are asleep. Santa won't come otherwise."

As Gwen held her nose, I wrote down instructions for how to get to Mom's place. "If you have any questions, just call. We'll meet around ten for breakfast and then we'll open presents. Thanks again for dinner. We'll see you tomorrow."

Gwen couldn't get out of there fast enough so she and Jay could get to their hotel.

It was quite a production having everyone pack up their suitcases and load all the food for Christmas dinner in Mom's car. Mom and Mork schlepped Lucy, Claire, and Josh over to their place with Charlie, Stu, and boys following behind them. Luke, Amber, and I stayed to pack my car with all of the presents and stocking stuffers from both Santa and us.

By the time we got to Mom's, the kids were in their pajamas but were running around filled with so much energy it was like they were high on uppers. I, on the other hand, was ready to sleep for fifty years. I desperately wanted the kids to go to bed so Santa could come and I could get the rest I desperately needed.

Like I said before, my mother was off her rocker

when it came to Christmas. Her home looked like a Christmas bomb had exploded in it. Wreaths decorated nearly every door, a sparkly red garland wound its way down the stair banister, figurines of snowmen abounded. Poinsettias could be found in every room. Mom had Christmas wall decorations in every room, Christmas dish towels in the kitchen, Christmas candles, a Nativity scene on the mantel of the fireplace, and a Christmas tree so full of ornaments it was miraculous that the branches could hold them all. Mom had Christmas-themed dessert plates, mugs, and serving ware. If Santa ever retired, Mom would be the first person in line to interview for his job.

"Amber, you take the pull-out couch downstairs," Mom said. "Charlie and Stuart, you take the guest room. Luke and Emily, you take Emily's old room. The kids will take Amber's old room. The boys can sleep on the bed and I've got an air mattress for Claire and Josh. Won't that be fun, kids? You get to sleep on air, just like a cloud!"

I got the kids into bed and kept the door open a crack so I could check on them to ensure they were asleep. When I stopped by ten minutes later, they were still whispering. Twenty minutes later it was the same thing. After forty minutes had gone by, they were all fast asleep—the adults could finally swoop into action. Like a SWAT team, Luke, Amber, Mom, Mork, Charlie, Stu, and I put out all the presents under the tree and stuffed all the stockings. We left the Christmas lights on and headed to bed ourselves.

Luke fell asleep in moments, but I couldn't sleep. I kept changing positions, but I couldn't seem to get comfortable. I was exhausted, but I was too jittery to sleep. I had that same feeling I got before I had to give a speech in front of a large group or before I went on a job interview—I knew I was going to be judged and I was terrified that I was going to fail. Finally I gave up and got out of bed and padded through the dark house to the family room where Amber was.

When she saw me, she sat up. "Emily?" she asked in a whisper.

"Hi."

"Couldn't sleep?"

I climbed next to her on the pull-out bed. The mattress was thin and lumpy and had such deep potholelike dips in it a person would need hiking equipment to get out of bed in the morning. "Ugh. This is awful. It's worse than I remember." I giggled.

"Why are you snickering?"

"Because. You have to sleep on the couch that will leave you with back pain for three days."

"That's funny to you?"

"No. What's funny to me is that I will always get to be the older sister. I'm just remembering that bed you had to sleep on when you and I shared a room. Remember? The bottom slats of the frame were broken, so you had to sleep at an angle?"

I made a gesture with my forearm so that my hand was forty-five degrees lower than my elbow to indicate the ski slope Amber used to sleep on.

"I'm glad you find the danger to my ergonomic health to be so amusing. I'm really sorry about your house."

I sighed. "It's OK. We'll get it fixed . . . Although, we're going to have to win the lottery to pay for it."

"Well, tomorrow Mom will tell us we're all oil barons worth millions. No, *billions*."

I laughed. "Yeah, *right*."

Amber started laughing, too, in that sort of way you get when you really need to catch up on your sleep. "Mom's not really going to tell us that we're fabulously rich, is she?"

"I *highly* doubt it," I said, laughing even harder. "Mom isn't exactly above trying to manipulate the facts for her own purposes. Do you remember that time we went and visited her sister in Albuquerque and the three of us were sharing that giant king-size bed in the guest room?"

"Mom was reading *Disclosure* by Michael Crichton, and she was so into the book she refused to turn off the lights."

"You and I were nearly hysterical from lack of sleep because we didn't get to New Mexico until four in the morning, but the lights in there were so bright it was like some sort of torture they'd use on a political prisoner. You'd have your eyes closed and the light went right through your eyelids as if they weren't even there. We kept begging her to turn off the lights or go read in the bathroom with the door closed, and do you remember what she said?" I was laughing so hard now I could barely speak. "She said . . . she said, 'I had a very difficult childhood. You should let me read my book.' She actually said that! I told that story to Luke and he didn't believe me. But the best was your response. Do you remember?"

Amber was laughing so hard I was afraid she might wet herself.

"You said, 'You're making us have a difficult childhood *right now!*'"

Amber and I laughed until tears streamed down our faces. We finally stopped laughing. For a moment, life was good. Then the olfactory memory of my home assaulted me like a punch. "Ohhhh," I moaned. "I just wanted everything to be perfect."

"Nothing in life is perfect. We love you despite the fact you're not perfect."

"I know, it's just, I really want Gwen to like me. She's always slipping in these comments telling Claire that she's such a beauty just like her mother or talking about how Elizabeth was such a great cook or whatever. Gwen actually told me that I should smile less because it was giving me crow's-feet."

"You're kidding."

"I'm not."

"She really wouldn't approve of our antics tonight, would she?"

We both laughed again.

"Don't worry about Gwen," Amber said. "She's just one of those people like Dad who can only see the bad things in people."

I nodded. "It's so tricky with Dad because he seems like he's always so positive about everything but then when you're least expecting it he just comes in and zaps you."

"Gwen and Dad are just insecure and they're taking their insecurities out on you. You can't kill yourself trying to be perfect for people who will never see anything but the negative."

"I know I can't be perfect."

"You may know that logically but you still go crazy trying. It's just like how you always drove yourself nuts trying to get Dad's attention with good grades, thinking you could get his approval if you were perfect. Dad's just a self-absorbed guy."

Maybe I was a tiny bit of a perfectionist, but Luke was the main guy in my life these days, not

Dad, and Luke loved me despite my flaws. My attempts to be perfect for Luke weren't because I didn't think he wouldn't love me otherwise, but because I loved him and wanted to be a better person for him. I wanted to do my best to make him happy.

I shrugged. "I guess you're right," I admitted. "I love you, Amber."

"I love you."

I wrapped my arms around her thin frame. We held each other close.

"This is just like when we shared a room when we were growing up," I said.

"Except back then we bit and kicked and tickle-tortured each other."

"Well, right, it's just the same except for that."

I fell asleep on the spectacularly uncomfortable bed next to her. In the morning, we were awoken by the sound of the children's voices. They were allowed to see what had come in their stockings before the adults were awake because the stuff in their stockings wasn't wrapped. After comparing stocking stuffers, they spent a great deal of time speculating about what might be contained in the wrapped boxes around the tree.

I got up and went in search of caffeine. Mom had already made a pot, I could tell by the smell of coffee in the air. Unfortunately, the pot had already been finished off. My mother always takes apart the coffeemaker the second the coffee is gone and puts all the pieces in the dishwasher. This was annoying for several reasons. For one thing, it was very challenging to stagger out of bed and be forced to go on a coffeepot scavenger hunt, looking for parts among the piles of unwashed dishes in the dishwasher. Trying to assemble the pieces (the lid had two separate parts, for God's sake), was like trying to diffuse a bomb—it was complicated and extremely difficult without any caffeine in my system. After much frustration, I put the coffeepot together and started another pot. I was much happier when I had a cup of coffee in my hand.

"Good morning, dear. I was just about to put the quiches in the oven," Mom said.

"Need any help?" I asked.

"Why don't you set the table for breakfast?"

I nodded, finished my cup of coffee, and poured myself another.

"Coffee," Amber said as she stumbled blearily into the kitchen.

"I just made a pot," I said. "Help me set the table."

She nodded. I grabbed plates and forks and knives and with Amber's help, we set the table for nine and set up a card table for the kids. I hopped in the shower and did my hair and makeup. When Amber and I were little, the tradition had been for us to open presents in our pj's. However, now that I was an adult, I understood just how long Christmas pictures lasted, and I was through having greasy hair and puffy eyes photographed and lingering in perpetuity.

Gwen and Jay arrived and we had breakfast despite the kids' begging that we open presents first. The kids went nearly insane as we made them wait even longer as we washed the breakfast dishes. I smiled, remembering just how endless time became when I'd been young and there were presents to open.

"Oh, Emily," Gwen said, drying a frying pan, "did I tell you that I invited Carol over?"

The coffee mug I was rinsing slipped out of my wet, soapy hands and went clattering to the floor, breaking into dozens of pieces. "No. No, you didn't mention that."

"Carol was a childhood friend of Luke's. She's just moved to the area recently and doesn't really know anyone around here," Gwen explained to Mom. "She's just going to pop in for a little while. That's not a problem, is it?"

"Of course not!" Mom said with a smile.

Wordlessly, I went to the closet where Mom kept the broom and dustpan and silently swept up the shards of glass.

My "perfect" Christmas was turning into Perfect Hell.

Luke was not at all like my father. I trusted him completely. He was a good, honest, trustworthy man. Still, I felt a tremor of fear. If Luke and I got into a fight . . . if it had been a while since we'd had sex . . . if he was *wasted*—most of us had had a few drunken experiences where we ended up messing around with someone we never would have messed around with when sober—was it *possible* that he *might* cheat on me? *Stop it, Emily. Luke is not your father. He would never hurt you like that.*

After I cleaned up the broken mug, I met the others in the living room. Mork played Santa and handed gifts out to everyone and we took turns opening them. I opened the gift from Gwen with trepidation. Last year she'd gotten me a nail kit to help me with my "dry, unkempt cuticles and unruly fingernails." For my birthday she'd gotten me a boxed set of hair care products to help me with my "frizzy, lackluster hair."

I opened the box to reveal several skin care products nested in straw in a wooden box.

"The instructions are inside," Gwen said. "Ideally you would have started using these when you were about sixteen, but better late than never, right?"

"Wow. Thank you. Are these . . . all for my face?" I unfolded the instructions. I was an intelligent woman, but reading this was like trying to decipher the directions for how to build a nuclear weapon. "I'm supposed to use all of these products *together*?"

"Twice a day, although you only use the eye cream at night, and you only use the SPF 15 skin-drench in the morning. These will help slow the progress of all your fine lines and wrinkles."

"Thanks, Gwen, that's very generous of you."

It was a fairly big achievement for me to wash my face twice a day. I might slather on some wrinkle-defying eye cream at night, but FIVE different face lotions twice a day? As if.

Beautiful, sexy Carol probably used five face lotions every morning and every night. Was that what it would take for me to keep my husband faithful? Nonstop moisturizing?

Mork handed me a gift from Mom. Last year she'd gotten me a neon purple scarf–hat combo thingy that made me look like an eighty-year-old Polish immigrant woman in a babushka. I always wore dark, muted colors like black and gray, so why she thought I'd suddenly like neon purple was beyond me.

The card said:

> *Remember to take some time for yourself. Life's too short. Make time for the things you love.*

I tore off the wrapping paper and smiled. It was a book of puzzles and word problems. It had been a long time since I'd taken the time to do puzzles. My mom got me a gift I actually liked—it was a true Christmas miracle.

"Thank you," I said.

"You're welcome." She smiled warmly.

The moment of mother–daughter bonding disappeared in a flash when the doorbell rang. My heart stopped.

Gwen leapt up. "That must be Carol."

The door swung open. Gwen squealed. "It's so good to see you! You look fabulous."

I took a deep breath and looked up, not quite believing what I was seeing. I had envisioned Carol to be a long-limbed, colt-legged beauty with a Ms. America smile and hair cascading down her back. The real-live Carol was nothing like I'd imagined. She wasn't unattractive, but she wasn't a beauty, either. She was thin and petite—probably barely 5'1". That alone would make it difficult for me to imagine Luke—who was 6'3"—with her. Her nose had a large bump that came straight out and then hooked downward sharply. It was so prominent, all of her other features became virtually unnoticeable by comparison.

"Carol, this is Luke's wife, Emily," Gwen said.

"It's nice to meet you," I said, extending my hand.

"It's nice to meet you. Luke just raves about you. He just can't stop talking about how wonderful you are."

"Really?"

"Oh, my gosh, you've put a spell on that man." Carol smiled at me. "I hope I'm not bothering you. I don't mean to interrupt. I hope I'm not in the way."

"No, no," I said truthfully. Luke went around

raving about me? I'd put a spell on him? "Do you mind watching us open gifts?"

"Not at all. It sounds like fun."

Mork handed me a small box with a card. I opened the card first. It was from Luke. The cover of the card had a Christmas tree with glittering ornaments and lights. Inside, the card read:

I already have the greatest gift anyone could receive because I have you in my life.

Beneath that Luke had written:

I know life has been challenging lately, but you've embodied the expression "grace under fire." You've kept a sense of humor through the tough times. Through it all, you have been a woman of uncommon beauty. This gift is intended to remind you how gorgeous you are and to remember the beautiful things in life even when times seem dark.

I blinked back tears and smiled at Luke, then I opened the small box and gasped. Inside was a stunning emerald ring.

"Oh, my God." I took the ring out of the box and slipped it on the ring finger of my right hand. "Luke, thank you! It's beautiful. It fits perfectly."

He smiled. I leaned over and hugged and kissed him. Though the gift was beautiful and I was touched by the sentiment, a flicker of worry flashed through my mind that we really couldn't afford a gift as extravagant as this. Then he said, "I got my Christmas bonus and I wanted to spend it on you. I know that things haven't been easy lately, but you've been amazing."

"You didn't want to use it to buy a motorcycle?"

He smiled. "The thought did cross my mind. But then I remembered that there was this woman I was crazy about who wants to be sure I live well into old age in one piece, and I figured she was a lot more important. I *was* thinking about taking some race-car driving classes, though."

I buried my head in my hands. "Oh, God."

He laughed. "Just kidding."

When it was Gwen's turn to open the gift from Luke and me, I held my breath. "Luke said you used to have a complete set of these but they were ruined when your house flooded." I hoped I hadn't chosen wrong.

She opened the box. Inside was a vintage collection of *Good Housekeeping* magazines from the 1950s. Gwen's face lit up. "How did you ever find these?"

Actually, thanks to eBay it had been quite easy, but she didn't need to know that. "I just kept an eye out."

She flipped through the pages of one issue with a smile on her face. "Thank you so much. This brings back so many memories of my childhood when I'd flip through my mother's *Good Housekeeping* magazines."

When the magazines had arrived, I'd taken the time to page through them to try to see just what the appeal might be. The collection of old magazines offered a fascinating slice of Americana. The 1950s were a time when politicos wanted the women, who had gotten into the workforce to help fill the jobs of the men fighting overseas in WWII, to get back in the kitchen now that the war was over and the men were home. Cleaning the house and making dinner were made to seem as complicated as sending a man to the moon. Buying a gift for someone who already had everything, as Gwen did, was no easy task. When Luke told me about the flood, I figured I'd found the perfect answer, and apparently I was right.

"I'm really touched, Emily."

"Thanks."

The kids received a ridiculous number of gifts from Luke and me, Santa, Mom, and Gwen. It was wonderful watching their faces light up as they opened their presents. Even small, inexpensive toys brought them tremendous joy. At least, that is, until Claire unwrapped her final present. Her excitement fell away and she frowned.

"What's wrong, Claire?" I asked.

"Santa didn't get me Baby Anna."

"Your birthday is coming up in just a couple months," I said. "Maybe you can get a Baby Anna then."

Claire shrugged. It was as though the huge stack of toys she'd received that day didn't matter to her at all. "Why didn't Santa bring me Baby Anna? Didn't you send the e-mail?"

"Of course I did. I didn't want to tell you this, but I got an e-mail back from one of Santa's executive assistant elves, and the elves said Santa's workshop was out of Baby Anna."

"But can't Santa do anything?"

"Uh, well, sure, but they were out of stock, you see, so . . ."

Thankfully, just then Tim handed her one of the Styrofoam Jedi-like "swords" all the kids had received that day. "Let's go play."

Claire studied the sword for a moment. When the boys ran off to play in the rec room downstairs, she followed grudgingly behind them.

I watched her go, feeling disappointed myself. I

was sure all the child-rearing books in the world would tell me that kids shouldn't get everything they ask for, and I agreed with that, but I'd really wanted to get Claire that doll. She'd been through a lot, and it seemed like a small, simple thing I could do.

I went to the kitchen and got a large cutting board and arranged an assortment of exotic cheeses, crackers, bread, grapes, and strawberries. I also took out the spinach dip I'd made the day before and popped it in the oven to heat up. It had only been a few hours since we'd eaten breakfast, but over the past month my stomach had grown about three times its normal size and now it expected regular feedings every couple hours.

I set the appetizers out on the coffee table, opened a bottle of wine, and poured all the adults a glass. Except for the fact that my home smelled like an outhouse and Claire was more disappointed about the missing Baby Anna than I'd anticipated, I thought things seemed to be going pretty darn well.

Of course, things are rarely what they seem, are they?

Chapter 21

Amber

Christmas

I'd spent the entire afternoon drinking wine and eating fattening cheeses and spinach dip, and without a pause I went right to drinking more wine at dinner and stuffing my face with the meal Emily had painstakingly prepared. She'd made glazed ham, scalloped potatoes, cauliflower au gratin, stuffed mushrooms, and spinach salad with candied walnuts and blue cheese. Emily had never been much of a cook, but she'd outdone herself today and she'd done it all completely by herself—she hadn't even let me help set the table. For dessert, she'd made a traditional apple pie served with vanilla-bean ice cream.

While the kids were down in the rec room watching *The Chronicles of Narnia* DVD that Santa had brought for Tim, the rest of us were in the living room drinking hot apple cider spiked with rum.

Gwen and Mom were talking. Maybe it was just because I was in a food coma and wasn't fully awake, but I was having trouble following their conversation. In my trancelike state, I remembered how Mom had said she'd had something important to tell Emily and me. After spending three days with a total hunk and then being thrown to the familial lions for the last few days, where I'd been kept too busy to re-member to pester Mom about her big secret, I'd forgotten all about it.

As soon as there was a break in her conversation with Gwen I said, "Mom, what was the big secret you wanted to tell Emily and me?"

"What?" She had a guilty look on her face, and her eyes were just slightly unfocused because of the wine.

"You told me that you had something you wanted to tell Emily and me in person, and that's why I needed to find a way out to Colorado. What was it?"

"Did I say that?"

"Yeah, Mom, you did. Emily, tell her."

"You did, Mom. You told me to tell her that you had something you wanted to tell us and we had to be here in person."

"Oh. Right. That." She took a long sip of her wine. "I just wanted to say that I loved both of you very much and I'm so glad we could all be to-gether for the holiday."

I bolted upright. "Excuse me, I *drove thirty hours* to hear you say that you love me? I know you love me. I don't need to *drive thirty hours* to hear that." Of course, it had actually been quite an enjoyable thirty hours for the most part and I hadn't wanted to be alone for Christmas anyway, but Mom really had manipulated the situation for her own bene-fit. Now she'd been caught and was feeling guilty and I was going to milk the situation for all it was worth.

"I'm sorry, honey. I just wanted to think of a reason compelling enough to get you out here. I know you have lots of friends back in New York you probably could have been with . . ."

Mom was saved when there was a knock at the door. Eyebrows furrowed, I looked at Emily questioningly.

"I have no idea who that could be," Emily said.

I stood. "I'll get it."

Either I'd had far, far too much wine and had started hallucinating, or Scott was standing just a couple of feet in front of me with a smile on his face. My heart jackhammered. It took me several seconds to find enough air in my lungs to produce words. "What are you doing here?"

"I missed you."

"How'd you find me?"

"You told me that your mother had remarried Jesse Moss. He's in the phone book. When nobody answered at your sister's house, I thought I'd try you here."

"And if we hadn't been here?"

"I would have kept trying your sister's place until I found you."

"But, Christmas . . . What about your family?"

"They understand. The deal is, Amber, that you're the most beautiful, smart, funny, interesting woman I've ever met. I know you think I'm too young for you, and I know that for some reason you don't have any faith in men, but the thing is, I'm in love with you. I felt something special on the first night we met. When I saw you working at that German place, I mean, I just . . . And then when Chrissie said you needed some way to get to Colorado and I'd been planning to head West for the holidays anyway, it seemed like fate. I just felt like . . . We were meant to be together. I've never met another woman like you."

I didn't know how to answer him. He was saying everything right. "Come in." He stepped inside. "Everyone, this is my friend Scott Cardoza from New York. He gave me a ride out here. He was in the neighborhood . . ."

My mother stood up from the couch and extended her hand for a handshake. Scott wasn't having any of it and pulled her in for a hug.

"Oh!" Mom laughed.

"Scott," Emily said with a smile as she stood and took her turn hugging him. "It's very good seeing you again. Amber's talked a lot about you."

"I guess you're going to need a place to stay," Mom said. "We don't have a ton of room left, but you're more than welcome to stay the night."

"Thanks for the invite. I'd love to crash here."

"Can I get you something to eat?" Mom asked.

"Thank you, Mrs. Moss, but I'm not hungry."

Scott hugged the other women and shook hands with the men. I couldn't believe he had flown all the way here on Christmas Day just to see me. It was an adrenaline rush, plain and simple. The plane ticket must have cost him a fortune. No guy would do that if he was just out for a one-night stand.

Scott looked at me and smiled; I realized I'd been staring at him. "Uh, so, I was just going to bring this stuff into the kitchen." I grabbed some of the appetizers that were on the coffee table from earlier in the afternoon.

"I'll help."

I took the platter of cheese; he took the nearly

empty bowl of spinach dip. "My sister's house flooded," I said, putting the platter into the sink and taking the bowl of spinach dip and soaking it in water so it would be easier to clean later. "That's why we had to come over here. A pipe burst or some sewage thing, I'm not quite . . ."

Scott's piercing gaze shut off my attempt at casual conversation. "I haven't been able to stop thinking about you," he said.

I looked at the floor. He put his fingers under my chin and tilted it up a little so my gaze met his. "I feel very strongly about you, Amber."

I looked away again. His gaze was too intense.

"Can we try this?"

I looked at Scott. He had heartbreaker written all over him. I wondered if Emily was right. Had I pushed guys away so I wouldn't get hurt? In my fantasies, I had a great job and had a man I loved and lived happily ever after with. In real life, people got fired from jobs every day and men were always leaving their wives for other women. The fantasy world was so much safer.

"We should go join the others," I said. I started toward the living room. In the doorway, Scott took me by the arm. I turned to look at him and my eyes followed his, looking up to see the mistletoe hanging overhead. He smiled and cocked his eyebrow.

I couldn't say I wasn't terrified, but this time, I didn't let myself think about all the potential pain and heartbreak that might lie ahead, I just leaned in and kissed him. It wasn't my fault. It was the danger of mistletoe.

Chapter 22

Emily

Christmas

I sat on the couch in the living room next to Luke and Mom with a smile on my face. It might have just been that I'd had too much wine, or it might have been that I'd miraculously managed to pull this holiday off despite unexpected visitors arriving a couple days ago and my home being bathed in fecal matter. It might have been the look on Amber's face after she'd opened the door to find Scott standing there after he'd flown all the way from California on Christmas Day to see her. It might have been the dinner that turned out well even though I never did manage to find the time to take cooking classes. It might have been the fact Gwen actually seemed to like the gift I'd gotten her. It might have been the shiny reminder that Luke loved me, and only me, despite my myriad faults.

Just now, as I sat on the couch with the people I

loved most in all the world surrounding me, I felt blessed.

Getting through this holiday made me feel a little like I had after final exams in high school and college. Before the test I'd stress myself out and work my butt off and always tried my hardest. After it was over, it was such sweet relief. It was the feeling of not having to beat my head against the wall after weeks of battering myself into a pulp. Back in school, the rewards had been clear-cut: right answers and good grades. Today, as I sat with my family and friends, I realized the reward had nothing to do with how cute my house was or whether I could cook a good meal. The reward was that I had family to sit with, right here, right now, bathed in the glittering lights from the Christmas tree, warm and safe and loved.

Chapter 23

Amber

Christmas

Scott and I rejoined the others in the living room.

"Would you like some spiced cider?" Mom asked Scott.

"Please."

Mom took a mug and poured him a glass from the teapot she'd kept warming on a hot plate and handed it to Scott. Scott was sitting just a few inches away from me. I could feel that my cheeks were flushed, and it wasn't from the warmth of the cider. I couldn't wait until everyone went to bed and Scott and I could get back to kissing.

"So, Scott," Mom said, "Amber tells us you've been in some movies."

He nodded.

"That's wonderful. How did you get started in acting?"

"I actually wrote and directed plays with neighborhood kids when I was just a kid myself."

"Amber used to do that," Emily said.

I nodded. "It's true, I did."

"And I suppose you were in all the plays when you were in high school," Mork said.

"I was."

"Just like Amber," Mom said. "So what was it like to film a movie?"

"Actually, most of it is just waiting around until the lights and camera guys are ready for you. The actual filming only lasts a few weeks, but it's a very intense few weeks. It's a lot of fun but a lot of work."

"Have you ever met anyone famous?" Gwen asked.

Scott smiled and recounted crossing the paths of various famous and semifamous Hollywood movers and shakers. He didn't brag about the parties he'd gone to or the people he knew. I wasn't sure I'd ever met a guy who felt less of a need to impress people. He was self-confident without having anything to prove to anyone. It made me like him even more.

When Gwen said she was getting tired and she and Jay were going to head home to Pueblo, I couldn't have been happier. After we said our good-byes to them, Mom said, "Amber, help me find the sleeping bag downstairs. I'm sorry, Scott, but the kids have already claimed the air mattresses, Amber has the pull-out couch, and Charlie and Stu and Emily and Luke are in the bedrooms. I'm afraid all I have to offer you is the floor."

"Don't worry about it. It's nice of you to let me stay here at all. I'm the party crasher, after all."

"The floor is more comfortable than the pull-out mattress on the couch anyway, trust me," I said. "I'm going to need to do some serious bartering for back massages with Chrissie to recover."

I followed Mom downstairs to the basement. It

was nine hundred square feet of pure storage space. My entire apartment was about half the size and the only storage space I had was in my oven. If I ever did cook, I simply took the stack of books out of the stove temporarily. So to see all the shelves lined with stuff Mom probably never used was something of a marvel to me.

"Now, where is it?" Mom asked, scanning the metal shelves that contained homework from when Emily and I were young, the French horn I played until my sophomore year in high school, a dusty sewing machine, various house supplies—the list was endless. "That young man is very attractive."

"Yes, he is."

"Are you two dating?"

"Not yet. I think we're going to give it a shot, though."

She turned to me and smiled. "Good for you. Ah, here it is. Would you mind?"

The sleeping bag was on a shelf that was too high for my petite mother to reach but that I could easily manage. I pulled down the bag and together Mom and I went upstairs, where everyone was saying their good nights and heading off to their respective rooms. Mom fetched an extra pillow from off her bed and I pulled out the mattress on the couch and spread my sleeping bag out like a regular blanket. Scott set up his sleeping bag on the floor beside me.

I spent extra time in the bathroom brushing my teeth and washing my arms, neck, and armpits. I quickly shaved my legs in the sink and brushed my hair and I put on a pair of shorts and a tank top that clung to my breasts.

As Scott took his turn brushing his teeth in the bathroom, I got under the covers of the sleeping bag on the pull-out mattress, my heart beating double time. By the time Scott joined me in the living room, the house was dark and quiet.

Scott got into his sleeping bag. "Good night, Amber."

"Good night." I waited for him to say something else. When he didn't I said, "Are you all right down there? Are you comfortable?"

"I'm fine. I used to go camping as a kid and with buddies when I was in college. This is much better than having some rocks jabbing me in the back. And at least here the ground is even."

"Good." I bit my lip. *Think, Amber, think.* "You know . . . If you are uncomfortable, you can sleep up here. We slept in the same bed the other night and, you know, that was fine."

"I don't think that would look very good if one of the kids woke up or if somebody needed to come downstairs for a snack or something and found us in bed together."

"Sure. You're right." I sighed in disappointment. I closed my eyes, but I was wide awake. I was much too aware of just how close Scott was to me. His coming to see me on Christmas was by far the most romantic thing a guy had ever done for me.

"Although . . ." Scott began.

"Yeah?"

"I guess maybe I could join you for just a little while."

"Sure. If you want to."

He climbed up in bed beside me and slid under the sleeping bag. I shivered.

"Cold?" he said.

"I'll be fine. You just let in a little breeze when you lifted the sleeping bag."

"I could try to help warm you up. Body heat and all that."

"That's how you're supposed to survive if you're caught in a snowstorm, isn't it?"

"I think so."

"It's worth a try."

Scott slid closer and wrapped his arms around me. I buried my face against his warm chest. After a couple of minutes, the heat from his body hadn't only warmed me, I was starting to feel almost uncomfortably hot, but I didn't want to move. Scott's fingers touched my neck. His lips lightly grazed mine. His hand found a breast and my back arched to meet his touch. He slid his hand down my stomach to the sweatpants I was wearing, and I spread my legs, welcoming his fingers that pushed their way inside me. Several times I buried my mouth in his chest or shoulder to keep from moaning aloud.

"I want to make love to you," I said.

"I want to make love to you." He began pulling off the shorts he was wearing.

"You can't be naked!" I whispered. "Someone could come down at any time."

"I'll hide under the sleeping bag."

I nodded, and in moments we were under the covers making out. The only problem was that the sleeping bag was supposed to keep us warm even if we were in Alaska at negative 30 degrees Fahrenheit. Beneath the sleeping bag, the temperature was approaching the core of the Sun. With Scott pressing his body against mine, it was even hotter. Sweat broke out across my forehead, neck, and upper lip. I felt like molten lava broiling in an angry volcano.

"I'm dying under here." Scott pushed off the sleeping bag.

"No! You can't!" I said. "If somebody walks in on us, at least we'll be covered up. We can pretend like we're just hugging."

"As I thrust my body into yours?"

"You want my mother to see you inside me? Cover up!"

"Hang on a second." He reached into the back pocket of his jeans and pulled out a condom. "I've got a whole box of these in my suitcase," he assured me. "I didn't want to seem presumptuous or anything, but I was . . . *hopeful.*"

He put on the condom and pushed himself inside me. I gasped. For the first couple minutes, it felt so good I wasn't even aware that I was roasting beneath his body and the thick sleeping bag, but pretty soon I couldn't deny that I was going to pass out from heat stroke. He felt amazing, but I was so damn hot I didn't care. "Get that sleeping bag off you!" I demanded.

He tried to toss it off, but it got caught on his left foot. Watching him trying to shake it off just like a dog lifting its leg to take a pee was hilarious, and I cracked up. "What?" he asked.

"Nothing." I couldn't stop laughing. Something about the whole scene made me feel like I was back in high school again. "Sorry. I can't help it. You feel really good, I promise." And then I laughed harder.

He laughed and collapsed on top of me. He pulled out, and for a time we just lay in each other's arms. When I was finally able to stop laughing, I reached down and got him hard again.

"I don't want you to feel uncomfortable," he whispered. "We can wait until we get back to New York and we're alone in your place."

"I can't wait," I whispered back.

He pushed himself back inside me and I let out

a moan before realizing I was in a house full of people and I had to be quiet. I sunk my teeth into his arm instead.

"Sorry, sorry," I said, removing my teeth from his bicep.

"You're fine," he said. "I think it's sexy. Do you want to get on top?"

"What if someone walks in? It'll be too obvious."

"Amber, we're naked from the waist down. I think they'll figure out what's going on either way."

He was right. I climbed on top and came almost instantly. I bit my lip and slapped my hand across my mouth in an effort to quiet my moans. He followed not long after. He tried to wrap his arms around me for a postcoital snuggle, but I wasn't having any of it. "There is no time for snuggling! Put your clothes on!"

I pulled on my pants and pulled the covers on top of me as fast as a firefighter putting on his uniform before leaping on the truck to get to a fire. Scott got dressed, went to the bathroom to dispose of the condom, then came back and tried to snuggle again.

"Did you hide it well?" I demanded.

"Of course. I was a high school student once, you know. I know all about the ninja tactics required to have sex when there are parents in the house."

I laughed. He wrapped his arms around me. I kissed him and, now that we were fully dressed, I pushed the covers off and fell happily asleep in his embrace.

Chapter 24

Emily

The day after Christmas

Christmas night I slept like the dead, almost making up for the last few weeks of sleep deprivation and stress. When I woke, I urgently needed a dose of caffeine, so I went downstairs to make coffee and found Scott and Amber wrapped in each other's arms. I smiled.

I made coffee and then returned to the guest bedroom to track down a plumber. I found one who was willing to come right away, but the price he quoted me was so astronomic I felt certain I could do better elsewhere. I called several more plumbers, and their estimates were just as bad or even worse. When it came to having a home flooded with sewage, getting it fixed wasn't exactly optional, so plumbers could charge whatever they felt like. I finally hired someone. He promised he'd be over at the house in the next few hours. I sent Luke to go to the house to wait, hoping that the plumber might not be as willing to rip off the man of the house as he would the woman of the house.

After breakfast, we helped Charlie and her family pack up their car. We hugged and said our good-byes and waved them off.

Then Mom, me, Amber, Scott, and Mork sat around watching DVDs. Every few hours we'd pluck leftovers from the refrigerator and munch on those.

Luke called late in the afternoon just as I was eating a sandwich with thick slices of ham. He said that the basement had been pumped free of water and the tree root that had blocked our pipe should be cleared by the end of the day. The odor would take a few days to dissipate, but we would be able to move home soon. Fortunately, nothing of importance had been ruined by the flooding in the basement, since we stored anything we cared about on shelves. My old coffee table had been ruined, as had my cheap old four-person table with matching chairs, but we hadn't needed that furniture anyway, so it was no real loss.

Claire and Josh played quietly with their new Christmas toys all day. It got dark early now that it was winter—by five PM it was pitch-black out—so when I went to check on them to see if they were hungry, even though it was early in the evening, it looked like it was the middle of the night.

I found Josh playing in the guest room by himself. "Where's Claire?" I asked.

He shrugged.

"Claire?" I called. "Claire?" I checked the rec room in the basement, the other guest room, and both bathrooms, calling her name all the while. I was just about to head to the basement when Luke got home. His cheeks were flushed red from the cold.

"Hey, baby," he said. He went to kiss me, but I turned and he missed my lips. "Is something wrong? You seem distracted."

"It's just . . . I can't find Claire."

"She's here somewhere," he assured me.

Luke and I searched the house. I checked my mother's bedroom, looking in the closets and under the bed. I even looked in the hamper.

I nearly crashed into Luke in the hallway. "Have you checked the garage?" I asked.

He nodded. "She's not in the car, she's not in the trunk . . ."

"Trunk?"

"I don't know. I just wanted to be on the safe side."

"What about outside?"

"She's not in the yard."

"We need to fan out. She can't have gotten far. She's got to be in the neighborhood."

Luke nodded. "We'll have your mom stay with Josh—Claire will probably come back here before we can find her anyway. I'll drive home to see if she's there."

"That's six miles away."

"Well, maybe she's headed that way."

I nodded. It seemed plausible enough. "What about her friends? Have you called her friends' parents?"

"I hadn't even thought of that. I'll call them on my way home."

Mom handed out all the flashlights she and Mork had, which was three. Luke had one in the car. Amber, Scott, Mork, and I each took a flash-light and headed out on our own into the dark, cold, starless night.

For several minutes, I could hear family members calling out Claire's name, but soon the sound of "Claire? Claire? Where are you?" become more and more faint, until I couldn't hear anyone at all. I walked down the streets with houses cheerily decorated in Christmas lights and tried to think where I would go if I were a seven-year-old girl. There was a playground nearby; maybe Claire had found it.

I walked in that direction but when I got there, the playground was empty. I needed to think.

Could Claire have been kidnapped? Did she run away? Why would she run away? She'd been upset about not getting Baby Anna, but running away seemed a little extreme.

I sat down on a swing and gently swayed back and forth, pushing against the ground with my feet as if I were in a rocking chair. Claire had seemed a little distant at breakfast this morning, but I'd thought it was because she was tired from all the excitement of the past few days.

I closed my eyes. This wasn't about a doll or being tired. Claire was upset about spending yet another Christmas without her mother. Her mother's grave wasn't that far from here. Could Claire possibly have gone to the cemetery? A seven-year-old in a graveyard at night? She was a brave kid, but I was thirty-four and I wasn't that brave even now. Still, I didn't have any better ideas, so I took off in the direction of the cemetery, first at a sprint, then at a jog, and then at a fast walk as I pushed at the cramp in my side that cut through like a lightning bolt. I had eaten much too much today and, seeing as I hadn't done anything more aerobic than pour a bowl of cereal in the morning for the last four months, I wasn't exactly in the best shape of my life.

I could see the graveyard up ahead. I tried to re-member exactly where Elizabeth's grave was. I'd gone with Luke and the kids on the anniversary of her death last year. I'd hung out several yards be-hind them as each of them lay a bouquet of flow-ers on her grave and Luke had said a prayer. Josh was too little to understand exactly what it was that he'd lost. But Claire, who seemed so much older and wiser than her years, remained stoic that day, not letting out a single tear to reveal just how sad she felt.

I remembered that Elizabeth's grave was near an ornate tomb and that the tomb, which was dec-orated with a statue of an angel holding a cross, was by a large tree. Unfortunately, there were many large trees, as this cemetery had been around for more than one hundred years.

So I just walked, hoping some internal divining rod would lead me in the right direction. I ap-proached the first tree I came to, but something didn't feel right and, indeed, it wasn't the place, so I walked on. I passed a couple more trees without ever seeing the aboveground angel tomb, but then I saw a tree that looked familiar. Even from dozens of yards away, I could see the angels' wings and the top of the cross. I quickened my pace, ignoring the cramp in my side.

"Claire? Claire?"

There was no answer. When I got close enough, I could see Claire sitting with her knees tucked into her chest, her back resting against her mother's gravestone. She wasn't wearing a coat. She sniffed as tears ran freely down her face.

"Claire, you scared us." I took off my coat and wrapped it around her shoulders. She didn't move or say a word. I hugged her tight. "We were so worried about you. Everybody is going to be so relieved you're all right." I pulled out my cell phone.

"No, please." She put her hand over the phone.

"Claire, everyone is scared out of their minds. I just want to let them know you're all right."

"No."

"OK, OK." I kept the phone out, though. "What's the matter, honey? Why did you run away? Why did you leave without a coat?" I was pretty sure I knew the answer, but I wanted to hear her say it.

She just shrugged. "I never get what I want. I thought Santa would bring me Baby Anna."

I didn't say anything, hoping she'd keep talking. She didn't. "Claire, I don't think you're crying because of a doll. I don't think you ran away because you didn't get a Baby Anna."

At that she cried harder. I held her close with one arm. With my free hand I text messaged Luke:

found her. shes fine. tell others. more ltr.

As covertly as possible, I put my phone on SI-LENCE and slipped it into my back pocket. I held her tighter with both arms now. She was sobbing so hard her body shook.

"This isn't about a doll, is it Claire? It's about your mother. You miss your mother."

For nearly a full minute she didn't say a word and then, almost imperceptibly, she nodded.

"You know what, Claire? That's OK. You're going to miss her. That's normal."

I held her in my arms and let her cry. Eventually her sobs quieted, but tears ran down her cheeks. I brushed them away gently. I was half-afraid they would freeze right there on her soft face.

"I'm sorry I yelled at you," she said. Her voice was so quiet I wasn't sure I'd heard her correctly.

"You were upset. I understand." I exhaled. "Claire, look, I know I'm not your mother. I know I can never take her place. But I do care about you. I love you. As your stepmom, it's my job to help make sure you're all right. Sometimes I'm going to make mistakes. There might be times when I forget what day it is and I don't pick you up from school on time, but that doesn't mean I don't love you."

"Would you tell me the rest of the story?"

The change in topic was so abrupt, I had no idea what she was talking about. "What story?"

"About Clarisse and the pebbles."

"Oh . . . Oh, of course I will." I started to stand and she pulled me back. "Don't you want to go home where it's warm? You've got to be freezing."

She shook her head. "No. Here."

"Oh." I settled back down and held Claire to my chest. "Uh, so . . .

Ever since the witch had saved Clarisse, Clarisse felt a little less lonely and a little less scared when she was alone and her father was at work in the woods cutting trees. Clarisse decided she wanted to do something for the witch, so she went to the witch's house. Clarisse marched up to the witch's house and rang the doorbell. As she stood there, she suddenly felt afraid. Before Clarisse could lose her nerve, the door to the house swung open. Clarisse peered inside the dark house. The ceilings were high and the rooms large. An immense staircase spiraled up to another floor. Clarisse couldn't help but wonder what was up there.

Clarisse jumped when the witch suddenly appeared in front of her out of nowhere.

"I've been expecting you," the witch said, pointing to a table filled with an assortment of cakes, cookies, and brownies. "Lemonade?" the witch asked.

"Oh, no, I'm fine," Clarisse said.

"So," the witch said, "What brings you here today?"

"You can see into the future," Clarisse said. "I'm sure you already know."

"True, true. You want to help me as I've helped you."

"I'll do anything. Just tell me what to do."

"Clarisse, my child, you are already doing it. You're already doing the one thing you can do for me."

"What? I haven't done anything. I can do your dishes. Sometimes I help Dad cook dinner—I could cook for you. Or maybe. . . ."

"I can snap my fingers and the dishes will be as clean as new. I can simply wish for a succulent dinner and it will appear on the table. The one thing I can't conjure from thin air is friendship, companionship, and love. You bring all of those things to me."

"The witch is really her mother, isn't she?" Claire asked.

"Ah . . ."

"I've been thinking about it. Probably her mother was turned into a witch when Clarisse was born because Clarisse was born out of wedlock or something."

Out of wedlock? How did seven-year-olds know

terms like that? I vowed not to let Claire or Josh watch the broadcast news until they were in their thirties. "No. Her mother really did die."

"Oh." There was so much disappointment in Claire's voice, I wondered if I should have given her a different answer. But I also didn't want Claire to think it was possible for her mother to magically come back to life.

"The witch was just a woman who cared very much about Clarisse and wanted to be sure the little girl was safe and happy."

"She was? She wasn't really a witch, then?"

"She *was* a witch. She had all these magical powers after all, didn't she?"

Claire nodded. "So was she a bad witch or a good witch?"

"Well, she could be a little bit of both. She loved Clarisse very much and wanted to be sure she was safe, but sometimes she could be the grouchy old lady so many people seemed to think she was."

"So what happened?"

"What happened was that the witch and Clarisse stayed friends, and when Clarisse found herself in a really tight bind, she would ask the witch for help. Clarisse learned that just because someone can be grouchy sometimes, that person might still have only the best intentions. That person might love you very much."

Claire didn't say anything for a minute or two. "I liked that story."

"I'm glad."

"My mom didn't like to tell stories, but she'd read them to us."

"Maybe next time you can tell *me* a story."

She nodded. I wasn't sure what had happened

between us, but I felt like an invisible barrier was starting to come down, some new and tenuous connection was maybe, just maybe, starting to grow.

Claire didn't call me Mom, and maybe she never would, but she did pull me a little closer, hugging me just a little tighter.

"Merry Christmas," I whispered into her ear.

"Merry Christmas," she whispered back.

Chapter 25

Amber

Two days after Christmas

Sometimes in life, what seems like the worst thing that can happen to you turns out to be the best thing. A little more than a year ago, I got laid off from a decent-paying job and, since I didn't have any better ideas, I decided to go to school to become a massage therapist. At school, I met a crazy girl named Chrissie. Months went by, the weather turned cold and the skies turned gray, and one lonely night, as I worried about money and how I'd afford a way to get home for the holidays, Chrissie brought over a friend of a friend named Scott. This Scott just happened to be driving through Colorado over the holidays. If I hadn't been broke, if I hadn't abused my credit cards passed the point of no return, if I hadn't gotten laid off, if my business hadn't been off to such a slow start . . . If any one of these things hadn't happened, I wouldn't be sitting next to Scott on a plane, holding his hand as we flew back to New York.

It wasn't that I wasn't scared anymore, but if the universe was going to so much trouble to see that Scott and I were together, I figured I'd better at least give this relationship a chance.

I smiled at Scott. He smiled back and gently squeezed my hand.

Buy These Calder Novels by

Janet Dailey

Shifting Calder Wind   0-8217-7223-6 $7.99US/$10.99CAN
Chase Calder has no recollection of who he is, why he came to Fort
Worth...or who tried to put a bullet in his head the night that a cowboy named
Laredo Smith saved his life. Laredo recognizes him as the owner of Montana's Triple C Ranch—but according to the local papers, Chase has just been
declared dead, the victum of a fiery car crash. The only person Chase can
trust is his level-headed daughter-in-law, Jessy Calder. Helping Chase brings
Jessy into conflict with headstrong Cat Calder, and into an uneasy alliance
with the mysterious and seductive Laredo. And when another family member is found murdered on Calder soil, Chase resolves to come out of hiding
and track down a ruthless killer...before the killer finds him first...

Green Calder Grass   0-8217-7222-8 $7.99US/$10.99CAN
Jessy Niles Calder grew up on the Triple C ranch, six hundred square miles
of grassland that can be bountiful or harsh, that bends to no man's will—just
like a Calder. As Ty Calder's wife, Jessy finally has all she's ever wanted. But
even in the midst of this new happiness there are hidden enemies, greedy for
the rich Montana land, and willing to shed blood to get it. Not to mention
Ty's ex-wife Tara, causing trouble wherever she goes. And soon Jessy will
be faced with the fight of her life—one that will change the Triple C forever...

Calder Promise   0-8217-7541-3 $7.99US/$10.99CAN
Young and beautiful, Laura Calder isn't content to live on a Montana ranch.
Touring Europe with her "Aunt" Tara brings her into contact with the so-
phisticated world she's craved...and with the two men—and ultimate
rivals—who will lay claim to her heart. Boone Rutledge is the son of a Texas
billionaire and used to getting what he wants. He wants Laura...and so does
a Sebastian Dunshill, Earl of Crawford, a handsome, sexy Londoner with a
few secrets he can't share.

Available Wherever Books Are Sold!

Check out our website at **www.kensingtonbooks.com**